SINFONIA BULGARICA

ZDRAVKA EVTIMOVA

FOMITE
BURLINGTON, VERMONT

ISBN-13: 978-1-937677-59-6
Library of Congress Control Number: 2013949939

Fomite
58 Peru Street
Burlington, VT 05401
www.fomitepress.com

Cover photo - Galina Cloutens

MONI

PERHAPS I BEHAVE so foolishly on account of my confused childhood and the endless July evenings when I was alone with my enormous mass.

The trucks loaded with scrap iron would roar at night, reeking of diesel, shaking the windows with the reverberating sound of their engines, and I could not sleep. I had the feeling that a line of two hundred trucks crept along my aorta and would burst into my heart; I had always imagined it was a defective organ that would put its owner in jeopardy. The trucks were my father's; he was ruining himself to make a bright future for me, exporting pig iron from the metallurgy plant in the town, importing scrap iron — meaning heaps of rusty iron wires stolen every now and then from different places. In general, he was killing himself quite successfully. Thugs had shot at him a couple of times. He was no less a thug than they were, but he had a convincing excuse: he loved his fat daughter very much. But why should he love me? I was a greasy bulldozer for whom the seamstresses had to sew special jeans into which a hippopotamus could comfortably crawl.

Bombs exploded twice in front of our house. On one of the occasions my mother's upper arm was wounded: a scratch. She then spent twenty-five days in the hospital. After that incident she left us and went to live with the doctor who had healed her wound. My mother was a very beautiful woman with green eyes that contained falling oak leaves in autumn and sprouting oak trees in spring. Actually, there was a whole calendar in her eyes, but it wasn't so much her eyes as her endless legs that compelled the doctor to fall head over heels for her. I have inherited her green eyes, but in my case they are almost always invisible under the hills of fat that surround them. I have inherited something from my father as well — he was enormous, with a broad back and a popping belly.

My mother left us before the trucks started rumbling at night. After she ran off with all her belongings and boxes and bottles of makeup, Daddy made up his mind to become the biggest, richest player in town so Mother would drown in a lake of misery asking herself, "Why did I kill the hen that laid golden eggs for me?"

My father could read a little and was quite familiar with the multiplication table, which was just enough for his business. Perhaps it was the hardness of his skull that made him the proud proprietor of two hundred completely different trucks with which he sold iron, cucumbers, potatoes, condoms, medicines and the rest. Mother used to tell the story of how, before she married my father, other guys used to beat him up at least twice a week. Later, she seemed to take a certain twisted pleasure in this memory, seeing nothing in the man she married, that enormous semi-literate oaf, but a swamp of love and sympathy for me, with nothing left over for her. That must have made her furious. I was his only child and had heavy breasts under which the greasy pillow of my belly began; below it my gigantic thighs jutted out, jiggling like bowls of congealed soup. Let me not speak of my behind whose volume probably put to shame that of the sand in the Sahara.

For quite a while my swollen body didn't get me into trouble; even when we were poor, my father left rolls of one hundred dollar bills in the drawer of the kitchen table. He never counted them, saying the money was mine. Mother, whose name was Kalina, (I guess her name hasn't changed yet), used to nod her head enviously remarking that the wad of bills in her drawer was smaller than the one in mine.

She had everything. The best massage expert in town, Maria by name, came to take care of her beautiful figure. The most distinguished beautician was responsible for her face — — the most famous artist in Pernik, a bearded phony with a bald head and the manners of a well-trained pug, had already drawn seven pictures of my mother in different poses. Her flesh twinkled on the canvas. My father would rush towards her, with his eyes first, then with his body, flowing hurriedly to her. She was a shrewd woman, my mother was.

She got a degree in law from the local university, even before she left us, and started integrating herself into the cultural elite of the town. Perhaps she is integrating herself perfectly in the house of her new husband. Doctor Xanov was one of the richest surgeons in the region, younger than she, and very tall. He worked in Pirogov Hospital, had a staggeringly large number of private patients, and unlike my father, he never swore.

Doctor Xanov made great efforts to diminish the fat under my skin; he was unaware of the fact that my lard thawed whenever I looked at him. My father often fought with other guys when brandy turned his brains into soup. Even when his chauffeurs, time and again, brought him home bashed, thrashed, and very bloody, he looked at me as if I weren't a fat, female colossus, but the most beautiful girl in the world. Sometimes, in the evenings, he used to put his enormous hand on my head. His palm was the size of a small pillow and had an inordinate number of notches, scars, and wounds from his fights, but on my head it felt smoother than honey. My father didn't say anything, just looked at me, peacefully. I suppose he might have felt sorry for me, for he knew women well, and felt that a fat one like me had no chance whatsoever. He simply loved me as a dog loves its puppy even when it is ugly.

In happier days, when the guys brought Dad home drunk and squashed after his regular sprees, Doc Xanov would come to our house to patch him up. Of course, he got juicy fees for his services. My mother helped and did her best handing him bandages, little squares of gauze, or disinfectant. It was perhaps at that time that they fell in love but that was not the subject of my curiosity. It was curious for me that, after my father was shot, Doctor Xanov and my mother stood by my side at his funeral, looking so sad, as if they both suffered from a horrendous toothache.

It was at that time that Doctor Xanov let his hand drop on my shoulder; compared to my father's paw it felt like a slimy hen's beak stuck in my hair. Doctor Xanov's eyes were brown, the color of frozen leaves fallen long ago from their autumn branches that had just begun to decompose in the first warm days of spring.

As Doctor Xanov examined me, he stuck his forefinger into the lard of my belly showing my mother that the finger sunk in to the knuckle. His forefinger certainly did not sink into my mother's belly because her belly is flat and hard as brass. Her green eyes were of the same quality and that was why I avoided looking into them.

The police didn't find out who shot my father and that was only natural. They almost never did unless the victim was some big shot whose widow would be willing to speak to the press about it. Mother was not at all willing to do that. Perhaps Father had thrashed and flogged many of his enemies for before he died somebody set fire to the café he had built, and twice bombs exploded under his Mercedes. She might have been upset, but she didn't show it. Finally, they killed him without dramatics; two bullets in the forehead and that was that.

Doctor Xanov thought I went off my hinges, but he didn't use those exact words when he diagnosed me. "A permanent shock" was how he put it. The truth was I was not scared of blood. At least once a week Father was brought home dripping and stained with blood. I was suddenly aware I would never again see his brown eyes that looked at me as if I were a perfectly normal seventeen-year-old girl. I would have done anything to make him come back to life.

He loved me as the sparrow loves its little sparrows, not with his brains (for is it possible for a human brain to love the equivalent of twenty-five frying pans of bacon?). He loved me with his blood, which had spilled and splashed onto the pavement.

My mother and father used to sleep in a spacious bedroom situated very far from my own but on the same floor of the house. In the middle of the night, I often heard screeching sounds and moans, so it was evident they made love. I would feel my blood howling in my ears. I would take a shower to cool the flaming lard of my body, but instead of getting cooler I had the impression that the water evaporated at the touch of my skin. The bathroom had mirrors on all its walls; Mother had wanted it to be that way so that every square inch could reflect the perfection of her pearl-like body.

Sometimes, I stayed with her while the masseuse labored diligently over her thighs, feeling transfixed, enchanted by her beauty. She looked at me with green jungle eyes, with liana vines that strangled my throat. I could not imagine how she looked in the spacious bedroom with the marble floor and pictures drawn by dubious painters who pawned their splotchy works of art off on my father at incredible prices. How would he know what a good painting looked like?

My father's father owned seven nanny goats and one cow; my father's mother, big and strong like the motor of a BMW car, herded the cow non-stop, silent, severe and grim. One day she remarked to my father gloomily, "She will be the death of you," meaning, of course, my mother.

I could not imagine Mother under the silver canopy of their matrimonial bed. But she might have been very good, for she conquered the most prestigious catch, Xanov the surgeon, seven years her junior.

Doctors, artists, and teachers in the provincial high school I attended fawned before my father. The brilliant female teachers in the private college I chose to study at did exactly the same because he paid them well to teach me the latest dances — rock-and-roll and tangos — me, under whose steps the parquet floor in the dance hall became unglued. My father couldn't spell the word "address" correctly, but he had all those rolls of one hundred dollar bills which were stronger than any doctor, policemen, or teacher, more powerful than the whole group labeled "the elite". He had money to burn. So did I.

I had never bought porno DVDs or magazines. I once found some Italian ones, which my mother kept at the bottom of her chest of drawers; I looked at them for no more than ten minutes. The next night I ran a temperature, felt giddy, and threw up. And that was not an insignificant event considering my imposing mass. It was that night that I made my decision: what I could not achieve by myself, my father's money would secure for me. How could I invite a man to my room considering the fact that in all four suburbs of the town everybody worked for my father? The drivers of the 200 trucks, the petty scrap iron traders, the owners of car services — my father watched everything closely, businesses throve under his shadow, the city cops and the best lawyers worked for him. How would I find someone who didn't know my father — and how much would I have to pay him to keep it quiet?

My father had appointed a brawny man named Dancho for my personal chauffeur and he drove me in my jeep wherever I wanted to go. He was always with me, my shadow. Once my jeep was shot at because the attackers thought my father was inside. Bullets splintered Dancho's left shoulder destroying some nerves making his hand droop like a rag. He couldn't raise it to the steering wheel. He couldn't even make a fist. But he drove on, blood pouring from the wound, more concerned about what my father would do if he did not get me to safety than about his own skin. It would not be easy escaping his shadow.

I would have to get out of our neighborhood of tall houses with courtyards and swimming pools. I could only find the man I needed where the eight-story flat buildings were; there lived the sacked workers from the steel plant that went bankrupt three years before. Most of the men were unemployed now. My father hired a few of the lucky ones and the rest stayed in the rooms of their small apartments in the daytime and got drunk in the evenings at The Last Penny, a cheap pub run by my father where lousy alcohol was sold.

In those old blocks of flats I hoped to find my man. Although rumors about my father and about me and my fat haunches sprang up almost every day, and songs about Mother circulated — with the occasional pornographic lyrics and inaccurate descriptions of her body parts — and flooded the town, the people from that area had never seen me in person.

I told Dancho that I was going to the town library, but I snuck my way to one of the dozens of little shops selling second-hand clothes. Most of the town's population bought their shirts and trousers from there, but who would ever think that the only daughter of Bloody Rayo would go shopping in the sleazy districts that smelled of sweat and urine? I dropped in at exactly eight neighborhoods like this and intentionally hung around in the sleaziest one. The cellar of one building was flooded; the water in it had turned into slime and pond scum. Half of the first floor was abandoned and in one of the remaining empty rooms there was a second-hand clothes shop. I guess it would be more accurate to say *fifteenth* or *twentieth*-hand shop. It was evident that the shop assistant didn't recognize me.

She was very dark and there was dirt under her nails; her face was wrinkled and hidden below a layer of makeup some miles thick.

"What do you want?" she asked me, adding acidly, "You are very fat and I don't know if there are any clothes that will fit you."

"I'd like a skirt," I explained to her.

"Um, uh, you'd be lucky if I found any dress for you at all. I haven't got a skirt that big. Try this dress on, but it is expensive, mind you. It's the only one I have that large."

She wanted one lev for the dress. For the first time in my life I was told that something that cost one lev was expensive. I paid her without any hesitation; the woman gave me a dragon's grin, causing the make-up to melt, and it flowed, mixed with sweat, down her cheeks towards her wrinkled neck. In a flash, she offered me two more dresses, as enormous as the previous one, but this time she said they cost ten levs apiece. She showed me a pair of shoes as well, so warped and torn that you could only use their heels to hit a stray dog on the head with or simply throw them in the trash.

"Wonderful merchandise," she boasted. "You can walk with these shoes for six years. They're already patched up so you won't need to bring them to a cobbler."

I did not buy the shoes. I chose a pair of slippers instead, which hardly clung to my heels, and gave her five levs for them. The woman grabbed at the money, stuck it right away in her bra and scratched her hand as if the bill had burned her skin. Then she jumped up, squeezed my arm, and dragged me to the upper floor; where she had "posh merchandise for big babes like you, love." She showed me a bathrobe mended in seven or eight places, worn and frayed as if a combat tank had driven over it several times. Then she unlocked a chest of drawers that was full of blouses — yellow, green, pink and faded as if all that *posh* merchandise had been soaked in sulfuric acid.

"Five levs apiece," the woman announced generously without letting go my hand. Her palm was very warm.

Then she took hold of my shoulder with both her hands and offered me a pair of underpants the size of a tent. I bought them for ten levs which made the woman gape at me. For maybe a whole minute she stood dumbfounded, then she hugged me and kissed my cheek.

"God bless you", she whispered, her mouth dripping with saliva. "God be with you every minute of your life!"

At that very moment it dawned on me that I could ask if she knew of a guy for me.

"What's your name?" I asked. Suspicion shone immediately in her eyes, black and slippery like a skating rink.

"Why do you ask?"

"Because I want to come back to shop from you."

"My name's Natasha," she answered. "But my true Gypsy name is Fatma."

I thought about the fact that I could buy all of her posh merchandise, the whole block of flats, the cellars of slime and mold with the smallest of the rolls of money my father had given me. The woman had sunk her black eyes into mine and refused to let go of my arm.

"You want something else. I can tell that by looking at you."

"Listen, Fatma. Can you find a man for me?"

She went on plunging her eyes deeper into my head.

"You want a man?" she repeated slowly.

"Yes" I answered.

Her eyes left mine and crept along the hills of my breasts, balanced on the greasy pillow of my belly, and then descended to my thighs. After that her hands let go of my shoulder, patted my stomach and back and, without any decorum whatsoever, groped my ass as if it were a vast unexplored part of the globe.

"You are fat," she clicked her tongue several times. "Very fat, I tell you. Tell me when you want to marry him and I'll tell you how much it will cost."

It was clear she had not understood. Her words were sharp as a result of which my belly and the cushions of lard above my waist wobbled like sacks stuffed with cabbage.

"You're really fat," she went on. "Are you sick? Is it some illness that makes you so fat?"

"I'm healthy."

"Then you eat too much. That's good. It means you have a lot of food at home. Don't you, eh? You bought so many things. I wish I were fat myself," she sighed and groped me once again, this time on my belly. "Can you breed?" she asked.

I didn't answer. The whips of suspicion lashed me.

"Does your monthly blood flow regularly?" she added.

"Yes, it does."

"What sort of a guy do you want, scrawny or a fat one like you?"

"I'd like a skinny one. But..."

"What?"

"I don't want to marry him."

"What!" she hiccupped heavily then surveyed me carefully, her face underneath the make-up so deep in thought that the wrinkles stretched and shone like parallels and meridians on the globe of her cheeks. "Oh, yeah," she patted my arm once again and winked at me. "Oh, yeah. I'll bring a married man to you, and you'll give him something for his kids. He'll be pleased and you'll be pleased. Kiro has five children. You'll have to fetch two doughnuts for each kid. I know a bakery where they sell them cheap."

"No. I don't want a married man."

I thought about my father, about me, my mother, and suddenly I was out of sorts imagining the children and the doughnuts from the cheap bakery. "I want to get to know a guy well," I lied to her.

"Oh, come on," Fatma winked at me. "Do you want him now?"

I was not ready to make such a quick decision, but I thought that I might not be able to free myself from Dancho the next day. Mother had invited a brilliant family of lawyers to dinner. She was in her second year of studying law and a number of bright constellations from the law universe were always visiting our home. Any barrister or notary was flattered to be her guest, of course.

She had not yet graduated, but tributes were sung in her honor noting her particular legal talents. I still cannot explain why she forced me to attend these dinners; my father usually stayed with us for no more than eight minutes — that was the length of time he could endure without cursing — then somebody would call him on his mobile to sign an important business deal.

It was Mother who always arranged this, carefully selecting the person who would telephone my father. She chose my attire for the dinners as well. "We'll hide your thighs with this," she would murmur, slipping a black skirt on me; her theory was that the black color concealed the extra fat. Alas, under the black skirt my legs were like mountains of the Himalayas. "And we'll hide your belly with this. Can't you suck your stomach in a little?" she would ask, very concerned; in those moments I hated her. "We must find a dancing partner for you."

Now Fatma, who perhaps was my mother's age but looked three times older with the plaster of make-up on her face and the parallels and meridians under it, repeated her question: "Do you want him now?"

I had to make up my mind.

"I want him now," I answered, meditating no further. "But where will we get to know each other? I can't bring him to my home."

"Your parents will object, eh?" Fatma winked and patted me on the cheek. "Your folks have fed you well, that's why they protect you so much. And they're right. If you don't mind using one of the dresses you bought to spread on the floor, you can get to know him within a minute."

Then she scrutinized me from head to toe. "Honey, step out of my shop," her chin pointed at the old cardboard boxes full of rags. "You might steal my merchandise while I'm gone. Wait for me outside. I'll bring the guy in a minute."

"How much will it cost?" I asked her. My father always started any negotiation with the question "How much? US dollars, British pounds or Euros?"

"I want five levs. You can give him … well, that's something between him and you. Work it out for yourself."

Fatma took me out into the corridor. People must have been living there, for there was a picture of a family on one of the boxes; a father, a mother and three kids, boys whose hair was cropped to the very bone of the skull. I figured they'd had lice. There was purple wallpaper on all the walls with some variation of a horrible flower pattern that had surely brought both parents and children to the edge of insanity. The strips of wallpaper were ripped off and stuck desperately to the floor; the cracked brick masonry covered by thick patches of mold was visible under them.

I thought about the wallpaper in my room, about the marble floor and my bed, which my father had bought for me from Austria. There was a button I could push that would lift it to a certain angle whenever I wanted to sit up; there was another button that made the bed sway like an ocean liner. I had a waterbed as well that Mother had bought for me during one of her excursions to North America. I took out one of the dresses I had acquired; it was dark red, faded and frayed at the hem. Mother wouldn't even have allowed me to throw it into our waste-bin for fear it was full of nits, tapeworm, ticks and other vermin. I could spread that dress on the floor, but where? Suddenly I was scared.

What was I doing?

It was summer. My father had made plans to go to Austria and import a new batch of used automobiles; he intended to import two tractors at a very advantageous price. He was a successful international businessman. What was I doing in this narrow walkway? The scorching heat outside had made the ground split the way men severed the bones of a slaughtered pig. Even the flagstones of the sidewalk had become unglued from the sweltering sun, but the slime in the cellar had not yet dried up. A suspicious stink reached my nose.

"Men are wicked and envious, love," Fatma had remarked when we entered the room I was to wait in. "They want to ruin my business, so they throw dead puppies in the flooded cellar. It's not dangerous. No one from this block of flats has died yet. Some guys coughed a little on account of the smell, but then they forgot about it."

After a short time of waiting I heard footsteps along the flight of stairs that reverberated like slaps in my face. After several seconds Fatma appeared, her make-up smiling greasily, for it was evident she had plastered on another layer of it and had erased the sweaty streams leading to her withered breasts.

"Here he comes," she announced, leading by the arm a mere strip of a man whom she pushed towards me. "He's very scrawny, it's true," she admitted. "But the guy is tough and strong, mind you. Every night he unloads marble slabs at the station in Pernik," she looked at me closely, slapped my cheek and suddenly snapped,

"Spread your dress here and don't make the guy wait. I won't let you in the shop, you might pilfer anything, just anything," then she turned around, the slaps of her steps echoed down the stairs of the flooded cellar.

The string — the thin streak of a man that unloaded marble slabs at the station — and I were alone. He was much taller than me, lanky and narrow-shouldered like a shoe box, and his hips were as broad as my upper arm. He was wearing a dirty lilac T-shirt and a pair of jeans that were cut off above the knees, and from there a net of tousled threads hung loosely to the concrete floor. The maypole immediately took off his cut jeans.

His eyes were muddily green, almost yellow; then he took off his dirty T-shirt and flaunted his lusterless puny chest before me. I remembered the men in the pictures of my mother's porno magazines which I had peeked at; their muscles had been taut, bulging like fighter aircraft, while the muscles of the maypole were practically invisible. It was impossible to miss the detail that the man wore nothing under his jeans, and it felt awkward staring at the part of his body that interested me most.

He came toward me and didn't make any efforts to undress me. My blouse had pasted itself with sweat to my paunch. It turned out I was incapable of taking off my skirt, so I let him help me. His efforts were great and futile, which made me doubt that he could actually unload marble if he couldn't manage somebody's backside — even if it was my backside. I took hold of his shoulders, which felt brittle beneath my fingers.

"Say 'I love you,'" I ordered.

"I love you," the guy repeated obediently.

"Say 'You are the only girl I love in the world,'" I commanded.

"You are the only... It's too long," the maypole complained and added, "I want ten levs."

"Okay."

"I want them now."

"No. After."

My father's favorite saying was "Don't pay beforehand if you want good service."

I touched him, the place on a man's body I had always dreamt of touching. My hand burned. He groaned. My father's groans were the same: like when a bone gets stuck in a cat's throat and the cat tries to spit it out. It was strange I didn't feel the pain I had read about. It didn't hurt at all; it didn't feel so great either. I simply had to live through it and explore the sensation again. The man's eyes had become purely yellow and shone like crystals of cracked mica on his dark face. He clung to me, a drowning rat clutching at the skin of a whale. It felt as if he were driving nails into a bag of down, rocking slowly, his eyes of mica hidden under shut eyelids.

His narrow shoulders could sink effortlessly into every part of my big body; I myself sank pleasantly downwards into the concrete floor, nurturing a vague idea that I'd carve a hole in it any minute.

Suddenly the man relaxed with his eyes still closed. Saliva ran from his mouth resembling the glitter of the mica I had noticed in his eyes. The bulk of my buttocks pressed a little pool of blood to the concrete floor, which did not make any impression on me. Theoretically I had been prepared for it. I could already report that in practical terms no matter how fat I was I had become a woman. The sliver forgot to get down from me, yawned, and fell asleep in the comfortable nest of my blubber. Even though he was scrawny, I could feel his weight heavily on me, so I budged and his head hit the floor. The guy was startled, but only for a moment, then yawned again, revealing a lake of saliva shining in his mouth, his dark hands clinging to me, like pencils writing the enormous sentence of my body.

Suddenly the beanpole broke into a sweat and started slithering onto me, and then unexpectedly his lips grounded inaccurately upon mine. I don't know if I could count this as my first kiss with a man, but since I hadn't experienced an event like it before I decided I might as well accept it as such.

This happened when my father was still alive.

I felt overwhelmed with happiness and wanted to get out of there before the happiness melted like everything else that came my way, so I shook the guy who slept quietly on top of me and whispered in his ear, "Say 'I love you.'" The tone of my voice was the same as my mother's when she talked to the notaries and lawyers, offering them her perfect profile or a glimpse of her pearly leg. I couldn't explain how an intonation like that was born in my throat.

The beanpole did not obey. His yellow eyes hung over my face, his mouth pressing mine. I had some money in the pocket of my blouse. It was very hard to thrust my fingers in the silk pocket glued to my skin. It took several minutes to extract a ten-lev banknote, which I left on the floor saying, "Take it."

"Wait a minute," the man said.

His hand, rapid and scorching like lightening, grabbed the money, then he left me on the dress I had bought from Fatma. At that moment I sensed the stink. Fatma was probably right; her neighbors had thrown dead puppies or worse in her cellar.

After five minutes the guy returned carrying two bottles of beer and a package containing the cheapest possible, suspiciously rosy-colored, sausage a man could buy in the cheap shops, squeezed in cellars and bungalows along the Struma River.

He opened one of the bottles, poured half of it down his throat, burped and gave it to me. I tasted a gulp of the liquid and was about to drop dead instantly; the beer smelled no better than the puppies ruining Fatma's business. The man ripped the sausage into two equal pieces, not bothering to peel its skin, tearing it with his teeth as if he hadn't eaten in four years. I felt nauseated watching the beanpole eat the sausage; I suspected I might have to drive him if not to the morgue, then at least to Pirogov Hospital.

"Eat," he said. "I bought the sausage for you."

"And spent all the money," I snapped angrily.

He made no comment on my remark, just went on chewing with his mouth open and stuffed with pieces of the cheap sausage soaked in the nasty beer. Then his head dropped to the ridge formed by my breasts. He pushed aside the last piece of sausage and turned again to me.

It felt so good that for a moment I thought, "God bless you, Fatma!"

Before I went home I remembered only the guy's scrawny ribs bulging like piano keys in his chest. My mother had had her heart set on making me play the piano and wasted heaps of money on teachers. Dancho, my father's loyal chauffeur, would drive directly from the Academy of Classical Music in Sofia to my music room.

I reached almost to the man's dimpled, stubbly chin. He let his hand drop on my head; his fingers felt like my father's, although some of the nails were crushed and warped. He ran them through my thick, toothbrush-bristles hair and mumbled, "Your hair's red like a bundle of carrots."

My hairstyle resembled a helmet and Mother criticized me severely on that account. How was it possible, she asked rightfully, that a young promising lady would get her hair cut like an infantryman? I was fat, and the hair baking my skull in its red-hot furnace made me feel hotter.

The lanky man's hair was black, dirty, tousled, and covered his shoulders. I didn't ask what his name was.

As I walked down the stairs to the cellar full of bilge water, slime, and pond scum, his steps behind me did not sound like slaps in the face; they reminded me of the first drops of rain after a two-year drought.

"Hey," he shouted. "When will I see you again?"

When? I wouldn't be able to get to this shabby suburb in the near future. All over the district the eight-storey flat buildings jutted out from the sidewalks with drab balconies covered by necklaces of drying clothes and linen. Among the blocks, cars, trucks, even several buses were parked and between them stray dogs sauntered, lolling out their tongues, some sprawled like corpses under the buses parked on the asphalt, which melted in the heat.

I didn't think even for a moment that my father would ever allow me to come here. If Mother learned that her daughter had been wasting her time in this lair of thugs (let alone the fact that she had visited the building with the flooded cellar and dead dogs!) she would convince my father to buy a house in one of the upscale districts of Sofia, the capital city. I wouldn't be able to see the lanky guy ever again.

"Listen," I told him. "Come to the Snowdrop Café tomorrow evening at seven. Then I'll tell you where you can meet me."

There could be no doubt that I would be seeing this man again.

There could be no doubt that it had been the most marvelous day of my life. In my chest of drawers I had a lot of money; if I bought a small flat, a flat with one single room and a bathroom — one rotten flat in this swamp of crumbling buildings — then everything would be all right. If I spread an old mattress on the concrete floor I could invite the beanpole and no one would know anything about it. Even Fatma wouldn't. Where could I buy the small one-room flat? It would be best to choose one in the center of town, near the library, for what sort of place could be honored by the visits of Bloody Rayo's daughter but the library?

My father would often remark, "Read, my girl, read. Science was out of my reach, but it will be within yours."

My mother paid the best teachers in English, in computers, modern and Latin dances, and good manners to train me. Most recently, she stumbled upon the idea to get a German teacher as well: a spinster with withered cheeks who always visited our home in smashingly expensive shoes. My mother adored her for that — she could adore only expensive things. That was the reason she had been so impressed by the young Doctor Xanov who patched up my father after his drunken sprees.

Yes, the only place I was allowed to go was the library. I never visited any fitness clubs; I was too fat, so my father built a gym onto our house and hired a personal trainer to set my targets and measure my progress. But my father, no matter how generous he was, wouldn't be allowed to buy the public library even though he had donated a dozen grand to repair the broken roof tiles. I doubt, however, he was interested in the books for himself, rather his interest in one of the librarians could account for the generosity: a puny woman with the unhappiest eyes you could imagine, as if someone beat her non-stop around the clock. I wondered why my father liked small women with eyes as sad as death itself. The only exception to this rule was Mother who was neither sad nor small, but she left him all the same.

Well, my point is that I had more than enough money to buy a rotten one room flat. If I did buy it myself, though, the news would spread through town like fire. I had no friends I could trust. The second most beloved saying my father used was "Money is the most loyal friend to man." I could ask a lawyer to acquire the flat for me. If I added two or three rolls of bills to his fee everything could be arranged within twenty-four hours and any lawyer would willingly keep as quiet as the eel in Doctor Xanov's aquarium, an animal my mother often admired.

"Don't you want to do this again?" the lanky youth asked, pushing his dimpled chin into the bristle of my thick short hair.

"I'll tell you tomorrow," I answered. "Seven o'clock at the Snowdrop Café. I'll give you more money."

"And we'll buy beer and sausages," he snorted happily.

All this happened before my father was shot, perhaps half a year before his funeral. Neither he nor Mother had any inkling about my decision to take money from my drawer.

THE APARTMENT WAS DESPERATELY SMALL. An empty room in a block of old flats, with its window facing north, a roof made of worm-eaten logs, crumbling plaster on the ceiling, a small empty kitchen, and a bathroom so tiny that I had to enter with my shoulder first to relieve myself. There was electricity, but unfortunately there was neither hot water nor any heat whatsoever. I bought a mattress and a cheap blanket, then I invited the maypole whose name I still didn't know.

The room was as narrow as a coffin; the lawyer was so curious about why I wanted it so badly that I had to lie to him. I told him that I intended to house my German tutor there. The lawyer smiled, which, according to the code of judicial behavior, meant, "Bloody Rayo's fat cow has a screw loose, no doubt about it. Her father has stuffed her so full of money that it's interfering with her brain."

Well, I didn't give a damn about his inferences.

I became the owner of the room with the mattress in less than twenty-four hours. This event once again confirmed my father's thesis that money would do more for you than your best friend. I didn't have any friends.

Before the battered entrance door banged shut behind his back, the beanpole had taken off his jeans and his dirty lilac T-shirt, the same one as before. And, as before, he did not have any underwear on.

"What's your name?" I asked him.

"Simo," he said.

"Don't you want to know what my name is?"

It was evident he didn't and so he clung to me instead, a thin rope spiraling about the masts of my endless buttocks.

"Aren't you interested in what my name is?" He didn't answer, and couldn't possibly do so because his mouth was full of saliva that shined in the light like mica. My mother had a diamond necklace that shined like that and a diamond ring, and there was a diamond on the belt of her formal evening dress. My father had brought it to her from Austria. So I decided that the saliva in his mouth wasn't mica, it was diamond.

"Okay. My name is Moni. Did you hear me? Moni. Here's the money. Take it."

He didn't look at the money because his body had already started swinging over me. I pushed him aside, which wasn't difficult at all. He banged against the floor, but his reaction surprised me.

"You're pretty," he said. "You are pretty."

It was at that moment that I understood how the other women felt: my mother, my classmates in the private school for girls, my tutors in English, German, modern dances, fitness and good manners. The other women whose boyfriends told them they were pretty, that they weren't fat bulldozers but simply pretty women.

"You are off your rocker," I objected, but he didn't hear me.

ON THE FORTIETH DAY after my father's funeral, Mother paid for a solemn church service and invited all the intellectuals and financial elite of the town. Or, I should say, all the people that Mother considered elite. The church service was an excellent opportunity for her to show off her mourning attire. On such occasions (and by "such occasions" I'm referring to opportunities for my mother to show off) she always hired the cook from Casablanca, the most expensive and posh restaurant in Pernik.

All were enchanted by the menu she offered and by her fashion. I was already very familiar with the cook's menus because Mother abided by her sacred law: once a week, on Friday, to take me out to dinner to Casablanca. I had the feeling that the waiter knew when we were about to arrive by the sound of my mother's jeep. The same very tall and attractive man always met us at the door, taking my mother's hat or cape and bowing gracefully, down to the last vertebra in his spinal cord, and whispering very sincerely, "You look just wonderful, Madame!"

The words would rattle like pebbles in his mouth, his eyes following my mother with such demonstrative admiration that I suspected he was ready to kiss the pavement beneath her shoes; it was hardly surprising when she would leave him fabulous tips.

Then the waiter would take my hat or coat and bring the menu, his eyes shining proudly for he had again anticipated what my mother would order. "Shall it be shark's loin prepared in the Saragossa way, Madame?" My mother made it a special point for all her guests to be aware of the fact she ate shark's loin in the Saragossa way.

She had grown up in a family of waiters. My grandmother and grandfather, her parents, experts in this trade, had nurtured several generations of drunkards at The White Elephant restaurant, and after the establishment went bankrupt, they set up a pub in one of the most backwater suburbs of the town. My grandmother Shar (I suppose it was an abbreviation of "shark") was slim and still had her sharp green eyes even though she was getting on in years. Compared to her, my grandfather resembled an obituary notice. He made cheap cocktails behind the bar, but more often drank quietly and sadly with his regular customers, not giving a damn about the rest of the world. His only daughter, my mother, had money to burn and was therefore happy. Grandfather was given to noble charity, ordering free drinks for his old friends, a bunch of poor pensioners with receding hair who poured the cheap cocktails into their brains, blessing him day and night.

Grandma Shar looked at them with disdain, burning them with the green flames of her eyes. In her rare fits of wrath she would throw my grandpa's friends out of the establishment in a most ignominious manner, but this happened once in a blue moon so they waited for death peacefully, full to the brim with brandy my grandfather sold to them cheap, for although my grandfather was a drunkard with thinning hair, he never swindled his old pals.

As my mother entertained her guests, barely remembering the reason for the occasion, I was wondering if it was a good idea to introduce Simo to my grandfather.

*** *** ***

BECKY ANEVA

THURSDAY WAS THE DAY of the week Becky detested. On Thursday she made Theo Anev's acquaintance and a month later he became her husband; her son was born on Thursday. Too late and too sadly she lost her virginity on Thursday. It was cold and windy April and the sky was sick with rain. She lived in a prestigious neighborhood of the town, no stray dogs roamed the streets, and discreet bodyguards were on the alert in their gables on the top floor of her house. Becky knew the man on duty; he was her husband's loyal guard dog and his eyes descended to his shoes whenever Becky happened to be around.

She was twenty-five when she married Theo. He was eleven years older than she. Becky had studied law in Germany and was accustomed to punctuality and discipline. She guessed her father's money came from some shady petrol trade and was convinced it was none of her business. She always made careful use of her bank accounts; she had seen people dying in squalor and their helplessness disgusted her. Why should her father push her to marry so young! Her mother harped on the same old string: their enormous house was empty without grandchildren. Becky accepted Theo, thinking he was the next pen pusher, fawning all over her father, an obedient worm she could easily manipulate. She was wrong.

Her intense loathing for Theo made her choke on her own tongue the minute her father introduced her to him, his most brilliant expert.

Two hours after they had met she told Theo she would like to invite him to her place then she took him in her car. She had a Toyota, so she took him to her house in Boyana, the most prestigious neighborhood of the capital. She made Theo wait for her in the street as she undressed, then she ordered the guard to summon him. She told him "Come on." She had never yet had an intimate contact, and the thought of it sickened her. She was struck with revulsion at the sight of his hairy hands although she had drunk a glass of Sauvignon Blanc. She vomited when he touched her. It was Thursday; the fog outside the windowpane had killed the sky.

The contact with Theo was painful. His body scalded her unpleasantly. It was not necessary for Becky to pretend she enjoyed sex. She was pleased he finished quickly and did not torture her with explanations of how beautiful she was. She appreciated the fact he did not look at her and kept his mouth shut.

Theo did the thing she had summoned him for. In the end, she crawled over his hot belly, went to the bathroom and called out, "You can get dressed."

"Would you like something else, Miss Becky?"

His voice made her think of disintegrating heap of potato peels exuding unpleasant smell. Becky imagined him calling her names.

"Would you like something else?" he repeated.

"Yes," she answered. "I want you to marry me."

That was the price her father wanted and Becky paid it however much she wanted to go back to Germany! She hated it when she had to speak to her mother when the middle-aged lady was not "with her young friends," the men she paid to share her company. Her mother had read somewhere that sex with young men prevented aging so she hired a new bodyguard every month.

It was Thursday again. Becky Aneva had a son who was two years old. Her father had died under vague circumstances in Red Lion hotel in a comparatively small provincial town. Her mother didn't have enough money to hire new bodyguards, and the reason was Theo. Stingy and immaculate, dressed in a perfectly ironed gray suit — Becky detested gray — he imposed himself upon her mother on the first Thursday every month, handing her a bunch a bank notes. It seemed he took evil pleasure in her mother's humiliation, giving her banknotes one by one, and never failing to remark, "Elinora, I do not want you to make a laughing-stock of me." His voice was cold like the trigger of a gun. He never shouted and the words he used were an even and smooth speedway that led her mother to insanity.

At the very beginning her mother screamed, "You mean upstart!" Theo took the money back in his pocket and left the room. This scene had been repeated in the course of two months and Elinora learnt to hold her tongue. It appeared Becky's mother was capable of putting up with the upstart's arrogance; she was tough, vital, and treated humiliation as an insignificant addition to her rich experience. Nothing could destroy her.

Elinora was a beauty. She had blue eyes, hazel-hair, fair complexion, she was generous to her present boyfriends and poisonous to her ex ones. She regularly showed up at her daughter's front door, her chauffeur opening reverentially the door of her BMW for her. Then Elinora went to the cot where Theo junior slept, left a cheap present at his pillow, and repeated again and again to her daughter that she needed more money.

Becky asked herself lazily if her mother had not been at it with Theo, but this issue was of no interest to her. The intense hatred she felt for her husband was quite normal in her daily routine, which contained items like the vase of flowers on the table in the living room, and the mute bodyguard at the front door of the house.

"My dear," her mother said one day. "Theo was a sleazy law student who didn't have money for his lunches. At a certain point he crawled into favor with me and I introduced him to your father. Now I regret it." Elinora had nodded her head. "He is a man of brilliant physical vigor, but I think you can hardly appreciate that. God..." She looked at the ceiling as if the Almighty could peer over the chandelier. "Unfortunately God has deprived you of a sense of love."

Theo came to Becky's bedroom on Thursdays as punctual as the news broadcast on the National Program of the TV. She didn't bother to pretend sex with him was a pleasure. His body had become uglier, the contact with him was more repellent; the only positive development in this respect was the fact that every Thursday he left a roll of bank notes under her pillow.

"Sometimes I think you like your masseuse better than me," Theo remarked one day, and that was true, but Becky did not find it necessary to confirm banal truths for him.

"Why don't we get divorced?" she had asked in an expressionless voice.

"You are pretty," her husband answered. "And my son needs a mother."

There was grayish wallpaper in the bedroom that Theo had chosen, dark gray window frames, and gray carpet. His eyes, popping slightly, covered under the carefully sliding eyelids, were gray as well, and the gray press of his presence exhausted all her patience. Perhaps he found pleasure in humiliating her and in the physical suffering he made her experience every Thursday. Becky had invented a protective device against Theo's clutch: she had a secret account in the bank. She had learnt to spend very little, and she had learnt to ask Theo, "Can you leave me some money?" at the moment he was about to go out of her room.

She informed her husband she took private lessons as she emphasized her endeavors to play the piano although she couldn't care less about music. The vague circumstances enveloping her father's death and her mother's humiliation had revealed to Becky that money was of crucial importance. She wanted to go to Germany. Begging for money was not a source of remorse. On the contrary, it was not so much the money, it was the joyous thrill she had wrenched it from Theo that made her happy. The roll of banknotes under her pillow was the material evidence she was more resourceful than he.

"Look me full in the face," Theo said one Thursday evening and she obeyed him. "I know you are not interested in money. Why do you constantly want it?"

"I want to go to Germany," Becky said. She did not attempt to lie. Theo could always pay the best detective agency; fighting him made no sense: each word Becky dropped unwittingly prolonged his presence in her room and that was the worst case scenario for any Thursday night.

"You don't give a damn about what is happening at home," her husband went on, as if reading her thoughts. "You lack ambition. You are not hospitable and friendly. You are pretty and that's your only asset. No, you will not go to Germany. I'll buy a house for you here, in Bulgaria."

"Can you give me money for that house now?"

"You want money again."

"A house costs money, Theo."

"You don't take good care of our child. You go check on him when I remind you to."

"Yes," Becky answered.

The only tone of voice that Theo adopted as he communicated with her was the imperative one.

"I will not give you money for the house," Theo declared.

At that moment Becky's hatred for him soared to the sky, but she knew she had to keep it to herself. So she just looked through the window. It was raining, a typical April torrential rain. Her life was like this useless and cold day in April.

"You will stay here." Her husband's gray voice crept towards her but Becky was not afraid. She did not fear anything. "You will attend the meetings with my partners. You must be dazzlingly pretty any time I summon you. I know you are not clever, but the other people don't know about that. Your beautiful face beguiles men into thinking you possess refinement you have always lacked. I might summon you at 10 pm, at 9 am, at midnight — you must be pretty all the time. Your job is to be my pretty wife."

"Yes, Theo," Becky answered. "Beauty costs money. Equitation, fitness, stringent and healthy diet."

"You want money again."

"Yes. I need money."

"I had asked your mother to convey a short message to you." Becky did not respond and Theo gritted his teeth. "I don't like your silences when I am here, with you."

"What was that short message about?"

"About a lady I spend much time with at the Escalibur Hotel."

"O, yes. My mother described that lady to me in great detail."

"Didn't you fly into a rage?" Theo sounded interested, his gray eyes on her face.

"I was enraged," Becky answered.

Her husband took off his gray jacket. This action did not portend anything nice or pleasant.

"I need to go out," Becky ventured.

"You want money, don't you?" his voice thickened, clambered up her skin chilling her breasts. "Take your clothes off."

Becky bristled up. Theo was a patient man; he watched her undress, his eyes squinting. On Thursdays she put on several layers of clothes to put him off. Her movements were rapid and graceless as if she were plucking the feathers of a dead bird. It was evident Theo got excited by that too. Becky had the feeling his fingers trembled, intent on ruining her, but she would survive that. She could survive anything. Theo's gray eyes licked her breasts, studied her pelvis, then he stood up and the thick asphalt in his voice filled up the pores of her skin.

"Lie on the floor," he commanded.

His orders had never frightened her.

*** *** ***

Di

Di's mother, Arma, knew Di did not go to teach Becky Aneva French. She did not approve of her daughter's ridiculous ideas; she thought that touching the shiny, often sweaty and greasy backs of strange people was dangerous. She was a researcher, an ex-associate professor at the Linguistics Institute of the Bulgarian Academy of Sciences, expert in Russian literature who took pride in the fact she was capable of reciting Lermontov's poems. Alas, these skills did not help her pay the bills for the central heating, electricity and running hot water. Nobody invited her to translate books and articles from Russian into Bulgarian anymore. She bought a coat eight years ago and its frayed sleeves could not persuade anybody that exquisite morality hid behind her high mysterious forehead.

Arma Kumova performed miracles in order to conceal the spots where her shoes were patched; her inventiveness was legendary: she had sewn eight new collars on her coat, putting out of sight the frazzled fabric at the shoulders with a gorgeous white shawl. If a friend asked her to a cup of coffee, she answered she was busy at the radio, and that was a lie. No one was interested in Arma

Kumova. Not a single soul with the exception of the retired senior executive from the Bulgarian Telecommunication Company — a bachelor, or perhaps a divorcee of many years who hinted that one day in the nearest future he'd start thinking about making Arma his Missus. In his opinion his pension "was ludicrously small," so he had bought some shops (Why can't *I* buy some shops? Arma thought bitterly) in the capital where he sold fashionable clothes, boxes of matches, socks, and lipstick. One day, he summoned up all his courage and asked Arma to a cup of coffee thinking that perhaps he'd bring her to his bed that very night. He had boasted he possessed "a magnificent apartment" plus a house he let, so the senior executive bought new sheets for the bed and had the toilet washed with a special disinfectant.

Arma had explained to him she was on her way to the radio; in fact, "the radio" was one of the picture galleries open at that early hour. There, she stared at the pictures hours on end. It was warm inside the halls and a few pictures really impressed her. Some of the curators noticed that the sleeves of her coat looked suspiciously frayed and were by no means becoming to her. Arma struggled with life and her battle resembled a grain of wheat that tried to burgeon amidst the sands of the Sahara, i.e. a project doomed to failure. Di, her daughter, had suggested a month or so before, "Mother, I can explain to you the basic moves of the relaxing massage. It is true people prefer young masseuses, but there are always lonely, aging gentlemen who gladly trust mature ladies with gray hair and golden autumn in their eyes."

"I can imagine their greasy backs," Arma sighed and added she planned to go "to the radio."

Several years ago, her husband, a man who claimed he was a

sculptor, but in fact repaired cars severely damaged in road accidents, abandoned Arma. He often told his wife he had to work in his studio, understanding "studio" as a young woman's place. The young woman was usually ready to share his solitude for a certain sum of money she had previously demanded and he had readily provided. Very often Di's father went "to his studio," and her mother "to the radio." That was the reason why Dilina, who had inherited her father's swarthy skin and her mother's dark eyes, was constantly alone. In the end, her father moved into his "studio" for good, living month in month out with each of his young girlfriends in turn. This situation did not stop Di from visiting him.

"I need money for my study at the university," she told him, not bothering to beat about the bush. She made friends with his girlfriends and if these haughty young women were in cheery mood, they bought her a dinner or a lunch at not very expensive restaurants.

"It is nice you study so diligently..." her father remarked leaving his sentence hanging dubiously in the air. "Find a job that will bring you steady income, massage for example."

In the beginning, Di massaged her father's girlfriends using the narrow room in the back of his improvised car service. The place was grimy, abounded in cockroaches, and smelled of lubricants, but Di had a natural talent for rubbing people's backs. Her father's girlfriends, whom he changed at a fast speed, appreciated the touch of Di's exquisite fingers. They all moaned with pleasure; the nervous tension ebbed away from their asses and shoulders as Di stood silent, enigmatically swarthy, taut as a bow-string, watching them with her inscrutable black eyes.

Later, if her father's girlfriends could read Di's thoughts, in all probability they'd accuse her of being a leech. Di dreamt of remaining as long as possible in her client's houses: it was warm there, the furniture was usually good, and the carpet felt soft, clean and thick.

In the one room flat where Di and her mother lived, the central heating was out of order and, for the time being, there was no running hot water. The refrigerator was damaged and in winter they stored their food on the balcony. It was a near-death experience to fight hunger while waiting for the pot of French beans to boil on the only hot-plate of the cooking stove whose metal frame had rotted. Her mother was grateful the stove had not disintegrated.

The first thing Di dreamt of was a lavish dinner; her whole being responded to the fragrances of food like Pavlov's dog. She had the impression that instead of blood her heart was full of saliva which flooded her mouth at the enticing smell of bacon. So, Di tried hard to be friendly, no matter that her mother despised the young women her father preferred to her. Slowly, Di's aversion to naked female bodies gave way to dull indifference; at times she thought she wouldn't turn down a massage of a cow's hoof if they gave her a good fee and dinner in return.

In the evenings Arma and Di almost never talked, but their silences were rich and cozy.

If her mother said, "It was all right," Di knew that Arma had sipped on a magnificent cup of coffee with a friend enjoying the warmth of the coffee house, the free apple pie. She had even seen a film on the satellite program — luxury that sounded absurd in their one room flat.

"She was horrible," Di would say, meaning that Becky Aneva had made her repeat the massage three times.

In Di's opinion, Mrs. Aneva was a queer fish. She kept silent and Di thought her tongue was a slab of marble demanding great efforts to set in motion. When her client wanted the massage repeated, she only stirred the forefinger of her right hand.

Her skin was snowdrop white; Di's dark fingers glided over it, drawing hot swarthy spirals. At the very beginning, Mrs. Aneva left a little pile of banknotes and Di used the entire strength of her will not to think about the money. Very rarely, Mrs. Aneva would call "Dora!" and another young woman, strong like a fortress, entered the room carrying a tray in her hands. Di didn't care a fig about Mrs. Aneva or Dora. She tried to divine what smelled so good on the tray: perhaps Viennese rolls and fragrant coffee? Perhaps lamb sirloins sandwich? The very thought about it made her dizzy and her dark fingers pressed harder on Becky Aneva's tender and sensitive flesh.

Di was constantly hungry, her stomach turned into a separate being that wanted to get full to the brim. That tray on the table looked so good! But Becky Aneva was mean, oh, how mean she was.

"You hurt me," the client whispered once and her palm fell onto Di's dark fingers. Then deliberately, like a guillotine severing the victim's spinal cord, Aneva reached out, took the cup and sipped tiny gulps of coffee. Di could smell cream in it. After that the client sank her white, even teeth into the sandwich, sighed and ran her tongue over her lips. Di had the feeling she was about to die. Mrs. Aneva did not offer her any food, she chewed slowly on, shredding Di's stomach and Di, in spite of her enormous willpower pressed harder the tender flesh under her fingers. How long did this torture go on? No more than two or three minutes, but for Di a whole era in the evolution of mankind elapsed. As Becky Aneva chewed at her sandwich, amoebae slowly evolved, turning into invertebrates, and finally roared like starving dinosaurs.

"You are hurting me," Mrs. Aneva whispered again, and this time she was not lying: under Di's dark fingers her flesh glowed red. At that moment Di woke from her stupor and lifted her startled hands from the obedient body. "Dora, bring something for the girl, please," Mrs. Aneva said.

After a minute, Dora the fortress rushed into the room again. There was something on the tray: three fish sandwiches, pieces of sausage and some gorgeous salad that threw Di into uncontrollable fits of palpitation. Then the fortress brought coffee in a tremendous pot, which probably held a whole lake of the aromatic liquid. The brilliant proportions of Dora's body were commensurate with her brilliant mind: she had sensed Di's hunger in the air, and had delivered a mountain of delicious food. Di was very grateful to her.

"You can eat now." Mrs. Aneva's voice was quiet as if she were praying or whispering sweet nothings in her boyfriend's ear. Di took a sandwich, her dark hand flying like lightning to the food. She forced herself not to chew too quickly or swallow at such an enormous speed, but her stomach, a crouching beast of prey, yearned for food, longed for food, wolfed the food. Di also planned to wrap up one of the sandwiches for her mother who that evening had to eat French beans cooked two days ago.

"Can I take a sandwich for tonight?" Di asked, turning a blind eye to the huge humiliation that cut her words and boiled her brain.

"No," Becky Aneva responded studying Di's face. "Eat and do not take too long. I'm waiting for my massage."

The beast in Di's stomach calmed down after the second sandwich, she felt an indefinable languor, but she knew: now was the time to secure resources for a rainy day. She gorged herself on the third sandwich, cramming it doggedly, methodically into her body with the help of profuse gulps of coffee. Becky Aneva's gray eyes followed her, but Di had learned to live with humiliation. It was her constant companion, like narrow pinching shoes, which she could put on and get out of the room.

"Why don't you buy food with the money I pay you?" Becky asked her once.

"I have to save it for my education, Ma'am," Di answered.

The white skin absorbed the agility of her dark fingers and turned pearly pink under their insistence.

At the end of the massage, Becky Aneva said, "You are pretty. Why don't you find a man to live with? He might be willing to pay for your education."

"I have never tried," Di answered and that was the truth.

She had grown up a lonely child; perhaps that was why she liked empty rooms, deserted beaches, empty buildings and even old deserted villages. She was twenty-two and was still a virgin, a fact that would provoke sneers among her acquaintances. Di had no friends. In school, she had always sat alone at the first desk by the window, surrounded by her immaculate notebooks in mathematics and in English language, which her teachers admired. In her home, the one-room apartment, everything was neat, orderly as if there was an axis in her mother's mind around which the scanty pots of flowers were arranged symmetrically like the coins of an ancient gold treasure. Sometimes, bearing no relation to her present work, Di suddenly thought of her mother: thin, exquisite like a porcelain ornament in the house of a new-rich slob, looking funny in her frayed brown coat.

Di saw her mother standing in front of a picture. Her face was pure, her admiration genuine; she had forgotten she owed the ex-tycoon from the Bulgarian Telecommunication Company one hundred levs.

The ex-tycoon was a funny type indeed. He kissed her mother's hand passionately as he explained he had eaten smoked salmon then assured her that on the following day he'd treat her to something very delicious: oranges stuffed with tender meat of river crabs.

Her mother was a proud woman, but not proud enough to turn down the invitation. Her mother even had ... well, it had happened during one particularly cold night when the snow had turned the streets into a wasteland of mud and icy lumps, Arma came home freezing cold and said curtly to Di, "I have already slept with him." It was the first time they had talked about sex.

When Di was in her first year at the university her mother was stunned to find her daughter with a guy.

This guy was the wretch of the neighborhood. His mother was a famous divorced gynecologist who had an imposing list of patients. Her son was big and passed through the doors, his head bent low. His abdomen had the form of a tank turret. His hips were wide, his chest was huge and no girl in her right mind took him seriously. He had a limp and was given to long silences during which he was insignificant like the dust on an old cupboard.

Di hoped he was the type of man who would not scoff at her; she was afraid of being scoffed at more than of hunger. It had happened once. Di had thrust a Valentine in the coat pocket of a guy in her high school. The guy summoned her in the break between chemistry and biology classes and tore the Valentine and most of her classmates were around. The Wretch could spurn her, too, but no one would know.

Di had met him in the street and told him, "Come to my place at four pm."

The Wretch pushed through the door shoulder first fearing his torso would knock down the walls. Di quietly led him to the kitchen. The only room of their flat where she and her mother slept was a place she would let no one in. Di didn't offer the Wretch anything to drink, she pointed at a chair, but he refused to use it; maybe he had already broken several pieces of furniture under his buttocks, Di thought. She pointed to a small divan that was transformed by her mother's ingenuity into an elegant bed, but the Wretch refused to sit on it as well. Then Di asked him to take a seat directly on the naked cement floor, and the gigantic mass of the Wretch fastened himself to it.

Di felt sorry for the beefy man and offered him her philosophy textbook and her French grammar; he could sit on these and feel more comfortable. Then she carefully kissed him on the cheek, then, still more careful, her lips descended to his mouth. The Wretch froze under her. Di did not want to hurt him. Her hand slid to his belt, but the Wretch violently shook, and Di was scared. She tried to soothe him, and kissed his mouth again. At that moment her mother entered the kitchen and froze in her tracks.

"You and the tycoon from the Telecommunication Company," Di had started, and her mother's face glowed red as if a million crimson carnations circulated in her blood. Arma coughed and lifted her hands to her breasts. Di felt weak and brittle like the grass in front of their block of flats that everybody trampled, people and stray dogs alike, as they tried to shorten their way to the bus stop. She felt desperate love for the thin woman standing shocked in her frayed coat by the door. It was a pity Di had not prepared any meal and had earned no money. She was kissing the Wretch instead, a man as big as a hill who burned with shame sprawling on her French grammar textbook.

From that day on Di saw the Wretch only in the old-fashioned cinema of the neighborhood. She kissed him, touched him tenderly as he sat frozen under her fingers, enormous and handsome in the narrow chair. Then the tickets in the cinema became unbearably expensive, and the Wretch waited for Di near the front door of Becky Aneva's mansion. In the beginning, he hung around the beautiful house jutting out like a colossal molehill, then one day Mrs. Aneva's bodyguard grabbed him by the collar and kicked him in the back of his head. The Wretch sank into the world of chaos and it was a miracle the doctors in Pirogov hospital could bring him back to life. He had suffered a severe brain concussion. The private detective the gynecologist hired shortly after the accident tracked Di within a couple of hours.

"You are blackmailing my son," the doctor declared, the ice of a frozen ocean in her voice. Di's body was numb and tingling. "I am familiar with the fact that you provide massage services for a living. I know that in the mornings you eat cheap rolls for breakfast. Your mother regularly resorts to food offered by charity organizations."

"Yes, Ma'am," Di confirmed. "Your information is precise."

"Of course it is precise," the doctor cut her short and quoted the sum of money she had paid the well-known detective agency. Di imagined the gynecologist would want to pluck out her ovaries on account of the crime she had committed. Sunshine spilled over the ice in the eyes of the older woman instead. "I'd like to bring something to your attention, Dilina."

Di sank into the blizzard that raged in the gynecologist's blue eyes. It was freezing cold there.

"I think you exercise a positive influence on my son's intellectual and physical development," the Wretch's mother said. "He had stopped being sheepish since he made your acquaintance. Now I see pictures of women in his room, a thing that has not happened before. He shows interest in girls, and that is a step in the right direction. I'd like to make you an offer."

Di did not say anything. Much to her surprise she survived the snowdrifts in the gynecologist's blue eyes.

"Aren't you interested what my proposal is?"

"I suppose you will tell me about it even if I am not interested," Di answered.

The meeting took place in the reception room of Doctor Metova's clinic. There were colorful posters on all the walls that advertised oral innocuous contraceptives that had no side effects.

"I suggest you continue seeing Peter." The gynecologist's categorical voce made efforts to drive a nail in Di's consciousness and rivet her to the floor. "It is highly recommended you perform an intimate contact with him. Of course, you understand the meaning of the phrase 'intimate contact'". Di was silent as the gynecologist, congealing further, went on, "Of course, if some problems or complications arise you can rely on my competent medical assistance. You know what I have in mind. The services in my clinic will be free for you."

Di kept silent, her dark skin pulsating, but Di was accustomed to pressures and was not scared.

"I can assign a certain monthly allowance to you to compensate you for your services," the gynecologist added in a business like voice.

Di stood up. She was a good listener and the lady's monologue held her attention.

"It was a pleasure talking to you, Doctor Metova," the younger woman said. "I am sorry your son suffered an accident and I sincerely hope the doctors in Pirogov hospital helped him. I cannot accept your proposal for reasons of a personal nature that I cannot share with you."

"You do not know what you lose by declining my offer, Di." The doctor's voice was all over the place and the reception room froze. "If you change your mind you can bid farewell to massage. You will forget about hazards of contracting skin diseases caused by saprophytic fungi."

"There are many beautiful girls who would willingly accept your proposal, Ma'am," Di answered thinking of her mother's frayed coat and the dead pipes of the central heating.

She saw the cooking stove with the single hot-plate, the bathroom in which most of the tiles on the floor were missing, the sink and the faucet, which dripped water. She thought of the pictures her mother loved, of the ex-Telecommunication Company tycoon who won her attention with Viennese rolls in glistening wrappers with inscriptions on them written in German. The Wretch was huge and handsome and meek. He'd collapse if Di told him she intended to break with him. "To break" — what a stupid verb! There had been nothing to break between them but a few films in the cheap cinema. She had not watched the flicks, she had kissed him instead as he waited scared and tractable.

Di was sure she couldn't find another boyfriend like the Wretch. She feared broken relationships. Her parents' marriage was a trap that weighed her down. Di would not get involved with any person. She had no relatives but her mother. She thought she'd be humiliated by a divorce, perpetual lack of money. A young child's misery filled her with cold panic. She would not let that happen. But the Wretch was sure to fall ill if they separated and she kind of cared for him.

His father was a gynecologist as well, owner of a prestigious surgery clinic; the Wretch's parents divorced a long time ago and probably they both loved Peter very much and had ambitious plans for his future. Lost in thoughts, Di instinctively squeezed the belt of her skirt and wrapped it tight around her forefinger.

"One thousand dollars a month," the Wretch's mother declared. Di went on squeezing the belt of the German skirt. If she had been chewing something at that moment she would definitively have spit it out. One thousand dollars was one thousand dollars no matter how one earned them. If she remained in that room a minute more, she would have accepted the offer, so she stood up and made her way to the door.

"Look here, if you had fingered that belt of yours ten seconds more, you would have heard two thousand dollars per month." The gynecologist's statement hit Di head on. She stood in her tracks. "Now I offer you one thousand. Take it or leave it."

Di turned around and looked the famous doctor in the eye.

"Peter was telling me that he had a two-story apartment. He said he didn't like it, because he felt lonely there," Di said slowly.

"So what?" Doctor Metova exploded, her face on fire. Di thought that there were ballistic missiles in her eyes.

"Will it be possible for my mother to clean that apartment?"

"Shall I infer Peter has already taken you there?" the ballistic missile exclaimed.

"Yes, he has. As your private eye has perhaps informed you, the central heating is dead in my flat. It is cold there. Perhaps my mother could clean the rooms for a modest remuneration."

"Instead of hanging around in the picture galleries?" the physician added in a scathing tone of voice.

"Yes. She can prepare low calorie food for your son as well."

"No," the doctor declared. "One thousand dollars. If you don't accept...and if you go on wasting Peter's time in that cinema, I warn you: there are dozens of methods to dissuade you from doing so."

"I understand, Doctor Metova," Di answered. "Where can I meet with Peter if I accept your proposal?"

"Of course, I cannot have you in my house," the Doctor declared, her face lighting up just the same. "I can see we are making progress. I have a small luxury flat two blocks away from here. You can use it."

"When shall I get the money you've just spoken about?" Di asked.

"At the end of the month," the gynecologist answered. "Of course, be advised that my son will inform me how you treat him, if you are friendly or not. Let me make it absolutely clear: by the adjective 'friendly' I mean not only purely physical intimate contact, but warmth and understanding as well."

In other words, apart from being his whore you want me to be his nurse as well, Di thought, then she said aloud, "I think you are right, but I am not sure if Peter will accept your plan."

"It is only natural he will," the gynecologist assured her.

Di remembered the quiet eyes of the Wretch, his waddling gait, and his futile efforts to repair the old tiles in the bathroom and then patch up her mother's old boots. The Wretch studied medicine and had flunked three exams.

Even before Di learned he was the son of famous doctors, she had seen the Wretch many times sitting on a bench in the City Park staring at beautiful women who passed by him. He was on that bench when she talked to him for the first time.

"I notice you are often here," Di had said.

At that time she had saved a meager sum of money and planned to have the obsolete TV set repaired; it had suddenly stopped broadcasting the eight free programs available in the country. The TV had gone blind like an old loyal dog in the corner of the only room they had.

"I have to bring a TV set to the shop to have it repaired. The shop is quite near. Can you carry the thing for me? I will pay you."

The Wretch accepted right away, but when Di handed him some money, which had turned wet in her palm, he refused to take it, assuring her it was a pleasure for him to give her a hand. Several afternoons after that Di sat beside him on the bench and kissed his forehead before she went home. The Wretch's skin flamed crimson from the forehead to the neckline of the enormous T-shirt that enveloped his stomach. Di liked that.

"Wait for me here again tomorrow," she told him.

To her surprise the Wretch not only waited for her, but also had bought a bag of popcorn and two sandwiches. Di told him about the backs she massaged, about her study at the university and, before she went home, she kissed his forehead.

"I will kiss you like that until you become a happy man," she said. "I want you get out of that dreary and lonely park."

"But then I couldn't see you," the Wretch said.

At that moment Di noticed his chest was moving as if it was a patch of earth rippling in a dangerous earthquake. His eyes were peaceful and happy. She took him to their one room flat where her mother had found them.

It turned out Peter had accepted his mother's plan. Well, what the hell! One thousand dollars per month sounded very convincing. Di didn't know why she felt so sick.

"HAVE YOU GOT A BOYFRIEND, Di?" For a second, Di could not understand the question. Her whole attention was dedicated to Mrs. Aneva's soft, sweet-scented skin. That lady was a quiet, exceptionally squeamish client, and that suited Di just fine. The acme of the massage session was approaching: the moment when Mrs. Aneva would dial a number on her cellular phone. That call would pull strings in the mysterious interior of the house and in would rush the young lady, unshakable like a medieval fortress, carrying the tray with sandwiches and an enormous coffee-pot. The thought of these made Di's hair bristle up.

She was hungry; quite deliberately she had not had lunch, leaving the plate full of stewed leeks for her mother.

"Have you got a boyfriend, Dina?" Mrs. Aneva repeated.

That was untypical of her; she was never curious about anybody's business. The answer to the question was a crow capable of driving its beak into your eye.

"You pressed me harder than a minute ago, so I assumed you were thinking about your boyfriend."

"I have no boyfriend," Di answered.

"Why? You are a pretty young woman."

Di said "thank you" and shut up, carefully avoiding the slippery path of long explanations: her mother's divorce, her constant fear she would be the object of gossip and ridicule. Was the Wretch her boyfriend? She had not yet taken the one thousand dollars from the gynecologist.

"Sometimes I suspect you have a peculiar attitude to me," Mrs. Aneva started, pursing her beautiful lips.

The air around Di solidified.

"You possess a remarkable set of professional skills, but of late you press me in a particular manner. Why?"

"I assure you I have no other concern but your highest satisfaction, Ma'am."

"You used the word 'satisfaction'. Why?"

"I assure you my desire is to make you feel satisfied."

"Only that?"

Di did not answer. She thought that today the sandwiches did not appear on time. It occurred to her that she was hot, so hot that she felt rivulets of sweat digging crimson canals down her face. Well, the fee she would get after the massage was over was quite attractive. Di and her mother would spend it on food.

"It is my pleasure to work for you, Mrs. Aneva."

"Aren't you my husband's spy?" The client's fine skin reddened furiously as she added, "Perhaps you know that the fee I pay you comes from his account in the bank."

"No, Ma'am, I didn't know that. And I am not Mr. Anev's spy."

"Aren't you?" the beautiful woman sighed.

Silver bells sang in her bosom, and her bright eyes the color of cornflower spilled their golden dust over Di.

"Please, repeat the last series of spirals on my back. Thank you. It is strange," the silver bells rang once again. "My husband had a serious conversation with me this morning."

Di felt the sweaty rivulets flow into her heart. Her fingers suddenly grew wet.

"Your fingers sweat," Mrs. Aneva remarked pointedly, but the golden dust in her eyes descended onto Di's swarthy face. "I don't like your fingers when they are wet," she added. "No, you needn't wash your hands now. Do you know what my husband asked me this morning?"

Di gave a start.

"He stressed the fact that I spend more time with you than with him. Then he asked me if I preferred your company to his. Don't stop the massage, please."

Di had instinctively lifted her palms in the air and Mrs. Aneva's skin recoiled like a frightened lizard.

"Do not press me so hard."

Di looked through the window. It was very cold outside. She thought that her synthetic leather boots would leak water. Perhaps she could get warm if she ran all the way home.

"My husband would like to make your acquaintance. It seems your popularity as a massage expert is growing," Mrs. Aneva said softly.

Di was silent.

"What will you say to that?"

Di said nothing.

"I would strongly recommend you decline the offer, but of course it is entirely your choice."

The eyes the color of cornflower weighed on Di's face then slid along a deep, blue parabola over the unobtrusive oval of Di's breasts. "So, you don't have a boyfriend and would not share with me the reason for that. Perhaps you wonder why I don't offer you sandwiches today. We both know their wonderful taste."

Di did her best to push back her sigh deep into her throat.

"I do not offer you sandwiches today, Di, because my husband will meet with you at six pm sharp. Please, don't press me so hard. Don't be in a hurry to finish my massage earlier than necessary. I'll decrease your fee if you do that. Do I make myself clear?"

*** *** ***

Moni

PERHAPS ONE OF THE lavish garden parties thrown by my mother marked the beginning of Gallantine's era of fame. He used to be and still is one of the exceptionally interesting types in our backwater town. When God created humankind He bestowed too many teeth upon Gallantine; I had the feeling he looked at me with his teeth and he never failed to notice the smallest details in people's behavior or clothing. My mother sighed and pined for him. After she had integrated herself in the city elite, she developed a taste for refined gentlemen and Gallantine was so refined that he could not recognize his own image in the mirror. Probably the bevy of young swallows (that was how the daughters of the elite families were dubbed), would stone me dead if they read my description of Gallantine. He was the delicacy dish on the menu of my mother's parties. It was at one of those parties that a male individual courted me in the most refined way. Of course, I sprawled in a custom-made chair the size of two easy chairs. I suppose my buttocks were overflowing in pessimistic waves toward the floor as my mother hurled the nets of her eyes to catch

Gallantine. That gentleman was a lawyer or was on the verge of becoming one if you judged by his great pains to stand out by the juridical terminology he lavishly used. So that remarkable legal functionary sat by my side, stuffed two hundred Latin wise sentences into my ear, then whispered, "May I have the pleasure of dancing with you?"

Had I been a more sensitive soul I would have eaten the carpet under his boots or at least would have jumped with happiness. But I imagined he would look like an exhausted exclamation mark at the end of the interminable sentence of my body. His smile consisted of sugar syrup that streamed down my breasts. That sobered me up.

"Yes, you may dance with me. I will be free in about twenty-five minutes," I declared with the hesitant voice of a beauty that everybody was dying to dance with.

"It will be my pleasure," Gallantine lied.

I went on studying the group of the intellectuals invited to my mother's party: two financiers, plus wives smelling sweet of French perfumes. My mother hung about them, rustling the skirts of her dress in a very concerned manner indeed. It was Italian and cost six thousand US dollars that my father had paid. I provide the precise price of the dress on purpose; my mother respected people who discussed how much her garments cost. She rushed enthusiastically to Gallantine bathing him in the golden torrent of her voice.

"Mr. Gallantine," she exclaimed. "I suspect you might be a little bored here. Could you possibly tell me what you think about..." and he ran to tell her what he thought, but returned to me very quickly.

After exactly twenty-five minutes he was holding me, trying to make me dance. I'd rather say I squashed him under my mass, the eyes of the whole party glued to us. I supposed that most of the guests were expecting I'd trip over the carpet and spread Mr. Gallantine in a thin layer on the floor under me.

"Do you know you are a very charming young woman?"

That was the young lawyer's first sentence and it sounded quite promising. It was evident he made efforts to smile at me as he intently watched Veronica in the meantime. She was a magnificent blonde who studied pedagogy; my father sponsored her scientific research when he was still alive, spreading himself too thin between his pedagogical endeavors and my mother's attractions. I suspected that in spite of his immense loyalty to my mother, my father indulged in pedagogy every now and then. Apparently Gallantine was attracted by that science as well. It would be my pleasure to stick a pin in his juridical ass, but the event that followed made me stare at my mother. It was the first time I had seen her as miserable as if she had been kicked out of the Institute of Social Sciences where she made titanic efforts to study law.

"I heard many people talk about your sharp wit," Gallantine added to the cologne of his flatteries. "In fact, let me admit I am a little afraid to tell you about the thing I have on my mind."

"There are no reasons to panic," I encouraged him.

Wild curiosity was eating me; what sort of a favor would he ask of my father? The compliment he presented me with made me think the man had set a very high goal before him.

"Will you marry me?" he said.

It was only natural I stopped dancing. Perhaps I had stepped too heavily on his toes, for his face blanched.

"Didn't your mother prepare you for our conversation?" Mr. Gallantine asked. "I asked her to."

For some incomprehensible reason Mother had failed to provide that precious information. My suitor's zest for life had obviously abandoned him.

"Will you marry me?" the lawyer repeated — this time he sounding rather more convincing than before.

"This is a topic of serious conversation," I remarked.

I had noticed that my prospective husband stared at the blonde pedagogue putting all passion and despair in the world in his eyes.

"I would like to discuss things with you in greater detail," I said.

His pale face grew almost as green as my eyes.

"You do not trust me," he concluded. After a second however he seemed to recollect something and added, "Okay. Now it's as good as any other time."

He touched my elbow tenderly, his palm sinking up to the wrist into my blubber, then dragged me towards the terrace. My father had bought marble from Torino, Italy, for Mother was delighted when the elite spoke about her terrace and marble from Torino. At such moments she felt like a full-fledged lady.

"It's so wonderful here!" the lawyer sighed and stumbled over a little naked statue of Eros in the middle of the terrace, around which Torino marble vases jutted out.

"Gallantine," I grabbed him by the hand and lifted him from the roseate marble he had hit his head against. "I will marry you."

My instantaneous consent to become Gallantine's wife made him very happy. He coughed and droplets of saliva flew at a considerable speed in all directions around his head.

When at last his jubilation abated he took a deep breath, looked into my eyes and said, "It is all right, dear. Now I'd like to list some conditions you have to bear in mind."

The denouement in the play approached: I was going to learn all crucial considerations on the part of the young semi-god who was making serious efforts to become my husband.

"I am listening," I reminded him.

*** *** ***

NORA

SEVERAL YEARS AGO there was a smudged piece of yellow linoleum on the floor in the corridor, but the memories of that time were lost in the present painful lack of money. Nora feared the minute when the corridor with the smudged linoleum would catch her in its stone throat. As she returned home, her twin brothers rushed to the front door and, though the two of them were already much taller than she, they asked, "Have you brought us something to eat?"

They were students in the local high school, the first boy an excellent one, the second much poorer; their mother commuted to the capital every day in the morning and in the evening. She came back home dog tired, hungry, and her face told them she had not been paid again. The regular story was that the boss had assured her she'd collect her salary "the following day". That "following day" had not come for three weeks now.

It was autumn in the gray wells of her mother's eyes. It made Nora stay in the narrow apartment; she remembered the time when the wallpaper in the children's room was still new. It was the same wallpaper, but the glue had turned into dust at places and it hung to the floor. Her brother's pictures were still visible over the faded flower patterns. Nora's father, a mechanic, unemployed for a year, had finally succeeded in finding a job in Dubai and worked as a plumber at a third rate hotel. He went there seven months ago but not a single dollar of his had appeared on their kitchen table, and there was no sign of his Dubai well being.

Nora worked as a waitress in The Greasy Café, a cheap café huddled under its dull asphalt roof. On her way to work, Nora saw the crows that hung like black rags on the branches of the poplars.

From the first day of its existence, the café had boasted gorgeous names: The Playful Jasmine, Jasmine being love number one of the owner; then, the establishment became The Playful Darina; after that, The Playful Ella and Cathie. As one could easily conjecture those were the first names of the irresistible ladies who captivated the heart of the proprietor at one time or other. Nora knew all four of them simply because they came and quickly went away at the time she was grilling the pork steaks in The Greasy. The patrons of the sleazy drinking house chose to accept Nora as its brand image.

In the evenings, after her brothers asked her if she had brought them something to eat, they expected she'd produce fried chicken wings or french fries, the cheapest delicacies in town, which smelled slightly of rot. Nora went to work very early in the morning when the Struma River did not yet stink of lubricants and oil; at the café, she fried chicken wings and chicken livers for the morning shift workers, thus adding a limited amount of money to her scanty remuneration. She often managed to furtively thrust some wings and livers in a plastic bag which she took to her brothers. They waited for her as if she were rain after six months of scorching drought. Evil tongues spread rumors that the chickens had died of fowl pox in Greece a month or so ago and one could eat them only after downing some glasses of cheap brandy dubbed "Stone-buster". Nora's brothers neither fell ill nor did their lymphatic glands swell, so they waited for the fried chicken livers their sister brought to them and chewed happily late into the night.

Even Nora's mother, known for her squeamishness among the tenants of their block of flats, ate the underdone chicken livers. Hoping against hope, she still expected her salary for several months and was ready to eat absolutely anything. Nora's fried livers made her a little dizzy, but the woman never spoke about that because she did not want to upset her sons. The boys left french fries for her, too, and she chewed at them slowly and painstakingly. Her teeth were no good; maybe that was the major reason Nora worked on as a waitress, brand image, cook, coffee maker and charwoman in The Greasy Café. She didn't know who would bring her mother and her brothers fried chicken livers if she quit her job.

Her father had rung up their neighbors and had mentioned that he could arrange for Nora to come and work at the same hotel in Dubai. She was such a beautiful girl, her father thought, and a good young man wouldn't hesitate to marry her there. But what would her mother eat in the evenings if there were no french fries to chew on with her teeth that were no good at all.

The proprietor of Greasy, a tall scraggy guy, as bald as an airport, had given his eatery a new name: Playful Nora.

"Hey," he turned to Nora one day as his greenish eyes gave her the once-over. "Would you care to have sex with me?"

Nora was making meatballs at that time and her boss's offer took her by surprise. Her hands sank wrist-deep into the pile of the minced meat. That question had a colorful history: first, playful

Jasmine had given a positive answer to it. The couple was quite happy for seventeen days, then playful Jasmine was fired. Playful Darina's, Ella's, and Cathie's love for Gozo, the owner of The Greasy Café, had developed in a similar fashion, so Nora assessed her chances of staying in Gozo's heart as no more than a fortnight.

"The meatballs you make look fine," her boss said thoughtfully. "I want you tonight at my place. You can be an hour late tomorrow. That will be your compensation."

"Tonight at my place" meant sex in the decrepit bungalow which Gozo used as a warehouse. He brought all his sweethearts to it and a day or two after the remarkable event, a new lady's name embellished the facade of The Greasy Café. Rumors had it that if Gozo wanted to make a woman his wedded wife, he'd invite her to his mansion that had a swimming pool in the backyard. Gozo's parents lived there and he was their only son and scion.

"You know that my father left our family," Nora spun carefully the thread of her refusal as she fought panic. "My mother gets no salary at all. In the evenings, I have to go home and cook dinner for my brothers."

"So your answer is no?" Gozo's voice hit her. "I suppose you know what that means."

"What?" Nora asked innocently.

"It means I don't want to see you here," the boss explained matter-of-factly, thrusting his big hand under his silk jacket.

A very positive feature of Gozo's inimitable clothing style was his love for silk garments. Although his suits were dirty without exception, they all were made of pure silk. He took out a ragged banknote from his breast pocket and threw on the table.

"Here is your salary. Take it and get out of here."

"I hoped there was something true and genuine between us," Nora muttered, trying hard to loosen the rope of the gallows which tightened around her throat.

Gozo's face was totally expressionless, and this was a sure sign that Nora's trick about "anything genuine between us" wouldn't work.

"The minute I entered your café I had been thinking about our love..."

Gozo made a step towards her and she calculated he could push her down onto the floor. He had already drunk half a bottle of strong Greek brandy.

That was the second positive aspect of his personality: he fought his bad breath drinking expensive alcohol.

"I have always been scared by the other girls who attracted you," she ventured.

Gozo snorted, said the other girls were all sluts and slowly pushed Nora to the wall. Not only his breath, but his eyes smelled of Greek brandy as well.

"I'd like to wash my hands. There's minced meat on them," Nora said trying to wriggle out of his grasp.

"I don't want you to do it with your hands," Gozo assured her as he buried his nose in her neck. "I don't like fat women. Ella, Stella... You are the first skinny one in the row. What are you waiting for, eh? Take off your skirt." He cursed the skirt and cursed her blouse. "You're more scraggy than a whip, chick."

At that moment, a big rasping voice echoed in the Creasy Gafé.

"I want a glass of Jim Beam."

"Fuck off," Gozo shouted.

"Now," the voice added calmly.

Gozo's hand let go of Nora's breasts and she took a deep breath.

"I told you very politely to fuck off," the café owner turned to the visitor. "If you carry a chip on your shoulder, that's all right,"

Gozo's hand sank beneath the counter and pulled out a heavy iron bar.

Nora sighed; she'd have to wash the blood from the concrete floor one more time. The naked concrete had started crumbling, and it was hard to clean it properly.

Months ago, when Gozo still had no crush on her, he ordered Nora to throw out the drunks who kicked up rows and fought in Greasy. Nora cashed in on their squabbles; the guys who were not plastered enough betted who would be the first to bleed in the fight. Nora passed through them collecting the money in an aluminum bowl, then selected the drunkard who was beaten black and blue, and quietly dragged him to the outskirts of the park. That was a patch of land strewn with squashed plastic cups and empty brandy bottles. Nora made her best effort not to hit the man's head against the stones. Sometimes, the patrons of Greasy gave her a handful of change before they got drunk for the evening and later she propped them up against a tree in return. The more well-to-do among them gave her a fiver and, after Greasy closed, Nora took the guys by taxi to their homes in the big blocks of flats. She left the drunk prostrate on the stairs, rang the bell, and hid behind the pillar in the corridor watching the wife open the door. The drunken husband usually smashed his nose against the floor of his own home. Some of the men thought Nora was a good-natured soul, but she strongly doubted that. She simply worked hard to get their money. The truth was she liked the drunks, but hated cleaning their blood from the battered cement floor.

"A glass of Jim Beam!"

The brand image, cook, charwoman, and meatball maker of Greasy expected another pool of blood, groans, and moans under the roof of the facility; Gozo beat his victims and, more often than not, broke their limbs. The drunks knew his ways and if Gozo's god-like figure loomed large behind the counter, they shut up, spitting reverently on the floor.

"Oh, welcome! Come in, please! Make yourself at home. Once again, welcome! I am so happy to meet you on my turf, Sir! Mr. Anev!" For the first time in her life, Nora witnessed a miracle: Gozo's voice turned into butter and its unctuous waves flowed towards the newcomer.

"That's the best whiskey, Sir! Here you are, Sir! Jim Beam is as clear as a baby's tear, which is what I have always thought. Perhaps you'd like a cube of ice?"

"Get out of my way."

"Of course, Sir! Here you are. The whiskey's as clear... I'll get out of your way immediately. I have a crystal glass here. Kept for my special guests... for my most special guests, Sir. It is made of German crystal, Mr. Anev, Sir. I brought it from Austria."

"Shut up."

"Nora!" Gozo shouted. "Quickly, move it. Come and bring the crystal glass to the gentleman!"

The man Nora was about to attend upon had spoken once on the local TV network and that was enough for the town population to swear at him for many years to come. That guy had bought the metallurgical combine, then took possession of the plant producing pipes and the glass factory, plus all collieries in the county. He was tall, narrow-shouldered; his gray leather jacket cost more than The Greasy Café, its patrons, their blood spilled on the floor, and the crystal glass for the special guests. Nora closely watched the new-comer's face: gray, narrow, and immobile. She brought the special guest's glass and placed it on the table in front of him. It seemed to her the greasy smudges on the faded plastic tabletop were enormous. That could hardly make the owner of the whole town feel at home. In fact, some of the new owners of other towns had made their fortunes out of the same cheap plastic tables, crumbling concrete floors, and people like Nora who cleaned the blood from the cement surfaces.

The expensive sleeve of Mr. Anev's leather jacket fluttered like an eagle's wing. His fingers grabbed the special guests' glass and chucked it onto the floor. The whiskey splashed over the floor and the glass burst into a handful of German crystal pieces.

"The waitress pushed my drink off the table," Mr. Anev declared placidly. "Bring me another glass. Jim Beam."

"But of course, Sir! Of course, Mr. Anev!" Gozo bent to the floor, his spinal cord a tape measure producing a soft deep bow before the illustrious gentleman. Nora dashed to the sideboard and brought another glass, an ordinary one this time. She poured whiskey into it and carefully set it in front of the great man.

He reached out his hand, his expensive sleeve fluttered again, the glass crashed against the concrete floor bursting into a hundred most ordinary shards of glass.

"Your waitress pushed my glass again," Mr. Anev complained. "She's very clumsy."

"Very clumsy, Sir!" the tape measure in Gozo's back bowed again.

"I'd like whiskey, please," the visitor ordered.

"Did you hear that?! You're incapable of serving a decent gentleman!"

Nora stood motionless. Anev's narrow face suddenly came alive, a Boeing aircraft that needed much free space to take off from the ground.

"You!" the Boeing said staring in front of him "Get out of here!"

"You heard him. Get out of here!" Gozo shouted looking savagely at Nora. "Shall I bring you another drink, sir?"

Nora was about to squeeze her way to the room where the meatballs and frozen chicken wings were stored. She suddenly wanted to bury her arms in the roseate heap of minced meat and beat it black and blue.

"The young woman will stay with me. *You* get out of here," Mr. Anev pointed his thumb at Gozo then watched his fingernails.

Gozo's face was suddenly a bucket of writhing worms. It was distorted and didn't know what to do. Nora watched. Gozo started for the door muttering excuses whose meaning was not quite clear.

"Nora, wash your hands first," Gozo grunted the minute he was about to leave.

"I didn't say you can go," Mr. Anev said, his eyes on Gozo's chest. "Bring a chair for that young woman and scram."

Gozo grabbed a chair and put it near the owner of the metallurgic plant.

Nora held the silver tray, the best object on the premises, a precious heirloom, on which she served Gozo a glass of brandy every evening before he left to go home.

"What's your name?" the important visitor asked.

"Nora."

The visitor sized up her legs, gazed at the mounds of her breasts, then again concentrated on the legs.

"Would you like to change your job, Nora?"

Nora did not answer. Answer him, stupid cow, Gozo would have hissed had he been here. The illustrious visitor took his glass and slowly poured some of the whiskey under the table.

"Nora, you are being clumsy. Look what you've done. Will you clean the floor, please?"

"I will not clean it, Sir," Nora said.

Then the stream of whiskey wetted the client's trousers leaving a stain, like a serpent's tongue, on the fine fabric on his crotch.

"I suggest you clean my slacks, Nora. Start, please." Nora stepped forward. "I'll appreciate your efforts."

After about half an hour, Mr. Anev's car roared along a dirt road. It was an epic sight: an expensive automobile creeping like a dung beetle through the ditches where fifteen-year-old Russian jalopies could be seen. Mr. Anev, the most important guest of The Greasy Café, the proud man who pulled the strings of the whole town, cut the engine and got out of his car. He was walking along the Struma River unbuttoning the six thousand dollars' worth of his jacket, no tie, no flower in his buttonhole. He trudged through the thorns, through the broken empty bottles and smashed plastic cups. Then he stopped to light his cigarette and spat into the water. He was dreaming: the Struma River made even the paving stones dream of summer sky. Now the zipper of his lips was undone, his face, a narrow piece of slate, looked content. The old scandalmonger, the river, ran too loudly in front of him, or Nora was skulking around so imperceptibly that Mr. Anev could not hear the low echo of her footfalls.

Nora slunk behind his back. Perfectly composed, as if she was about to buy a packet of cigarettes from the cheap stall at the bus stop, she produced a stone from the pocket of her apron. Her hand moved quickly. The round stone hit the pate of the smoking man, the most memorable visitor The Greasy Café had ever boasted of since the hour it was set up. The man collapsed by a heap of waste plastic cups. Nora chucked the stone into the river and walked slowly towards the nearby bridge. She felt like a million dollars. She thought she'd done a good job.

*** *** ***

Moni

I'D LIKE TO TELL YOU more about Gallantine. I knew he was waiting for me, exhibiting his athletic body (male athletic bodies are priority number one with my mother) on the divan my father had fetched from Italy. I supposed Gall would produce convincing arguments as to how sharp my wit was, how rich and colorful an imagination God had blessed me with, and how well I spoke English. I could only surmise that the attractive blonde lady, who constantly hovered around Gallantine and made it known far and wide she studied pedagogy, had probably written the text which Gallantine would use in order to declare how impatiently he wanted me to become his wedded wife. Well, her name was Veronica, the queen of pedagogic research.

Although I possessed the weight of a combat armored vehicle, I was well capable of getting on the nerves of little fluffy kittens like Gallantine. I had made him wait for me on that divan fifty minutes now and I hoped his handsome face was crushed like a doormat under the burden of his wounded pride. Who the hell dared make fun of him? I did, I, the fat heiress. He had perspired profusely, this was inevitable, and the smell of his first class sweat ruined the aroma of the deodorant liquid in which Gallantine swam every day.

It was a must with me that men had to be coerced into realizing how precious I was, so I intended to keep Gall on that divan an hour more. That was a trick I had learned from my deceased father, "A guy waiting in front of your door is a chunk of stale bread, my girl. A dog wouldn't sniff at it." The thought of Gallantine as stale bread breathed new life into me.

Somebody knocked at the door. It would be more precise to say kicked at the door as if he intended to wrench it out of its fixture and that, strictly speaking, was supreme arrogance. I would not allow a chunk of stale bread to ruin the property my father had bought at the price of his own blood. An anonymous bullet assisted Dad in successfully meeting his maker. My gentleman caller knocked repeatedly at the door made of yew wood my father had delivered from Belgium and I sent a maid to inform him I was not ready to see him. Then, Mother rang me up and spoke to me in a very concerned manner.

"Gall is coming to pop the question, dear," she sighed on the telephone. "Please, be friendly with him. You know how much that man loves you."

That man ardently loved all heiresses in town; he was a lawyer whose clients drove cars which were more expensive than the overall financial resources of our municipality. Gallantine had chosen me. That fact, apart from being an open acknowledgment of my father's money, was a topic that gave rise to unsavory comments about me.

I switched on my computer, riveted my heavenly eyes on the monitor, and called out, "Come in!"

"Good afternoon, my dear!"

I was right: his mouth did look like a worn-out doormat.

"You look swell today. Has your mother informed you what I intend to do now?"

"Yes, she has," I assured him, waiting for additional information.

"You are very beautiful," my prospective husband ventured and the doormat in his mouth cleaned my old sandals. It was obvious he wanted to appeal to me.

"I assumed you'd start with the assumption how intelligent I am," I interrupted him discreetly. "The intelligence of a human being is invisible. You can use that and be on the safe side."

"But you are really very beautiful."

My fiancé had evidently let his imagination run loose.

"Your eyes are green like..."

The comparison was too cumbersome to make and, willing to eliminate the awkward pause in the conversation, Gallantine pushed his lips into my mouth. In other words he kissed me, as a proper loving husband would positively do.

"You are an exceptionally intelligent woman and I really want you to be my wife."

He produced the same sentence several months ago as he tangoed around the excessive curves of my body at my mother's party. His offer did not surprise me at all. I was interested, however, in how much he would want in return for his self sacrifice.

"You are a person of rich and compassionate soul..."

"My soul is another good topic of discussion," I encouraged him. "It is invisible with the naked eye."

"I am serious... and I enjoy your sense of humor, too."

"Let's drop the unnecessary procedures."

My voice sounded dry like the sands of the Sahara.

"In spite of all your admiration for my soul, my sense of humor, my rich and colorful imagination, let us concentrate on my considerable weight."

"You are so pretty," my future husband repeated stubbornly. Gallantine lacked both inspiration and imagination, and reiterated, "You are so pretty..."

I remembered the scrawny gypsy lad who had used some very similar words. Suddenly, I badly wanted to be with that lean gypsy. He, the poor soul, frittered away all money I had paid him on those nasty sausages. I loved him.

"Yes. Yes, you really are quite... how shall I put it... bosomy. Yes. You are fat. And fat is fat. Well, you know it's important to get on with one's marriage partner from the spiritual point of view. In order to understand one's partner spiritually, one needs money."

"Gallantine," I said. "How much money do you need to understand me spiritually after you become my husband?"

"You are intelligent, I grant you that. And I appreciate the fact you speak to the point... no prejudice, no beating about the bush."

"Yes," I whispered changing the approach to our conversation. "You know what? I really thank you very much. You are such an attractive man and I am such a ... fattie."

The clouds in the sky witnessed my humiliation. They knew: I preferred gulping down the toads in all swamps of Bulgaria to uttering abject words about me. Well, my father used to say, "Let the brassy idiot clamber atop your head, my girl. Leave him there for a minute to check how deep into your brain he'll try to spit. Then squash him in the mud under your boots."

"Yes, you are fat," Gallantine agreed, the weighing machine in his eyes measuring the tonnage of my buttocks. "Yes, you are. You are positively familiar with the fact that your mother approves of me."

Yes, I knew she approved of him on Tuesdays and Fridays in the afternoon after she had had her lunch and the beautician had refreshed her face with pineapple juice. Gallantine, however, decided to explain to me what that exactly meant.

"Your mom's great... You will become my wife. You will be Mrs. Taleva. Can you imagine it? There will be only one Mrs. Taleva in the whole country. You will that lady. But, as you know very well, everything in the world has a price," he dropped the bait of his sentence and let it hang in the air as he inserted its sharp hook into my stomach.

I had to keep my mouth shut and my eyes glued to the parquet floor. If I looked at this hamster, his poor ass would burst into flames. Even Gallantine would sense I was about to shoot him dead.

"Of course, the price is high," the hamster produced the end of his statement. "Forty percent of your father's property, my dear, and you will become Mrs. Taleva in return. If you interpret this sentence from the standpoint of diplomacy, it means that you'll be welcome to all drawing rooms of the elite, although I find it hard to imagine what you'll talk to these people about. Perhaps you'll have to read some books on art or on law. I have built my reputation painstakingly for so many years now. You'll be invited to all major receptions and you'll have at your disposal..."

"Forty percent is too high a price," I blurted out, then I swallowed my rage and shut up.

"Apart from your sojourns in the elite houses of the capital, I will be in your bed once a month on a regular basis," Gallantine assured me.

It was evident he was not overjoyed to take this opportunity.

"Perhaps you'll get pregnant, although I strongly doubt it..."

If my father had heard about the young snail's plans he would have crushed his shell.

"Thank you," I whispered, carefully pulling open the drawer of my desk. "Probably the rest of the month you'll share my mother's company... or that of the blonde lady you study pedagogy with."

"Yes, you are quite right, dear. Man should not live in loneliness, don't you think? You and I can often talk on the telephone — for example, Mondays in the morning. Let me sum it up: forty percent, and let us decide on the date of our official wedding ceremony. If you conceive a child by me, dear, all doors of legal entities and institutions will be open for him. I personally will introduce him to a number of eminent families. His photographs will be in all newspapers. As for you...you are his mother anyway."

"Perhaps all that deserves fifty percent of my father's property," I whispered.

Anger burned a tunnel into my brain, but a fat young woman like me should never drive the sledge of anger.

"What will you say about sixty percent?" I purred, sticking my eyes into my belly button. I had no desire to look at him.

"You know what? You are very fat, but you're cool," the hamster smiled encouragingly, making a pass at me. "Sixty is my favorite number."

"I don't need money," I lied brazenly. "All I need is your love. If I make it sixty five percent, will you visit my bed twice a month?"

Gallantine's face lit up inspired by the vision of our bright future.

"You are very cool! Very cool indeed!" he whispered. "If you want we can make love here and now!"

I had already managed to open the desk drawer, so I thrust my fat hand into it, and dragged out a Makarov pistol. Makarov is a good gun and I hope my father had made proper use of it before his competitors sent him to the world beyond. I lifted Makarov's muzzle to Gallantine's mouth, although the man had already planted his hand in the glen between my breasts.

"What about eighty percent?" I asked, pressing Makarov against his forehead.

My future husband choked as he gulped the air under his nose.

"Get...th...this gun aa...way!" he stammered chopping the words with the red saw of his tongue. "G..g...get it away!"

I hit his nose with the handle of the pistol.

"Would you like eighty five percent?" I repeated the question in a pleasant tone of voice.

Perspiration ran down his smooth forehead.

"I am a very good shot," I lied. "This piece of iron has got a silencer."

My future husband grabbed at his stomach with both hands, ready to throw up any minute now; a big blonde pile of legal knowledge stewing in his own juice. He had probably wet his high-quality pants.

"Tomorrow you will introduce me to the eminent families in the capital of Bulgaria and I will prepare your business program for the week."

He pressed his stomach with both hands and was on the verge of puking on the parquet floor my father had delivered from Spain.

"D..d...don't sh..shoot!"

"The day after tomorrow, December 20th, you and I will pay a visit to Mr. and Mrs. Anev."

The hamster groped for his heart. He had a sore throat, no doubt about that, for he tried hard to spit something out of his foaming mouth.

"Yes... y..yess, dear."

"Otherwise, you'll acquire an exceptionally interesting part of my father's property, a nice leaden bullet in the medulla oblongata. I hope it makes exactly seventy five percent of my father's assets, doesn't it?"

I was afraid that Gallantine was unable to calculate the exact percentage just now. The doormat on his face cleaned my slippers and Gall, the most prestigious catch at parties, trembled and shook like an aspen leaf.

"Dear," I croaked using all my compassion. "If someone learns how you asked me to become your wife — a proposal, which I have already accepted — I will make sure you won't survive to attend the next meeting of the lawyers' league. Do I make myself clear?" I pressed my father's Makarov harder against my future husband's forehead and got no reply, alas. That induced me to force a part of the muzzle between Gallantine's crimson lips.

"Well, will you love me loyally and with all your heart till death do us part?"

It is difficult for a human being to speak with a muzzle of a gun between his or her teeth, but Gallantine coped with this impossible situation.

"Yes, I will love you," his words did not sound sad, although I saw tears in his eyes."

*** *** ***

74

NORA

SHE WALKED SLOWLY, trapped in the shabbiness of her second-hand coat. The happy days of fried chicken livers and French fries in the old apartment on the fifth floor were over. Nora was no longer the brand image of The Greasy Café; she had become the brand image, waitress, charwoman, and meatball maker in another eatery, The Dove, whose owner was a belligerent middle-aged lady. That woman could draw blood from a stone, milk a snake, or sell the dust Nora had collected in the vacuum cleaner as powerful medicine for chest infections. Nora could not scrounge a penny from The Dove because the warrior constantly watched her, directing the searchlights of her eyes to Nora's hands.

It was snowing and the air was wet, cold and very unpleasant. Nora's boots leaked and her feet turned into ice in the freezer of December. Nora approached the drab facade of The Greasy Café, her lips a scared arc, then she plucked up courage, strode across the road to the eatery newly painted in a threatening red color.

She set the door ajar and was instantaneously aware of the fact that The Greasy Café had acquired a new brand image. That was the pimply new waitress, charwoman, meatball maker, and probably Gozo's new girlfriend.

"You must be Nora," Gozo's new beloved declared.

It was not necessary for Nora to answer in the affirmative; the girl rapidly pulled out an iron bar under the countertop.

"The boss said, "If she doesn't get out of here you throw her out."

The iron bar hung within a cigarette's length from Nora's intelligent face, but its menacing weight failed to impress her.

"Listen, bitch," the new waitress grunted, the avalanche of her voice advancing towards Nora. "He's mine, bitch. Is that clear?"

It was evident the new waitress was determined to clobber Nora's head, but at that very strategic moment Gozo's voice blared out, "Leave her alone!'

The pimply jaw of the new brand image hung desperately after she muttered something under her breath, then the girl dropped the iron bar onto the crumbling cement floor with apparent displeasure.

"But you told me to throw her out," Gozo's new beloved pointed out, hoping against hope.

"Get out of my way!" the owner of The Greasy Café bawled at her. "Beat it!"

Nora thought Gozo had changed: a straggly beard covered his face, his eyes shone like beacons at the seashore, and he was fatter of course. Nora recognized him by the oily smears on his apron and the pungent smell of his jeans.

"Oh, you dragged yourself here again, Nora," he grumbled.

"Good afternoon, Gozo," Nora greeted him, her voice wriggling its way to her ex-boss's heart, hard and invisible under his soiled apron. "I'd like very much to have a word with you."

"I knew you'd crawl in here," Gozo said and spat on the floor, the beacons of his eyes offering Nora a safe haven all the same. "Gozo's bitches always come back to lick his boots."

"I miss you," Nora whispered, ignoring the fact that none of Gozo's bitches had come back so far. "I really miss you," she repeated, her voice rising convincingly.

Her ex-boss's beard trembled with pleasure.

"Don't spin filthy yarns for me," he rumbled, just in case, then slowly, meticulously unbuckled the belt of his jeans. "You miss me, ah?"

Nora thought that his black beard would clog her mouth if he fancied kissing her. But probably he wouldn't do that; Gozo didn't go for sissy whims.

"Run to the kitchen," he ordered.

Nora did not start for the greasiest room in The Greasy Café, and its owner pulled her by the collar of her coat. He had torn her blouses a number of times in this manner.

"Take off that lousy coat," he said, then muttered it was too cold. "Okay. Don't take off the coat. Take off your pants and sprint. How can you ask me where! To the kitchen damn it!"

"Gozo..."

Nora felt her voice was not soft enough so she passed it through the mill of her teeth and the words went out frozen and dead like the skinned hares hanging on the hooks in the larder.

"What do you want?" he asked.

"Gozo," she tried to draw his attention, but he had focused his energy on the buttons of her blouse.

"What? You don't have your period now, do you? If you dragged yourself here leaking..."

"No. I am pregnant, Gozo. I am pregnant with your child."

Gozo's hand that had dug a tunnel to her breasts under her coat dropped dead. A second later his sticky fingers clutched at her throat.

"You bitch."

Nora kept silent. The scenario could be painful, even deadly for her. Gozo could crash his fist into her face. She had foreseen that possibility and hid her head behind the roof beam. He could kick her in the stomach and Nora was scared she would lose consciousness, but she had taken due precautions against his evil disposition. She would crawl under the table.

"Gozo, you are everything to me... to me and to the child. I love you."

There was no kick in her stomach, but this did not mean the danger was over. Gozo took considerable time before he grasped the contents of the information he had received. Nora doubted he understood the meaning of the phrase "I love you"; probably he connected it with two bitches in his bed and a bottle of whiskey by his pillow.

No matter that, she repeated stubbornly, "I love you, Gozo."

She had studied basic psychology in school and she had learned that dogs loved to be spoken to affectionately.

"You are the only person in the world I have ever loved."

It seemed her quiet voice had brought Gozo to one of the rare serene moments in his life. Instead of crushing her forehead, his hand perched on her head. Nora stood in her tracks: he could twist her hair around his wrist, then hurl her against the wall. Gozo had done that several times to his ex-girlfriends. There were smears of dried blood on the walls in the kitchen, the places where he'd broken Cathie's and Elli's head. But now Gozo did not intend to thrash her with his fist, at least for the time being. Instead, his hand descended towards her abdomen and pressed it hard as if he wanted to catch hold of the baby under her skin.

"Bitch," he cursed quietly, then concluded, "Your belly's beginning to swell. Shit. You'll get fat and swollen if you don't get rid of that bastard."

"Gozo," the voice of the new waitress crawled under the door. "Can I come in, Gozo?"

"Beat it, bitch!" he roared, his palm pushing Nora's stomach, squeezing. "You're pregnant, eh? And you love me. Shit. Love or no love, it's your problem. The bastard's yours. But you're cool. Take off that lousy shirt. Come on, it ain't that cold. Take all your clothes off."

"Gozo."

His hands were all over her breasts, but Nora wasn't paying attention to the pain.

"Gozo... look at me! I am a pretty woman."

"Yea. You're cool. Lie on the table. Cool. You've got a problem. Your bloody problem is none of my bloody business."

"I am the prettiest of all your women. Stop! Stop and look at me!" Nora almost shouted with pain. "I am the best educated one as well. The kid will be handsome like me. A boy. You'll have a son, Gozo. I'm clever and you know it. You know how much money you made when I worked for you. Five times more than you earned with the other women. And the baby is your son."

"Don't lecture me, bitch. Lie on the table."

"Gozo," Nora whispered, running the risk of getting kicked in the mouth. "I telephoned your mother. I told her I'm expecting a baby by you."

She suspected she could not evade the trajectory of the fist if Gozo wanted to squash her jaw, yet she decided to have another try. His red-rimmed eyes gleamed faintly. That was dangerous, extremely dangerous.

"Your mother wanted to meet me. She and your father talked to me."

Gozo reached out to hit her, but Nora was prepared; she jumped and his fingers grazed her face harmlessly.

"Look, that's what your mother gave me."

Nora pulled a necklace out of her pocket: a cheap, ugly necklace of stringed glass balls. "

She used to put this above your cradle when you were a baby."

Gozo grabbed at the necklace and held it close before his eyes.

"Your mother liked me and..." Nora ventured on, but the end of the sentence froze in her mouth.

"She won't like scum like you."

"I'm no scum. I am a pretty woman. A very pretty woman and if you don't see it, then..."

"Then what?" Gozo barked, but he was not interested in the answer.

"Marry me, Gozo," Nora said. "Your mother liked me. I'm not lying to you. Ring her up, ask her and she'll tell you."

"You brazen bitch...but you're cool. Cool. Cool."

He was already on top of her taking intense pleasure in plucking the golden hairs on her thighs with his teeth.

"Why did you quit your job at Greasy if you loved me?"

"A woman loses something first, then becomes aware how much she misses it," Nora answered, parroting one of Gozo's favorite sayings.

"So you moved your butt out and then understood what you

lost?" he blurted out and bit her breast. "Don't fuck with me."

"Listen. I can get rid of the baby. It will cost 500 levs with a good doctor. I can borrow about 70 levs from a friend. But I love you, man. I love you."

"Shut up," the owner of The Greasy Café ordered, his voice sinking below her breasts.

"Marry me, Gozo," Nora repeated. "You and I together will make five times more money than you earn now. Remember, your mother liked me."

The mop of his beard stroked her stomach pleasantly. He did not reply and Nora continued, "Listen, it's true the child is my problem, but it's your child. He'll be strong like you."

Gozo looked down at her and, for a second, Nora thought he'd hit with the back of his hand. His palm only gagged her mouth causing almost no pain.

As his hand moved to her breasts, Nora said, "I'll wait until January 15th for you to marry me. On the 16th, I have an appointment with the doctor. I'll have an abortion. If you don't want the child you can give me some money for the doctor. A good doctor costs a lot."

She paused then added quietly, "Your mother wants the child. Your father wants it as well. Do you know what they told me? 'This the child will piss in golden swaddling clothes.'"

Gozo rose. He did not kick her, just balled his fists above her naked body prostrate on the table.

"You're the coolest bitch I've ever fucked," he grunted. "Yes, you are. Lie down. Quick!"

Nora sank onto the tabletop with the greasy smudges on which she had made meatballs and cut the chickens into small portions.

Her back stuck to a puddle of congealing chicken blood. Her leg hung over the crumbling cement floor, then she suddenly felt his sticky fingers dig into her scared skin.

"You're cool. Cool."

"Marry me."

Gozo rose above her. Nora felt the sticky taste of blood in her mouth.

*** *** ***

ARMA

Her brown coat was frayed at the shoulders. She suspected the shawl that concealed its sorry appearance was not fashionable. Her make-up was cheap and too shiny; although she had done her best to use it thriftily, she felt so down and out she could hardly suppress her desire to retrace her steps back home. But Arma knew she should not think of going back. Her daughter and she still had some banknotes in the cupboard drawer, the most loved place in their one room flat, and they had to live on them until the end of the week. Of course, she could borrow some more from Mr. Spiro, the ex-telecommunications tycoon, however she had already asked him for a loan. It felt bad to undress in his enormous bedroom, his eyes gray like worm-eaten bark of a tree slithering along her emaciated body. He could indulge in affairs with much younger women, she thought, but perhaps he was too stingy for that. Each time the retired telecommunications director told her, "Forget all about money I've given you," he inevitably continued, "With 400 levs one can buy..." and he enumerated the kilograms of cheese, pots of yogurt, bottles of beer, plus the medicines for his ailing kidneys, so it was very clear to Arma he remembered every single penny she owed him.

"I want you to marry me," one day Mr. Spiro mentioned in between the kilograms of cheese and cartons of yogurt. "On Mondays we shall eat pork meatballs. Tuesday we'll consume no meat, it's no good for the kidneys. Wednesdays, cheese, potatoes plus tomatoes, Thursdays, well, that's the day to collect the rent from tenants of the flats I own, plus the stalls I have at the marketplace. Saturdays, we'll have fish for lunch, soup, custard and fruit for dinner. You are quite attractive, Arma, my girl." Then, the worm-eaten bark in his eyes touched her breasts which, Arma felt, hung like old pants on the back a chair. She was ashamed she had to talk again to that modern factory owner.

Arma remembered the sad poems by Lermontov and felt old-fashioned and hopelessly unemployed. She could not borrow money from Mr. Spiro. It was not so much the intercourse, but the cold obligation to engage in sex with that man on Mondays and Saturdays between 10 and 11 am on the fur of an old, unfortunate bear Spiro had killed as a young man, that made Arma feel plain.

"Mother," Di said one day. "I have good news for you. Mrs. Aneva is looking for a governess for her son Theo Junior. She provides good food, the house is warm,, and if she approves of you, she'd offer you a room to live in. You wouldn't need to stay at home and you won't be cold all day long."

Today, hidden under her frayed overcoat she attempted to conceal beneath her shawl, the most presentable part of her wardrobe, that made her feel ashamed as well, Arma was on her way to her job interview with Mrs. Aneva.

She refused to think about the cold wind that hit her scalp

and froze her fingers. She did not notice the trams as their metal wheels licked the rails. Arma believed losers like her used street cars that spread viruses in the cold. The more fortunate citizens whizzed past in their expensive cars; in all probability they had never heard of Lermontov, but that fact hardly affected their digestion. Arma walked.

She had a method of spending at least an hour or, if she was lucky, two hours in a warmed, well-lit room. She regularly read the cultural programs of literary magazines and knew that book launch parties were organized in the Town Hall Library. She waited there at an early hour, praying that the other visitors would not notice the frazzled collar of her coat. She hoped they would glance at her feet where her daughter's neat shoes gleamed. The mother and daughter had made a schedule and shared the pair of good shoes between them. In the evenings, as Di came back home after a series of elite backs, then went directly to bed and had her dinner there, enjoying the calories she had brought from Mrs. Aneva's house, Arma put on the shoes, still warm with her daughter's feet, and went to the following book launch party.

She listened carefully. It seemed to her the other visitors suspected that the cold wind had brought her to the library and she did her best to pay for the warmth she stole by asking the authors long poetic questions. They answered her, glowing with gratitude, as she looked into their eyes feeling the power of the central heating flow like silver into her frozen toes. She preferred poetry collection premieres; sometimes, very, very rarely, it seemed to her that a gentle stream rose from the thin book of poems and mixed with her blood, making her soar in the air above the dead sky. She lost herself in the soft magic world of metaphors where there were no electricity and telephone bills, no temperatures below zero, no empty fridges. At such moments, the woman was happy, so happy she drank half a glass of the wine the poets offered at the party. Then Arma did not know if it was happiness that made her feet fly like the happy sandals of a little child or she simply staggered because she was drunk. A little wine was enough to turn her head; Arma had meals twice a day: a little bread, some yogurt, one or two olives. She carried in her coat pocket a sachet of sugar. If she felt the earth vanishing beneath her feet and white sparrows circling before her eyes, she knew she was neither sick nor exhausted. She just had to spray some sugar in her mouth for additional energy and the world came back into place.

Arma could not but notice him: a man, perhaps a little younger than she. He came to the premieres dressed like Arma in the same clothes; a brown striped suit and a tie. Arma did not like striped suits; men in striped suits struck roots in her life and stayed there for a long time. A man of this sort had been a burr under her saddle for many years, besieging her at the time she worked for the Bulgarian Academy of Sciences, but after she was fired the gentleman lost interest in her.

The current man sported an intriguing tie, not an exceptionally clean fashionable piece with black and yellow stripes. His shoes, like Arma's, were immaculately polished. His eyes, russet brown, inquisitive, crept cautiously up the authors' faces, then regularly hopped over to Arma and paused on her shoulders. One evening, the man took a seat by her. A famous critic spoke about the strengths of a collection of essays as the man in the striped suit bent to her and whispered, "You are among the regulars, Ma'am."

The first thing that struck Arma was his bad breath. She felt exposed; her petty offence had been noted. To crown it all the man's eyes strolled towards the most frayed parts of her coat. There was no use pretending she could not hear him, the man familiarly nudged her in the ribs.

"I said that you and I are regulars, therefore we have similar tastes. I suppose we are kindred spirits."

"Well..." Arma answered.

The man bent lower towards her.

He'll sink waist deep into my ear, Arma thought, frightened, but he amicably whispered, "That fat guy is as rich as the Bank of England, my dear."

Arma didn't know who "that fat guy" was, but her neighbor did not bother to throw light upon that topic.

"His pockets are well lined." The man illustrated his ideas by outlining a large parabola over his own pockets. Arma did not react; instead of feeling discouraged, the stranger did his best to provide further details for her.

"The reviews will soon be over and there's going to be a lot of guzzling." The man's whisper wriggled its way under Arma's collar and tickled her skin.

"The guy's brought sirloin and smoked mackerel." The stranger reached out his hand and squeezed her elbow.

"You're quite thin, my love. You look pale to me... Well, it's all right. After the blabbering and the reviews we'll eat free sirloin. It smells good, doesn't it?"

Arma recoiled.

"I have to go, Sir."

She tried to stand up, but her interlocutor took hold of her hand and whispered in her ear, "Last time I stuffed almonds into my pockets..."

Arma remembered: a collection of poems, *The Wells of Salt*, written by a sad young woman. Her lonely stanzas had taken Arma high above the dead sky and she had again found Lermontov's quiet metaphors.

"I was watching you all the time, Ma'am," the man said. "You didn't take a single bite and I stuffed peanuts into a plastic bag for you. I beckoned to you, but you didn't see me. I'd like to be your friend...if you'd allow me to put it that way. Kindred spirits should communicate, I said to myself."

Arma could send him on a wild goose chase. If she were a lady she had to do that by all means, but she wasn't a lady any more. She could not endure the cold night air. The only roof that offered her security was the leaking ceiling of her one room flat where the hot water bottle turned into ice at night.

So Arma answered the man quietly as his fingers sank into her elbow, "You are very kind, Sir."

"You look weak to me," the man went on. "Probably the food they offer at the book launch parties is not enough for you. My name is Anton," the man introduced himself, and his hand kept its place on her elbow. "It will be my pleasure to buy you a cup of cappuccino after we have our dinner here."

His hand slalomed down Arma's sleeve and landed on her knee. She felt Mr. Anton's eyes size up of the frazzled spots of her coat.

"You are single, I think," the man inferred effortlessly. "I'll pay for the cappuccino."

ARMA STROLLED BY the shop window of the best grocery store in town, but she did not concentrate on the magic radiance of the sausages. If she did, the earth would jump under her feet and she'd be sick. She had eaten three slices of bread sprinkled with sugar, then she had wolfed down ten olives thinking she should have left more for her daughter. Arma believed she had eaten enough and she was surprised that the shop window made her swallow even though it was behind her back.

She doubted the smell of the food could reach her through the thick glass, but she could swear her nostrils swelled like the sails of a boat in the wind from the beautiful fragrances, especially of that smoked ham! She did not dream of travelling to Niagara Falls and she did not even think about the new production of *Swan Lake* at the opera house. All she wanted was to sit at a table with a white tablecloth and four bowls on it: the first one full of soup; the second of olives; the third filled to the brim with stewed meat and the fourth with fruits. Arma's spirit was not powerful enough to soar further than the second bowl. She'd rather stick to the bowl with the soup. But if she became the governess of Mrs. Aneva's son (Please, God, let the woman hire me!) she would enter that fabulous grocery store. Arma dreamt on, choosing different brands of cheese, hesitating how much — half a kilo or a whole kilo — she'd buy. The most audacious flares of her imagination launched her into the orbit of the smoked sausages. Everything depended on whether she could become the governess of Mrs. Aneva's son. Arma had to walk two more blocks.

Arma passed by the beauty parlor, the Mister and Mrs. Baby store, and peeked into Sylvester's Hair Paradise. She knew Sylvester personally: a handsome deaf-mute hairstylist capable of transforming a scarecrow into a Miss World 2013. He was a generous soul. Week in and week out, he paid Arma to sweep the floor of his studio. In fact, she bought the olives with the money she had earned cleaning the parlor's marble tiles and dear Sylvester cropped her hair free of charge. Arma was the only person that could endure Sylvester's company for a whole day. His throat produced deep gurgling blasts that sounded like they spurted out directly from his rectum. Arma learned to guess the meaning of his "Uh, uh, uh" and even tried to learn sign-language.

Arma passed by Sylvester's studio and the hair stylist waved his hand at her. She hoped to God that was a good sign.

On her way to the job interview Arma prayed with all her heart, the stray dog of despair cringing inside it. She promised the almighty being in the far-away universe, "Let me become governess of Mrs. Aneva's son! If she approves of me I'll never again talk to that man in the Library. Never!"

MRS. ARMA, IN HER FRAZZLED COAT the obvious defects of which she attempted to mask beneath the insufficient length of her shawl, stood in front of an imposing stone fence. A castle-like building was erected amidst the vast space encircled by the fence. For a moment, Arma imagined that the Sleeping Beauty would emerge from the shadows, followed by a suite of devoted pages. Alas, it was not the Sleeping Beauty who opened the gate. It was a sturdy young man. His hair was cropped so close to his skull that his bones glistened through the bristle of thick black hairs. The giant's cheeks were meticulously shaven and perhaps that was the reason why he looked bluish in the face.

"I gather you are Arma and you come to occupy the position of Master Anev's governess."

Lost in the shadow of the bodyguard's imposing figure, Arma felt stunned and totally useless. She feared she had lost the power of speech.

"Ma'am, I asked you something," the bodyguard's voice went up pressing her against the paving blocks in the street. "Can you hear me?"

"Yes, Sir," Arma came to her senses, relieved that she had driven away the white sparrows that circled before her eyes. She could feel the stone beneath her feet.

"Yes, sir," she repeated, willing to prove she was capable of speaking again. "I am Arma Kumova and I've come to occupy the position of Master Theo Anev's governess."

*** *** ***

Di

THE EXQUISITE BODY that lay on the special divan with the hard mattress was milky white, almost translucent, and Di's eyes were unable to extricate themselves from the smooth skin. The chisel of nature had worked diligently on the stomach, the breasts, the haunches, doing its best with the legs, which shone their pale symmetry, electrifying the air in the room. The unaccustomed observer would probably be spellbound before the perfection of that body, but Di knew the almost inaudible sounds, like the rustle of autumn leaves, that each square inch of Mrs. Aneva's flesh produced in the course of the massage. Di distinguished between the beats of the surf in the hardly visible waves of the stomach and the short cracking whispers of Mrs. Aneva's spinal column. These noises reminded her of the creaking wooden bridge which led to the Sunset Hotel. Di worked there in summer three years ago, taking meticulous care of the backs of German and Scandinavian tourists. In the evenings she used to walk their dogs by the seashore.

Mrs. Aneva's back cracked darkly under Di's fingers exactly like the grass under the soft paws of Mr. Weise's cocker spaniel.

Mr. Weise came from Dusseldorf, and gave Di large tips and radiant smiles when his wife was not nearby. Mrs. Weise stood six feet tall, a dazzling blonde column that barked orders to Di and expected heartfelt gratitude in return. Di smiled at her, bowed and scraped assiduously, and managed to touch her indomitable German heart. On such occasions, the massive lady waved her hand to Di and left a five Euro tip on the very edge of the table. Di appreciated Mrs. Weise's tips; she had bought an elegant suit for her mother on them and it was still fashion item number one in her mother's wardrobe.

Di's mother had put it on for her job interview. Arma had prayed to become governess of Mrs. Aneva's young son.

"I presume your mother will come on time."

The submarine of Mrs. Aneva's voice cut the perilous zone under the tips of Di's fingers.

"Yes, Ma'am," Di answered alert to the possibility of an imminent explosion.

When the lady was satisfied the waves of her stomach, small and warm, lapped D's fingers. Now they were beginning to rise and that meant one thing: danger.

"Your hands are cold today," Mrs. Aneva went on.

Her voice, as usual, was gentle and soft, but in its depths dark currents flowed and stalked Di.

"Yes, Ma'am, they are cold," she replied.

That was the safest answer, one that never failed to launch Di into the orbit of the sandwiches, a sign of gratitude Mrs. Aneva gave her in the middle of the massage. Di had already caught the tantalizing smell of baked ham in the dark recesses of the corridor. Her fingers jumped restlessly on the cathedral of Mrs. Aneva's buttocks.

"You know that your hands have to be warm enough."

The cold currents in Madam's voice went on driving Di towards a slow but sure wreck.

"I am cold and I have the feeling that icicles touch my skin."

"I will warm them up right away, Ma'am." That was the rapid reaction that Di had acquired while she worked for the blonde Mrs. Weise. Di had discovered the treasure trove of massage inspired by the severe German gymnast.

"Di, you can earn twenty-five Euros if you make efforts to rub my back in an adequate way," the gymnast had said one day.

Mrs. Weise's back could not compare to the pearly symphony of Mrs. Aneva's flesh, but Mrs. Weise did not want Di's hands warm; neither did she insist on her palms smelling sweet of Mystery, a French body lotion which Di's Bulgarian client adored. The German gymnast made it a point that the massage should invigorate her soul and tone up her powerful muscles. She was convinced that her masseuse had to make her burn as much energy as a quick swim and Di processed each square inch of her sallow skin with utmost force.

Di's life depended on the fees she took from Mrs. Aneva. Di dipped her hands up to her elbow in an aromatic solution and waited a minute, afraid that the aroma of the sandwiches might vanish in the maze of rooms and corridors. Then she dried her fingers on the towel, treated them to Mystery, and took a couple of steps to Ma'am. Her client had changed her body posture. The pearly luster of her stomach singed Di's face.

"I would like to see your fingers," the quiet voice ascended to Di. The masseuse extended her hands; the skin was a pale, dull color, the fingernails were short and unpainted. Suddenly, the client's soft palms covered Di's dark hand. Di thought she was a muddy street under the white snow of the other woman's fingers. She pulled her hand away, but the white palm heaped its snow on it again.

"You are trembling," Ma'am's slithering voice came to a halt. "You have to warm this hand of yours. Let me see it." For an instant Di's fingers fell into the tender white cave of Mrs. Aneva's hands.

"My husband…" Ma'am's voice trailed off, the tread of its self-assurance broke as her fingers crept hesitantly to D's wrist. "Yes, now your hands are pleasantly warm. Have you had a bath recently?"

That question threw Di into the fire of ugly doubts.

"Yes, Ma'am." She offered the usual reply, knowing that the act of washing her armpits with cold water could hardly be called having a bath. Di had deliberately cut her hair very short; her ears were naked and exposed to the severe winter colds, her black hair, less than one inch long, was an unyielding curly thatch. Di hoped it never looked dirty even if she hadn't washed it for a week. Well, one could never be sure with Mrs. Aneva. It was easy in summer; Di heated some water in two wash-basins on the balcony. The fact they lived on the top floor of the building was an advantage; the sun warmed the water quickly and Di poured it on her body twice a day.

"The smell you exude is not pleasant."

The words were insulting, but the voice that pronounced them swam in a tropical harbor redolent with palm trees and exotic flowers.

"I would like you to have a bath before you start the massage procedures."

The white narcissi of Mrs. Aneva's fingers blossomed for a second on Di's shoulder and descended slowly downwards, dangerously close to the unobtrusive hillocks of Di's breasts.

"You can use the bathroom over there."

It seemed the narcissi had enjoyed the dangerous vicinity and Di's embarrassment.

"I make it a point for my massage experts to smell pleasant. Do you think the fee I give you is sufficient to compensate you for the efforts you make?"

"Yes, Ma'am," Di answered and took a step backwards. Mrs. Aneva's eyes flew to her face, then touched the divan with the hard mattress.

"You can use my deodorant spray. I will not decrease your fee for this, Di."

"Thank you, Ma'am."

"You are hungry, aren't you?"

"No, Ma'am," Di lied with the few remaining shreds of her will, all cells of her body taking in the beautiful smell of food behind the door.

"Are you sure you won't mind if I have a snack in your presence?" The soft cobweb of the voice crawled on Di's naked arms. "We'll start the massage right from the beginning. First of all, I want you to have a bath. And please, do not put on that ugly turtleneck sweater. It smells bad."

The insulting words sounded unnaturally smooth as they slashed Di's throat.

"But Ma'am," Di objected weakly.

She knew objections were the most murderous step one could make in a massage parlor, yet she went on. "Ma'am, I have another client after you, and I am afraid I will lose a fee that is very important for me if I am late for her massage."

The walls of the massage room were lined with milky pink terra-cotta tiles. They reflected Mrs. Aneva's whiteness, gave Di the feeling that snowdrops had sprouted on the surface of a moonlit lake. A tall, immaculately dressed butler entered the hall. His white hair accentuated the copper tan of his face. Di tried to concentrate on his rugged features, but it was beyond her power to forget the fact that the old man had brought an enormous tray of sandwiches in the room. Di didn't have to glance at the tray. Her nose flawlessly puzzled out its contents: smoked ham, smoked salmon, butter. She gave up thinking about the remaining ingredients of the sandwiches; she was aware that the floor shook under her feet. She focused her attention on the white locks of the butler, the only thing in the room that did not smell of bread.

"Did you like my butler?" Mrs. Aneva asked.

She had sat up and was rearranging the sandwiches on the tray keeping her eyes locked on Di's dark face.

"Yes, Ma'am," Di answered.

She found out she could stare at the pink terra-cotta tiles on the floor and suppress her impulse to swallow ravenously. That fact reassured her. Uneasy silence descended on the room thick with the munching and smacking sounds that spurted from Mrs. Aneva's lips. Di knew she was sweating and knew her client had noticed that.

"It is a pity you are not hungry. Go and have a bath. Apart from the fee you earn from me, I'll pay you the fee you would get from your next client. What is she by the way?

"A doctor, professor in gynecology."

"Is she young?"

"In her early fifties, Ma'am."

"Does she ask you to take a bath before you take care of her body?"

"No, Ma'am. She insists I disinfect my hands and arms and use lavender scents."

Mrs. Aneva had swallowed three tiny bits of cheese; the other sandwiches lay on the silver tray on the small round table.

"My husband..." Madam's voice paused and unexpectedly set in another direction. "You have thick and beautiful hair. And it's curly. Why do you crop it so short?"

"I like short hair," Di lied, lost control, and swallowed convulsively a couple of times.

"My butler's hair is long and you told me you liked him."

"Yes, I do, Ma'am."

The white narcissi of Mrs. Aneva's palms blossomed on the tray with the sandwiches. She chose a soft piece of bread and kept it close to her lips.

"Di, you are an attractive young woman." The tight knots in the voice did not squeeze Di's neck too hard. "And you are not mean."

Di took the compliment silently, concentrating on Mrs. Aneva's elbow. She knew by experience that the best way to accept clients' compliments was to smile. However, Mrs. Aneva did not appreciate smiles. Suddenly the room reeled. The beautiful client had asked the following question.

"Has my husband made indecent proposals to you?"

"No, Ma'am, he has not," Di answered rapidly, unable to extricate her eyes from the pink terra-cotta tiles on the floor.

"You are lying to me," Mrs. Aneva's mysterious eyes smiled softly. "He is a brute, isn't he?"

Di did not answer. Her neck burned and her nose was unable to absorb the smell of the sandwiches. Her tanned, panicky hands fell into the white nest of Mrs. Aneva's fingers.

"Was he very rude to you? Did he make you do things that appalled you?"

"I don't know what you are talking about, Ma'am."

Mrs. Aneva stopped watching her masseuse in the course of the remaining relaxation procedures, and Di devoted all her attention to the slender back of her client. She had already completed the long distance run along the shoulders, down the fine basket of the ribs, and now was laboring on the curves of the waist, painstakingly careful not to touch the gentle dunes of the buttocks. The most difficult part was in store for Di. The legs were difficult: all their muscles had to relax, and achieving that was a demanding task. So far, Mrs. Aneva had insisted on Di's repeating the movements along the hips in order to eternalize their immaculate shape. Now her client lay lost in thoughts as if her soul had temporarily flown to the world beyond to meet a dear deceased friend.

These were Di's golden moments: no more massaging, the money waiting in the safety of her purse, her feet warm with the pleasant ambience of the well-lit room, the only unfriendly presence the January night sky.

THIS EVENING MRS. ANEVA made an unexpected move: she personally brought the enormous tray with the sandwiches to Di and said, "Help yourself, please. I counted how many times you swallowed this night: twenty eight."

Di made efforts to turn down the invitation, but the soft tiny loaves of bread were stronger than her will.

She was taken aback as Mrs. Aneva drew away the tray under her nose and declared, "I hope the reason you keep silent all the time has nothing to do with the fact that you dislike me."

"Ma'am, my desire is to make you feel good."

"Stop it!" the scissors in Mrs. Aneva's voice cut Di's hopes for peace and quiet. "You've already eaten my food. You had a bath and used my deodorant spray. Oh, come off it! I like your swarthy complexion better than your blush. I like you."

The client's cold palms did not fall onto Di's dark fingers. They paused on Di's shoulders, now free from the turtleneck sweater which, in Mrs. Aneva's opinion, exuded an unpleasant smell. For a split second, the white palms excavated two craters under Di's T-shirt. Di recoiled, shivering. Mrs. Aneva's fingers waited, offended, their disappointment cold and flat.

"Listen to me, Di. I am going to stay in Germany for two months and nothing in the world will make me give up my massages. Perhaps you still don't understand what massage means to me."

"Yes, M..." but Mrs. Aneva did not let her finish the banal answer. The unspoken phrase hovered awkwardly in the air.

"I want you to come and stay with me in Germany. Of course, I will cover all your expenses and I'll pay you much more than I do here. Do you agree?"

"I study at the university Ma'am. I'm afraid I will not be able to..."

The sharp pulsating impatience in Mrs. Aneva's voice slashed Di's answer.

"This is my only condition, Di. If you want your mother to become my spoilt son's governess, you have to accept. Is that clear? And there is something else you don't understand. Or perhaps you do."

*** *** ***

ARMA

THE SHORT STORY COLLECTION launch party was over. Mr. Anton had stuffed various delicacies into his pockets and into plastic bags he had prepared in advance. Amazed, Arma noticed he had sewn a dozen additional pockets on the inside of his striped jacket. A kilo of almonds plus sliced sirloin and biscuits vanished in a flash, sinking safely into the depths of his attire. Apparently, some of the pockets had a plastic lining; Mr. Anton crammed several pieces of strawberry pie in them. Arma was stunned by the amount of whiskey her new acquaintance succeeded in downing within a couple of minutes. Then he drank red wine and crowned his alcoholic triumph with four cans of Heineken. The man accomplished this spectacular feat clutching Arma's elbow — with the exception of the five times he visited the bathroom.

"Excuse me, dearest," he apologized. "It's the call of the wild."

After the actors finished reading the selected excerpts, Anton declared to the admiring audience that the short stories had warmed the cockles of his heart. That was a move he made at the end of each book launch party no matter if it was dedicated to a short story collection, a novel, a collection of essays, or a poetry collection. Everybody loved him. That evening he kissed Arma's hand and explained to her he'd like to take her to a "gorgeous café".

"We can eat some of our provisions there," he assured her. "Nobody will mind, I'm sure. Let me add it is a cheap place, dirt cheap, dear. You'll see."

The shape of the shack in which the café met its patrons reminded her of a garage. Its name was Playful Theodora. The only woman there was a pimply young waitress who vehemently swore at her male clientele. The thick cigarette smoke was impenetrable and Arma had the feeling she was sinking into the crater of a volcano.

"Two coffees, Teddy," Mr. Anton shouted, and the pimply waitress came swaying her powerful breasts towards Arma. The pox-marks on the girl's face made her think of a neglected car park.

"How's your boss Gozo today, dear?" Anton asked, to which the waitress responded with a fierce grunt. "Oh, take it easy, pretty girl. He'll fall in love with you again."

Anton comforted her and pulled the slices of sirloin out of his pockets, placing them — though crushed and distorted under the weight of his backside — in front of Arma.

"Eat," he encouraged her. "This is a high quality eatery. They call it The Greasy Café and the name is not a very flattering one, but it's okay."

The sirloin slices smelled of cheap deodorant and Mr. Anton smelled exactly the same. The smoked meat was sprinkled with shreds of cheap tobacco, but Arma noticed how fine and tender it looked and suddenly was aware of how hungry she was. She tried hard not to grab at the appetizing chunks, ordered herself to chew slowly and not stuff two pieces at a time in her mouth. She knew her new acquaintance watched her and was convinced he had counted the slices beforehand. At a certain point, Anton produced biscuits, baked almonds, and peanuts.

Feeling ashamed, Arma thought she had never tasted more delicious almonds in her life. They smelled of Mr. Anton and cheap tobacco, but at the same time they were magnificent, redolent of the moon and sea shores. It seemed she'd never get tired of putting food in her mouth. She savored every second as the biscuits melted on her tongue, each crumb leaving a miraculous trace in her blood.

"Eat! Eat, my love!" Mr. Anton chimed in every ten seconds.

In the beginning, his hand touched her elbow quite shyly. After Arma had wolfed three sirloin slices, his fingers plucked up courage, pirouetted down the sleeve of her coat and landed on her scared hand.

Arma wanted to escape from The Greasy Café, but the biscuits were there, smelling miraculously of treasures, knights, and fair ladies. She was not strong enough to go away. A man in front of her fell onto the floor between two chairs. Arma felt Anton's hand on her knee. Then she jumped.

"Well, well, well," Anton said reassuringly. "It's perfectly human, isn't it?"

Arma did not know what to say; she wondered how the man interpreted her silence. His lips cut his face into two halves, both unpleasant and angry.

"It's a compliment if someone makes a pass at you at your age, Ma'am."

"I am sorry," Arma blurted out. "I didn't want to be ungrateful."

The two halves of Mr. Anton's face produced a beaming smile.

"It's okay," he said. "We can go to my place now. I live nearby."

"But… maybe another time," Arma mumbled. The Supreme Being somewhere very far away — if he existed at all — knew she detested herself. Had she been a decent woman, she wouldn't have come here in the first place. Now she managed to wrench herself from the gravity of the biscuits, but she wanted her warm corner in the sleazy café.

"Please, Mr. Anton. Let's leave that for another time," she said.

"Oh, dear! Perhaps you think I'll drag you to a pigsty. No, my love! You don't know the Captain!"

The hands of the self-proclaimed Navy officer settled down on Arma's shoulders. A couple of seconds later, his fingers touched her knees.

"You are pretty, my love. I don't know if anyone has told you this before me, but it's true."

A dribble of saliva flowed at the corners of the Captain's lips.

"Listen, my girl, the Captain has a big apartment and lets it to three foreigners. They pay him handsomely to keep their butts warm in it. Do you understand, my love? The Captain is rich. He wallows in money and he has another two-room flat: French furniture, a Dutch fridge, and a tub in the bathroom where I can help you take a warm bath. Can you imagine the juicy rent I collect from the fat foreigners? 'Eine kleine Nachtmusik' by Mozart, love, and that means a little night music. A masterpiece!"

"I am convinced you are a charming man," Arma forced herself to say, twisting her knees away from Mr. Anton's hands. "I am convinced that…"

"I spend almost no money on food, my love. All these literary launch parties are a satisfactory source of delicious foods and I acquire cultural knowledge as well." The man belched, waved his hand and touched her cheek, then added, "And I meet interesting women. To be honest, you're not a charming piece of nature, my love. Why are you trembling? I won't hurt you. You've never been married and you aren't accustomed to a strong man's love. Love is the best thing for you, believe me. You may come and spend the night with me. It's warm in my flat. Your fingers look bluish, so I think you've got no central heating in your flat...They fired you, didn't they, love? If another woman were in your shoes she'd thank God on her bended knees she'd met a guy like me."

"Maybe another time!" Arma said.

"See you tomorrow, then, six pm, in the Library Hall. Another launch party: *Narrow Sky*, a novel or a poetry collection, I forgot what. I know the author personally. He is a penny-pinching skin-flint, but I hope there will be cheap whiskey and peanuts. I don't believe he'll bring good wine. I like good booze, my dear! See you tomorrow, 6 pm."

The captain jumped from his chair and quickly kissed Arma. His lips, thin and cold like the brim of a porcelain cup, jabbed the skin above her mouth. His tongue was insistent and hard. It crushed Arma's resistance and stayed in her mouth. She felt sick. The cement floor vanished beneath her shoes and white sparrows circled before her eyes. Now she didn't have a sachet of sugar. Nobody could help her. A second or a minute later she swam out of weightlessness.

God, Arma thought. *I'd like to meet a good man, God, a normal, kind man. It doesn't have to be someone who's heard of Lermontov. He doesn't have to be able to speak English. Let him be good. Let him love me. Let him hate sirloin and biscuits, God!*

*** *** ***

DI

"DID YOU CLEAN YOUR HANDS with lavender cologne? I see you have. You smell as if you have been soaking for a week in a swimming pool of lavender spirits."

The woman was big, broad-shouldered, powerfully-built, and had careful, bluish eyes which, in Di's opinion, ricocheted off all objects.

"Would you like me to start, Mrs. Metova?" Di asked as she approached the hard mattress on which her client's body jutted out like a castle.

"Professor Metova!" the woman corrected her acidly. "You know, Di, if I make a point of something, I'd rather people take it into consideration."

"I am sorry, Professor Metova," Di responded rapidly, trying to concentrate on the woman's shoulders.

"I am surprised that today you have not visited my son, although you took your monthly fee from me."

"I am sorry, Ma'am."

Di hoped she sounded miserable enough, but she had no reason to be sad. There was a fat bundle in her purse; the money was three times more than she had expected to get from Mrs. Aneva. The sandwiches she had eaten had lighted a pleasant fire in her stomach, which illumined her whole being.

"I don't think your excuse could be of use to anyone," Professor Metova commented. "I am positive that Peter missed you. He called me twice and wanted to know if you had come for my massage."

Overwhelmed by thoughtless courage, Di suggested, "Professor Metova, I can give you back the fee I received from you." It was a stupid thing to have done and she bitterly regretted it. Professor Metova's response was prompt and blunt.

"Very well, Di. Give me the money. I am convinced that relationships should be regulated by strict financial standards. Please, do not press me so hard."

"I am sorry, Professor Metova."

"You can massage my legs once again instead of giving me back the fee. One important thing: do not disturb Peter. I have conveyed the meaning of what I want clearly enough, I hope."

Di did not answer.

Metova's body was as hard as a plastic chair in a cheap café. Her hands, strong and decisive, could shatter things and build walls. Her legs had an impressive mass of muscles.

"Why didn't you visit Peter?" the professor asked, the muscles in her voice ready to fight. Di could tell, judging from her client's skin, that Professor Metova was in no mood for being polite. She was intent on raising hell. Perhaps Di had to give the money back after all.

"Maybe you found another man to have sex with so you decided to jilt my son."

"No, Ma'am, I have not split with your son," Di answered.

The blue-eyed woman's weight had the effect of a guillotine on Di. She was afraid of Alexandra Metova and had an aversion to her.

"I had another client, Professor Metova. She asked me to repeat her whole series from the beginning."

"Perhaps your client was a he?"

"No, my client was a lady."

"You are a very discreet person so you are unable to provide her telephone number. Please, press my neck harder."

"I cannot give you her telephone number," Di answered, and her client stiffened under her fingers.

Professor Metova's muscles snapped and shattered the peace in the room.

It was nine pm; the city was coming to life and the dusk teemed with threats of unpleasant meetings. For a moment, Di forgot she was at Professor Metova's place. She thought of the autumn day when she and her mother switched off the central heating in the only room of their flat. They were in their beds talking in the dark, saving electricity, clutching hot water bottles in their hands. This happened rarely — very often her mother didn't come home. Di knew she spent the night with Mr. Spiro, the retired telecommunications tycoon. She did not worry; she knew it was warm and safe at his place. In the only room of the flat, Di saw her breath in a gush of white vapor, but she longed for the moment she got there. No sandwiches waited for her at home, at least not like the ones Di was offered at her clients' places. "At home" was the absence of legs and buttocks she had to massage, a hiding-place far from tender hands that furtively touched her shoulders. At home, the memory of Mr. Anev did not cause coughing spasms and her mother's smile lasted a century. At home, no beads of perspiration squirted out of beautiful pores and no dazzling women loved her. Roaches chased one another in the dark corners of the room and stray dogs wept at the front door of the building. There were old postcards which Di had sent her mother from the seashore resort, the southern paradise where Di had taken care of Mrs. Weise's haunches. There was also a letter from the only boyfriend Di had ever had, the enormous Peter, Professor Metova's son.

Peter had a place in Di's life, although Di was a realist and the cold scissors of doubt cut her thoughts of him into pieces. Peter could not be different from all the rest. He simply had not found a girlfriend from the elite where he belonged. Di didn't speak about him and her silence was a shield that protected her skin.

"I WOULD LIKE TO ASK YOU A QUESTION and I demand an honest answer."

Professor Metova communicated with people — especially those who did not bear grand titles — by exploding the verb "to demand" into the conversation. The blast hit Di head on.

"What do you think about my son, Peter?"

"He is a young man of promise," Di offered a standard reply.

"I know that very well."

The voice blasted an angry hole in the wall in spite of Di's efforts to appease it.

"I know Peter is smart, educated and very talented. I want you to rate his performance as a man."

"He is good-hearted," Di said. The conversation took a turn that embarrassed her.

"I know perfectly well he is good-hearted," the icy stream in Professor Metova's voice drowned all Di's hopes she could avoid the dangerous zone. "I wanted to ask you...well, have you already had an intimate contact with Peter?"

Di choked on her tongue and that prevented her from completing the smooth spiral pressure down her client's back. Silence felt like a haystack in her throat.

"Well, Di, will you answer my simple question — did you have an intimate contact with my son or didn't you?"

"No, I did not, Professor Metova."

"I have asked you to. I pay you a monthly fee to provide this service and you don't make efforts to earn the money I give you."

Di was an exceptionally patient person. She had saved money for her education because she had neither yelled nor hit anybody, especially in cases when people deserved it. Now she slowly counted to fifteen, a method which kept her from shouting. She saw a sheltered bay, the smallest one at the seashore near the town of Varna. If she was lucky, she stole some minutes and was free from her clients' elite backs. These were Di's happiest moments; she sat huddled against a boulder and watched the sea. She thought about the flowerpot and the paint peeling off the ceiling in her mother's apartment; at a certain point, she noticed the blue tapestry of the waves and the sky. So far, the sea had helped to forget she wanted to scream.

"Mrs. Metova," Di shaped her words into a cold pyramid. "I like your son. I cannot trap him in a relationship that is all wrong."

"I know you massage famous men," the professor said. "I suppose some of them want other services from you. Di, let me be open with you: I chose you only because I expected you would provide such services for my son. You do not do your job although I pay you."

This time the waves did not help Di.

"Ma'am, I do not want to see your son anymore." Only the appellation, "Ma'am," was a strained, high-pitched sound, and the rest of the sentence crawled on the floor as did most of her statements.

"You've been seeing him for a month," Professor Metova's muscles pointed out. "You are always with him. You waste his time, don't you?"

Di did not count to fifteen. She couldn't reach beyond six as she massaged the tight cape of healthy muscles, making efforts to send ripples across her client's back.

"Have you kissed him?"

"Yes, Ma'am."

"Does he give you money apart from the fee I pay you?"

"Yes, Ma'am, and he also buys coffee and croissants for me. From time to time, he brings an ounce of olives to my place."

"Please clean your hands once again. Use the bottle of lavender spirits on the uppermost shelf."

Suddenly, her voice took a sharp turn to the sky and hissed; obviously the gynecologist had noticed something wrong.

"Di! Show me your hands."

Di stretched out her dark palms: long, thin fingers like lightning in the air of the clean room.

"Cut your fingernails, please," the client insisted. "And clean the edge of each nail with lavender spirits."

Her eyes touched Di's thumb first, then climbed the tops of all fingers, letting off indignant fireworks.

"Di..." the voice reeled as if it had stumbled upon a muddy puddle along the way. "Has my son offered you something...something special...recently?"

Di thought, she'll instantly die from a heart attack if I tell her

Peter took me to dinner at the Casablanca. If she learns how much her son paid two nights ago, she'll die even if she has no heart attack at all. And that would be fun to watch.

"Yes, Ma'am. He invited me to dinner and I accepted."

"Anything else?"

"He wanted to buy a pair of gloves for me. I did not want them."

Professor Metova's x-ray eyes scanned Di's entire brain and spinal cord.

"That happened a fortnight ago," Di added quickly. "I have not accepted any money from him since."

"Really?" Professor's Metova's voice strode decisively forward. "Lying will not help you."

At that point her voice paused, assuming new power.

"I wonder how you have the nerve to come to my own office, to look me full in the face and behave so...so... The Bulgarian language lacks a proper word which can describe your brazen behavior."

"Ma'am." The waves in the sheltered gulf at the seashore ran dry. The sea ran dry as well.

"You married my son in spite of our agreement not to! I told you he's not your cup of tea. I explicitly told you that a number of times. What you did is mean and you won't get away with it, I assure you."

"Professor Metova." Di survived the deluge of the other woman's wrath. "I did not marry your son."

The ocean of muscles in the professor's body stopped roaring. Her eyes nailed Di to the wall.

"He told me he married you yesterday." Two forces struggled in Metova's throat: the bright power of relief and the dark one of ugliest doubts.

"Professor Metova, I assure you, Peter did not marry me. Perhaps he married some other woman."

"Really? Oh, really?"

Immense relief flooded through Professor Metova as she produced a beautiful sigh.

"I hope you are not lying to me, Di. No one would get away with that! No one, believe me!"

At that moment Di thought she loved the winter cold and even the hunger in her stomach. At that moment, she knew she loved Peter.

*** *** ***

NORA

THE DOCTOR WAS TALL, robust, and looked impressive in his immaculately clean white coat. His feet were squeezed neatly into narrow white shoes. Nora had wormed her way into the clinic, plunging straight off the crowd of nurses and doctors before she could even reach him; the personnel of the clinic were all important and austere. After they heard Theo Anev's name, their faces lit up and the severity in their eyes gave way to warm hospitality of two thousand watts.

"Perhaps you are Mr. Anev's wife?"

All nurses, without exception, had made the usual tentative suggestion and, having established that Nora was neither Mr. Anev's spouse nor his sister, all rapidly hid their eyes under the cobweb of contempt. Yet Nora made it to the Senior Manager of the clinic.

"What is the message you have to convey to me, Ma'am?" the man asked, not bothering to mask his suspicions as to Nora's credibility.

"I am Mr. Anev's employee," she lied without batting an eyelid. "I have to inform him about an issue of crucial importance."

"Mr. Anev's bodyguards told me they did not know you. I cannot let you talk to him. It is a private medical clinic, and you understand we all here endeavor to maintain its flawless reputation."

"I understand you, Doctor Simonov," Nora smiled, the dimples in her cheeks a trap the drunkards from The Greasy Café adored, and gave her generous tips for even if they were not drunk. The doctor smiled back at her then asked in an extremely polite tone of voice, "What can I do for you, Ma'am?"

"Could you kindly inform Mr. Anev that Nora Nikolova, this is me, Sir, would like to talk to him about the Satellite B Project?"

"I cannot promise you anything."

The manager came to his senses, forgot her dimples, and thought hard. After a while, he waved his huge hand and let Nora approach a long white corridor. A marble sign at its door read VIP. This meant she had made it. So far so good, Nora thought.

Theo Anev's hospital room resembled a pink carriage which was set in motion by three nurses and two doctors on duty. The walls were painted in soft bright colors which encouraged the patient to recover rapidly and completely. Theo lay in an enormous bed in front of which an expensive television set and a laptop were installed. Noble tunes of Vivaldi's "Spring" sounded from the ceiling of the room, and Vivaldi was a composer none of The Greasy Café customers had ever heard about. Mr. Anev's face and the pink terra-cotta tiles on the floor merged together; the man looked like a floor, too. There were bluish circles under his eyes and a scalp bandage was applied to the top of his head.

"Good afternoon, Mr. Anev," Nora said.

"Come closer," the floor in the man's face encouraged her.

He was making considerable efforts to speak to her.

"It's nice of you to visit me here. What do you want?"

"I heard on the radio about the brutal attack against you, Mr. Anev," Nora said. "I am very sorry about that. I have brought you something."

Her fingers delved in her jacket pocket and produced a bar of chocolate.

"Come off it," the patient cut her short, but it was obvious his heart had softened, and the terra-cotta tiles in his eyes smiled at her. "What is it? Tell me."

"It is difficult, Mr. Anev."

"Speak up. I like smart and rapid answers."

"Yes, but..."

"Come on. I liked you quite well in The Greasy Café. Tell me."

There were still life paintings on the walls: predominantly ripe fruit and bright flowers, all so lovely and sparkling that Nora felt like smashing them to smithereens.

"What do you want?" Anev repeated.

Nora examined the terra-cotta floor. The patient stirred the thumb of this right hand. Nora had learned from experience this was an order to participate more actively in the discussion.

"You either speak or I'll make the bodyguards throw you out."

The fruit in the still life paintings boiled and turned to jelly. The dazzling sun painted on the canvas waited tactfully. Nora stewed in her own juice as her face glistened in profuse rivulets of sweat. She looked at the patient, studied his bed and slowly, as if she tried to swallow a handful of sand, squeaked, "I am pregnant, Mr. Anev."

"So what?"

Nora did not say anything. She felt like looking through the window of the pink carriage; there were beautiful benches and a park outside, but Nora disliked hospital yards. Her mother was operated on a month ago and, thank God, the cyst the doctors took out of her was benign. Nora enjoyed watching a small stall from which a woman grilled meat because the woman's smiling eyes calmed her down. Actually, when she was in a bad mood, she imagined a sun-lit stall and boys who did not have money and stayed to smoke a cigarette together. She had thought up a boy whose name was Shalaman; in fact, the dog her father had brought home when she was ten was called Shalaman. Now Shalaman, the boy who had no money in his pockets, was her favorite.

"You say you are pregnant," Mr. Anev's voice hit Nora, and she winced. When she was a little girl a wasp had stung her and now she thought Mr. Anev's voice produced the same biting sensation of injury. But Nora was not afraid of stings any more.

"Yes," she said.

"And I should draw the conclusion you're pregnant by me?"

The sting in his voice tried to bite off a piece of her, but Nora had been working a year and a half in The Greasy Café amidst heaps of minced meat, cockroaches, and semi-frozen poultry that smelled bad. Her nerves were as stable as the Earth's gravitation.

"Yes," Nora answered.

At that moment, she imagined that a very expensive and powerful car hit Shalaman the teenager, but deep in her heart she was sure the kid would survive, he was not injured, he was only temporarily stunned. Mr. Anev's eyes were a terra-cotta cell in which she was supposed to gratefully withdraw. We will see about this, Nora thought. Mr. Anev examined her with the curiosity of an astronomer researching an unknown asteroid. He probably found nothing of interest there.

"Do you know how many girls like you claim they are pregnant by me?" he asked.

Three years ago, Nora would have run away. She could have taken no more humiliation, but she was a different girl now. She had heard obscene language and she'd dragged drunks beaten to a pulp every evening. Mr. Anev's swan song did not impress her; Nora was sure she had no crush on swans.

"I asked you a question," the terra-cotta floor said. "I was speaking of the girls who pester me with unfounded claims. You can imagine I do not find pleasure in listening to their lamentations."

At that moment, Nora remembered the quite cracking sound Mr. Anev's skull had produced as the cold weight of the stone sank into the bone. The vivid memory of that night made her shudder, then she was perfectly calm. She made up her mind. She had nothing more to say, so she simply turned her back on him; she had always known her back was beautiful and she was perfectly composed as she started for the door of the room that glittered, clean and pink, like a king's carriage. Her steps sounded like penny coins falling into a street musician's hat, but she did not think the man with the terra-cotta cheeks was much impressed by small change.

"Won't you ask me to give you money?"

The ropes in his voice tightened the noose around Nora's neck, but she did not fear any nooses; she was afraid of Theo's bodyguards.

"No, I will not ask you for money. I decided to keep the child," she said quietly without turning back.

"Why?"

"Because the genetic material he will receive from you will be of use to him."

Silence reigned in the pink carriage. "To reign": an old fashioned, pompous verb. It was as peaceful in Nora's mind as if it was midnight, and Theo's bodyguards could not harm her.

"Didn't it cross your mind that the genetic material the child will inherit belongs to a shabby drunkard? You simply made some money behind the café and got pregnant."

Even if Nora had gripped the vase with the expensive flowers, she wouldn't have used it against Mr. Anev. The battalion of body-guards and nurses would have immobilized her on the spot. She thought of Shalaman, the teenager, instead; he had just bought sandwiches and grilled meat and was quite content. Then Nora remembered the sounds Mr. Anev's skull had produced after the stone had hit, and felt much better.

"I do not make money in the way you suggest," Nora said.

"Then perhaps you've learnt the things you did for me from the internet?"

The terra-cotta on Mr. Anev's face melted and was now ordi-nary muddy clay. "You knew very well what you were doing."

"You did a number of things to me, too," Nora remarked.

She felt as calm and free as if she was having a stroll with little school kids.

The long thin fingers, of which the doctors would take good care first thing in the morning, dug their way into the pillow. A roll of banknotes gleamed in the man's palm, a fat bundle, as big as a molehill. Mr. Anev lifted the money in the air, his lips quiv-ering squeamishly.

"Take this and go away," he said and threw the money onto the floor.

The bills fell an inch away from Nora's feet. Nora had rich expe-rience with money being thrown at her and she knew there were no less than five hundred dollars on the tiles. She thought of her brothers, of her mother's operation which was still not paid for. Her heart rushed to the money, but she did not bend down, she did not take the banknotes. She made for the door, her steps ringing bells of despair. How she needed that money. But Nora had worked for the drunks in the Greasy Café. There were creeps among them. If you took a creep's tip he thought he could spit in your throat, he was sure you'd kiss the dirt under his old shoes. The creeps were impressed if you did not take their money, if you left the banknotes lie on the terra-cotta floor like an empty cigarette pack, like spittle, like dung. Let me see what a creep you are, Mr. Anev. Nora's hand perched on the perfectly polished silver doorknob.

"Hey, wait!" the voice of the patient jumped then crept. "I'll give you more."

Nora looked back. The patient before her was a heap of quality minced meat, a little bit bigger than the ones she had to defrost in the Greasy Café, the perfectly processed ground beef over which a dozen well trained bodyguards kept watch. Nora was not afraid of ground beef. She'd never been.

*** *** ***

MONI

"I AM VERY DISAPPOINTED, very disappointed indeed," my mother declared.

She had lost considerable weight recently like the aristocratic ladies from the soap operas and, also like them, she had made up the dark circles of despair under her eyes. She looked very pretty, I gave her that. Doctor Xanov, the man she lived with, rushed to her very concerned, offered her a glass of water, then held her hand for half a minute in a very soothing manner. He was deeply in love with her and made it a particular point that everybody took special notice of it.

"Your mother's disappointment has many aspects to it," the Doctor ventured tentatively, but Mother's green eyes flashed in a spiral towards his throat, making him shut up prematurely. "I mean, she will explain everything to you by herself."

"Of course I will. I'll discuss things with her, my love."

Of late, my mother had adopted the fashionable habit of addressing him as "my love," following the English example. She had very recently started drinking her tea with cognac and milk like the

English, had all her dresses sewn in the UK, looked up a massage expert capable of speaking fluent English, and hired a butler to iron her linen after the English fashion. The only Bulgarian thing she kept around was that supercilious doctor, taller than the nests of the magpies in the poplars and dangerously emaciated on account of his love for her.

"I am disappointed at your brutal attitude towards Gallantine. The poor darling described kindly for me your threats by means of which you wrenched from him a promise to marry you. Of course, that will not happen. Forget you have ever seen that man. Oh, poor, poor Gallantine."

"Poor" was another favorite word of my mother's. Whenever she was at a loss groping for an appropriate expression she instantaneously declared the gentleman or the young lady "poor".

"He, of course, will not marry you and you can be sure no one in town will unless you..."

"He will."

I was positive Mother would calm down.

"You, the lady of fashion and glamour, know very well why any man wouldn't hesitate to choose me as his matrimonial partner, even if I am fatter than you."

Awkward silence, as thick as steel, crusted the room. My mother was clever and businesslike; she had been accustomed to speaking to the point, but there was no remarkable point anywhere around her, so she made up her mind to shut up and look beautiful.

"Money is not everything in the world," Doctor Xanov stated very decisively.

"It is the better part of it," I agreed.

The room in which the three of us spent the afternoon amicably conversing was the magnificent Vienna hall in the new house that my father had bought before some bad guys shot him dead. Poor Dad had been beside himself to gratify my mother's whims. This afternoon, she was enchanted by everything of English origin, but in the past she wept for articles of trade produced or pertaining to Vienna — her car was bought from a shop in Mendelstrasse, the damask curtains in the hall originated from the most expensive furniture store in Vienna, even the straws for the fruit juice were dutifully procured from that glorious town on the Danube. The parquet floor was milky beige, glossy like a mirror, the curtains were cream-colored, the furniture even more cream-colored. My mother's face resembled custard in this sugar Odyssey. She had recently started drinking red wine. Doctor Xanov was an absolute teetotaler, so even his shadow smelled of disinfectants and detergents. I suspected he abstained from sex as well, if one judged by the acidic expression on my mother's face. It was very quiet in the Vienna hall and the colors all around me rustled in their colorful language of silence.

"It was not fair of your father to transfer all his property to your name in his will," my mother said, looking shattered indeed.

She was not the color of custard any more.

"He loved me so much, and he left me a ridiculously small amount of money."

I had no comments to make on this, so I went on sipping at the orange juice, expecting the logical outcome.

"Even the house in which we are at present belongs to you and you can throw me out whenever you please."

These words sounded so sad that if I didn't know her, I would be sincerely sorry for her for many years to come.

"Yes, I can," I heaved a deep sigh. "But I will throw out only Doctor X."

The Doctor bit his straw savagely, perhaps intending to drown his entire indignation in the glass of orange juice. His thin, oblong torso, in spite of being diligently wrapped in a godlessly expensive Versace suit, rushed towards my mother and clung to her shoulders like seaweed.

"You should not speak like this!" she objected.

Her voice shattered the peace and quiet, and several geysers of her wrath poured forth fire and brimstone. The Doctor clung to her and stared at me horrified.

"You are not throwing the Doctor out of your house!"

"Yes. I am throwing the Doctor out of my house." I reiterated very calmly. "Doctor Xanov," I addressed him courteously, "I can say it in French and German as well, but I expect you will not understand me. Get your ass out of my Vienna hall, Doctor X."

"But you are fat. Very soon you will suffer from high blood pressure and you'll ask Doctor Xanov on your bended knees to come and help you."

The geysers of wrath in my mother's voice discharged some more poison, the syllables of her words disintegrating in the crucible of her emotions.

"I can summon a doctor from Sofia on my father's money. Perhaps he could take better care of my blood pressure than Doctor X, don't you think so?" I asked her.

My mother tried hard to burst into tears. I had to admit she was very good at that. When I was a kid she used to cry very often and my father was so sad I thought the whole world was in store for a sorry end. She had the glory of winter snow in her tears and the color of sorrow in her eyes. I would do anything to cheer her up. After her performance, a new diamond ring would glitter on her finger, or a bracelet would glow on her wrist; it turned out that only precious stones were capable of discouraging the profusion of tears in her magnificent eyes. My mother was an unbelievable woman — that was true.

"Now, when I am poor," my mother sobbed, "you can do anything to me."

"Not to you," I said peacefully; even without a ring or a bracelet her tears had run dry.

She had grasped the fact that it would be unreasonable of me to buy her a diamond ring now.

"My respect and admiration for you will remain the same. You can always rely on me, I assure you."

Although my mother was exceptionally beautiful, her cheeks, chin, and forehead were not the color of custard as she glowered at me, swallowing hard.

"What! Rely on you for help? Me?" she exclaimed, her pearly white hand flitting toward her heart.

Even under the expensive layer of rouge her face had acquired a shade of green that was in sharp contrast with the creamy colors of the Vienna hall.

"You'll make your mother lose consciousness," the Doctor remarked dryly as he smoothed his Versace jacket over his chest with utmost dignity. "I will never forget that you prefer a doctor from Sofia to me, you can be sure of that."

I knew Doctor X was the most eloquent speaker in town so I turned my fat back on him, reached my fat hand to the desk, and pushed a discreet, almost invisible button.

After five seconds, my two bodyguards entered the Vienna hall: that was the usual consequence of the discreet cream-colored button. It was not necessary for me to speak. All I had to do was direct the tip of my fat chin towards the doctor. The two strong men grabbed Doctor X under the armpits and nodded their heads simultaneously to my mother as a sign of their deep respect for her exceptional mind. She followed their activities, the greenish shade of her skin becoming darker under the fine layer of rouge.

"Will you excuse us, madam?" they spoke out simultaneously as if they were the two twin throats of a two-headed dragon.

"Boris! Ivan! Let me go immediately!" Doctor X ordered them, but my fat chin sank low towards the floor.

The boys knew well what this meant, so they lifted the medical luminary complete with his expensive Versace and, dragging him in the air torn away from the stout pillar of my mother's love, carried him to the exit. It was my pleasure to watch the unnaturally long feet of the Doctor kicking the beige space of the Vienna hall.

"Boris! Ivan!" my mother commanded. "Put Doctor Xanov down and apologize!"

The two burly fellows froze in their tracks, but did not let go of the seaweed which fluttered and hung between the ceiling and the floor, clasped tightly under the armpits. A short clarification: Boris and Ivan were the bodyguards my father had hired to ensure my mother's safety — in fact, she had chosen them herself. It happened at the time when she had not yet demonstrated her inordinate preference for Vienna ways. To cut a long story short, my mother's requirements concerning her security were legendary: her personal bodyguards had to stand not less than six feet two inches tall and they all had to be younger than twenty-eight years. Their Zodiac sign was to be Taurus, which my mother adored because, according to her horoscope, she could maintain very stable social relationships with the representatives of this sign. It seemed, however, that the contact she established with them had gone rusty.

"Boris! Ivan!" she shouted imperatively, but my fat chin sank an inch further down towards the beige floor.

The bodyguards noticed that. Let me add that before my father hired them he could choose from forty-eight guys for each vacancy. He paid his employees generously. These two could make excellent astronauts as far as their health was concerned. My father had covered the costs of all kinds of medical tests in the Academy of Human Health in Sofia; he had checked if their grandparents exhibited any dangerous psychological aberrations or sexual perversions which might threaten my mother's well-being. My mother was to have the best quality of everything, and she did.

Boris and Ivan were intelligent enough to grasp that now I was the person who paid their salaries. It became painfully clear to them that I inherited my father's impressive property when I provided them with no remuneration for two consecutive months, the reason being insubordination concerning my orders. Apart from that, they were well aware of the fact that they would either show up a second after I had pushed the cream-colored button or I'd bid them farewell.

All this explained why it was unnecessary to say anything to them. My mother's lamentation hovered unattended over the desert of their sensibility.

One of the guys, who in my opinion was wittier than the other, asked, "Shall we carry him out in the street, Madam?"

Again, it was not necessary to speak; I pointed the tip of my chin towards the door and the sea-weedy doctor was transferred from the cream-colored atmosphere of the Vienna hall into the cold atmosphere of the frosty winter afternoon. You might not believe me, but it was still snowing.

My mother and I remained alone.

"You are appalling," she whispered, driving the green indignation of her eyes deep into my sense of guilt. "Why didn't you order them to kick me out, as well? Actually you don't need to do that, I'll go by myself."

"Mother," I spoke slowly and I could see her breath turn red. "You are welcome to this house, as well as all the other buildings that father left me in his will. Please, do not bring Doctor X with you. If I catch a glimpse of him in a place that belongs to me, I'll order Boris and Ivan to shoot at him as they do at thieves."

"Why?" she blurted out, then regained her self control, which, in my opinion, cost much more than the heaps of money my father squandered on beauticians, fashion designers, and shrinks who took care of Mother's emotional stability. My father adored the fact that his wife preserved her equanimity in all kinds of situations.

"You left my father and went to live with Doctor X," I answered and that was the truth.

"I will dispute the will!" my mother whispered.

Oh, you poor, poor lady, she would have exclaimed if she had to describe her own plight. She knew that through my father's money I had the best lawyers, the whole city in my hands.

"Oh, my God," she went on. "At times, I was sorry that you were so fat. Why on earth do you need all that money? It will not buy you people's love and respect."

"It will," I interrupted her quite delicately. "I can order a man to my bedroom by telephone or select one on the internet. I can do that immediately, in your presence, Mother; I can buy any man I have a fancy for. Tall, slim, and blond, or fat and squat..."

"That is outrageous... outrageous!" she thundered, then paused for she was a shrewd woman and knew she had to take into account my money in the bank, the rolls of banknotes that cost more than love, decency, and all compassion in the world. "You are a monster."

"I can order a girl to my bedroom if I please," I told her. "A beautiful one or a plain and fat one. I can order her to come after breakfast, at lunch, whenever."

She was silent. Her hands did not tremble. Perhaps her entire body had gone numb.

"But I will not do that, mother. In an hour, I will meet the men who used to manage my father's business. I want you to know that I am the new emperor of my father's small empire: the sleazy pubs at the marketplace, the second-hand shops, the dairies, the real estate business, the iron mill, everything. I will give you the house with the Vienna hall; I will let you have as much money as you need, within reasonable limits. I have one single condition. Leave Doctor X for good. Do you accept?"

"No," she answered.

The sun had crept under the cream colored wallpaper and now it was golden.

"He'll jilt you and you'll suffer," I told her plainly.

She was golden in the sunset and looked very pretty. "Who are you without my father's money? A beautiful, aging woman. A day will come when you won't be able to buy wrinkle creams. You will have no money to pay the massage experts. In the mornings, you will have to go clean somebody's office and a younger woman will ride your horse. I am convinced you won't find any other job, you will be a charwoman, and your beauty will evaporate within days. Do you think you will be the jewel that Doctor X will show proudly to his guests?"

"He loves me," my mother objected vehemently.

"There are many younger and more beautiful women than you, can't you see them? Doctor X is not blind either, I assure you."

She was quiet as the sun caressed her custard cheeks.

"Your father was shot dead," she said. "One day soon you will be shot dead as well and I will not regret it."

My hand, warm in its nest of lard, touched the discreet cream-colored button.

"Summoning Boris and Ivan to throw me out?" she asked contemptuously.

"No, I ordered them to bring in the next visitor. I would like you to see him."

Obeying the powerful cream-colored button, the door opened silently. I had the feeling that my father had enjoyed the wonders of modern technology. I had seen him gawking at computers, but he met his maker unenlightened on which button he had to press in order to turn them on.

A strikingly attractive man entered the hall in which everything, with the only exception of breathing air, did not come from Vienna. His shoes were dazzling and immaculate, his suit looked flawless, and the man's broad athletic shoulders were both dazzling and flawless, which annoyed me. The man held an enormous bouquet of expensive flowers. They were so marvelous that even the glorious Vienna hall was impressed.

"Gallantine!" my mother exclaimed. "Gallantine, you..."

My gallant visitor nodded in a very reserved manner to her then approached me.

"I come to apologize, dear, for my inconsiderate behavior. I was rude and I am very sorry."

He gave me the bouquet of flowers, which I left without further ado on one of the beige sofas nearby. My visitor caught hold of my hand. He kissed it so passionately that I suspected he had recently become an admirer of my short and chubby fingers.

"Mrs. Xanova," he bowed coolly to my mother. "Would you excuse us for a minute, please?"

"But... but I..." she started.

Gallantine had already turned his attractive back to her.

My mother made it to the door. I was sure her ex-bodyguards, Boris and Ivan, stood there, very attentive and concerned about my security. I supposed they had bowed to her; she had always been generous in giving help to men who admired her.

*** *** ***

BECKY ANEVA

IT WAS THURSDAY AGAIN and that meant at nine pm Becky Aneva's husband would visit her. He had emailed her, had called on her mobile, and had sent a fax message warning her to be in her bedroom exactly at that hour, but Becky hoped that at least today she would break the established routine. Theo had some important/ official meeting in Bonn and odds were that she would be in luck: he was already ten minutes late. She dreamt of going to Bonn herself; she loved the cold, humid air, the intimate fog hovering above squares and statues, the sluggish dark river, but, above all, she enjoyed the closed faces of people. Their cool, unobtrusive presence put her at her ease. She was wind or dust on the sidewalk and the feeling of solitude was sweet. She adored the loneliness of the houses; although they were arranged in strict straight lines, each one had an ancient facade and a little fountain which spoke of the owner's frivolity. The marble arches cast their quaint shadows on the squares full of legends and history. She felt the stares of men on her skin; their parasitics eyes delved deep into her flesh and sucked delicious juice from it.

Her husband's business partners were civilized enough, but Becky Aneva guessed that at the end of the day they had one of the expensive girls in their hotels. She imagined the services the men wanted and felt appalled. Thinking about men was an appalling occupation, for it made her remember Theo, her husband, and the Thursday nights he spent with her.

Becky hated Thursdays.

Bakalov, one of the business partners of Becky's husband, had so far behaved in a very friendly manner; he sent her discreet flower gift baskets on the mornings after each official dinner. At the last working lunch, the seventeenth in a long, tedious series, Becky mentioned something about the film *Titanic* just for the sake of participating in the conversation. Theo had warned her not to be silent like a statue even though she looked as beautiful as one. Out of pure politeness, Becky took part in the discussions. She dropped a question in the sphere of culture she had prepared beforehand — finance and politics was a perilous zone and Theo had cautioned her not to poke her nose in it, pointing out how narrow-minded her way of looking at things was. In general, he did his best to stress her overall inability to cope with anything outside cosmetics; because of that Becky asked Bakalov her well prepared question, "Have you seen the film *Titanic?*" Perhaps the question was downright stupid, but pronounced by her beautiful lips it acquired weight, and the businessmen, feeling the ennobling female presence, commented on *Titanic*. Unlike all the rest of them who kissed her hand and bowed silently, the bolder ones discreetly directing their eyes down the neckline of her dress, Bakalov, on the following day, sent Becky a disc with the film.

Then he sent her a novel by Barbara Delinsky, an author Becky abhorred, so she paid her son's nurse, a woman called Arma, to read the novel and provide her with a two page synopsis, plus analysis of the basic story lines. Becky had made up her mind to indulge in a small adventure with Mr. Bakalov. She needed neither sex nor the sugary porridge of love; Bakalov attracted her with the fact that he had not lowered his eyes to the neckline of her dress nor had he attempted to swim in the stream of the topic of how beautiful Becky was. He simply established a dear little tradition to send her modest bouquets of snowdrops on Mondays, Wednesdays and Fridays. Becky appreciated them all the more because on these very days Di, the strange girl, came to her house and massaged her body with such intense concentration, as if that was her most favorite occupation in the world.

When Bakalov brought Becky to his villa in the country, and she saw him naked, whitish, and flat like the undulating shapes of tapeworms she had seen as a schoolgirl in her biology classes, the iceberg of repugnance hit her throat. Becky did not want Bakalov; she imagined his hands, scraggy, overgrown with transparent hairs, touching her, then she saw his thin colorless lips closing down on her mouth, and she thought she would throw up. Bakalov caressed her and Becky was scared by his dry palms moving rapidly all over her, his unnaturally quick fingers planting warts in her skin as they touched her. The experience was all the more unpleasant because of the question that Bakalov constantly kept asking her, "Does it feel good?"

Finally Becky answered that it felt good, hoping that he would calm down, but he sank into her all the more intensively, leaving dry pain in his wake. There were thin grooves of saliva running from the corners of his mouth on which Becky concentrated. Yet she could gain considerable advantage from this situation; Bakalov's blue, almost transparent eyes swam in fog, his eyelids slid downwards, his mouth kissed her persistently as his body swayed on her like a buoy tied at the bottom of the sea. She could examine him closely and had the chance to experiment with him; she scratched his back, ready to avenge herself on his body for the humiliation and the splitting ache he gave her. Then she hit him.

Last Thursday night, while her husband Theo was making love to her, she scratched him as well; and he hit her. That was the only time he had ever done that to Becky and after, when he had gone, the money left on the bed for the week was three times more than usual. From that time on, Becky suspected he nurtured a vein of sneering and sadistic malice, he tried to humiliate her in public and, since she was not a woman given to procrastination and suspicions, she told him plainly, "Next time you hit me you're asking me for a divorce."

"You won't divorce me," Theo answered, his gray eyes hungry for her. "You need my money."

Becky did not object and did not explain anything.

"Try me," she said.

BECKY SCRATCHED BAKALOV'S BACK AGAIN, but instead of leaving her alone he blurted out, "You are great, you are great." He sounded credible, as if he really believed what he said. His saliva dripped on her breasts and she hated that, but the exhilarating feeling that she was a researcher experimenting with a species unknown to science never left her. She could push and scratch and beat and bite him. She could do anything to him and for a moment Becky was sorry her imagination was so poor she could not invent anything twisted and deviant.

"Stop!" Becky ordered him.

He ceased moving and sat up, whitish and undulating in his glass jar of acid where the tapeworms were preserved in her biology lab at school.

"I love you," Bakalov said, but Becky saw his shiny saliva and the whitish hairs piercing his colorless skin. "I love you. Marry me! Abandon your husband!'

She hit him once again, this time on the mouth, and instead of yelling, he tried to kiss her. At that moment, Becky saw in her mind the dark hands of the girl who massaged her and was unable to catch her breath.

Becky drove on the way back home and Bakalov slept, the streams of his saliva dripping onto the seat of his expensive car. She suddenly wanted to make him feel pain; her desire was so irresistible that she drove her fingernails deep into his wrist. Bakalov woke up and looked around expecting that somebody wanted to break his neck. Becky stopped the car. It was so cold and wet that for a moment she wanted to throw Bakalov out in the street and go on without him. She kissed him instead and bit his lip, bit it savagely, feeling the taste of his blood in her mouth. He shouted with pain and as Becky let him go he whispered, "I love you."

Becky thought about the hands of the girl who massaged her and remembered that it was Thursday again. That meant that Theo would be home at nine pm. His gray eyes — if the lewd gloss between his eyelids could be called eyes — would pick a spot on the floor, then he would order, "There!" Sometimes, he did not speak at all, but it made no difference to Becky. She accepted his visits on Thursdays with the same reserve as her appointments with the dentist: the sooner they were over, the better. Theo did not allow her to be a researcher intent on scratching, hitting, and dissecting him closely. Very rarely, perhaps one Thursday a year, her husband would snort, "You are pretty, damn it."

"I am cold," Bakalov muttered from the seat of his expensive car. "I am cold and I love you."

She had totally forgotten about him.

"I will not leave Theo," Becky said, and thoughts of the girl who massaged her every Thursday blissfully flooded her.

What a pity her husband had chosen Thursdays to make love to her. She wished the girl stayed after he went out to work in the city. She wished Theo never came back to her life.

BECKY HAD MADE UP HER MIND to speak to Theo this Thursday evening; she needed money, she wanted to stay three months in Germany. Of course, she had already talked Di into accompanying her. People in Germany were tactful and discreet; they did not care about the young man next door. The fine silver fog there would envelope that strange dark girl. Becky had to convince Theo how important it was for her to stay in Bonn. She would do anything, just anything to convince him.

Theo had invented another family ritual: before he left Becky alone on Thursdays, he made her spend time with Theo Anev Junior, their son. Theo took the boy and held him in his arms. Once, out of sheer curiosity, Becky measured how long this procedure took, and found out that Theo held the heir apparent to the family throne for forty-five seconds. Her husband was a man of disconcerting habits, and when the next time she measured how long he held his son, it was exactly forty-five seconds again. Having invested efforts in creating a familial atmosphere, her husband handed the baby triumphantly to her. When it happened the first time, Becky did not know what to do, just stared at her son's face, white as marble, a high forehead Theo was very proud of, gray eyes the same color as his father's, then she tried to give the boy to his governess.

"No," Theo stopped her. "Kiss him first!"

Becky kissed Theo Junior and that concluded the ritual. Once in a blue moon, her husband skipped the boring thing and went directly out which gave Becky a sense of relief, but he usually lingered half an hour longer asking Arma to make him some coffee.

Becky thought that since that woman became her son's governess, things at home went smoothly. Theo junior, a tractable, maybe not too clever child, played happily in his cot and smiled at the world most of the time, so Becky believed Arma had to do some additional work to be worth her pay. Becky made her read famous bestsellers or classic novels; it was a must for Arma to pick at least three particularly revealing passages from a book and then describe the plotline and analyze the contents to Becky in great detail. At the official dinners, Becky diligently repeated the quotations she had learnt by heart. Theo's business partners gawked at her awestruck, admiring, knowing deep in their hearts their wives were dirt compared to her. However, Becky was not interested in the wives. Bakalov's bouquets became desperately expensive, arriving in her bedroom with the frantic persistency of absurd love. Theo smiled grandly at the compliments the gentlemen paid his wife. What could be of higher value to a connoisseur of precious art than the consuming envy his business associates could not conceal?

BECKY HATED THURSDAYS. Unfortunately, it was Thursday again. She could, of course, summon Arma and ask her to say a few words about Dostoyevsky, Emily Bronte, or another famous author, but she did not feel like it. Arma annoyed her. Perhaps it was the smile with which the governess accepted Becky's requests to read the newspapers and inform her about the most intriguing articles in them. Was it because the governess's eyes gleamed very particularly as she looked at Becky? They were the eyes of a superior being who knew her own worth even though Becky paid her salary and without the money the governess would starve.

"Arma!" Becky yelled.

Arma and Theo Junior entered her bedroom together, the governess holding the boy in her arms. She carried him everywhere with her the way the frogman dragged his bottle of air.

"Yes, Mrs. Aneva."

"Can you call your daughter and ask her to come to my house? I'd like Di to be here as soon as possible."

"Is there anything wrong, Ma'am?"

"Yes, there is. I would prefer to personally inform her of it."

"Yes, Ma'am. But our telephone at home is out of order and today I forgot my mobile at home. Apart from that..."

The governess's voice trailed off. That was another thing that bothered Becky. She hated incomplete sentences. The Germans always finished their statements and made them short and clear. Arma spilled chaotic words in the air. The trails of incomplete thoughts she left behind her stayed longer than the smell of cheap deodorant or a heap of useless belongings.

"I'll order my chauffeur to drive you to your apartment. Come back with your daughter. Don't take too long."

"Who will take care of Teddy while I am not here, Ma'am?"

"Don't call him Teddy. I don't like that," Becky said. "I know what you're worried about: you get paid for the hours you are in charge of Theo Junior and I will also pay you for the time you are tasked to bring your daughter here."

"Thank you, Ma'am."

Then the governess gave a reserved little bow that exuded contempt for all parts of the human body from the pelvis to the top of the head that had bent down.

"Arma!" Becky said curtly. "Do not bow down to me in your disrespectful manner. Ask 'May I go now?' before you leave my room."

"Yes, Ma'am. Of course. May I go now?"

"Yes. Do not use the phrase 'of course.' I do not like it."

"Yes, Ma'am."

Becky's mobile phone played Beethoven's "Symphony Nr.9" to her. It was not necessary to be extremely clever to recognize who was looking for her.

"You are great!" the electrons of the cellular phone purred into her ear. "You are so beautiful!"

Of course it was Bakalov. He invited her again to spend an unforgettable evening in his villa. It was Thursday again. Becky detested Thursdays and she detested Bakalov even more.

*** *** ***

Di

"I KNEW YOU'D PASS your exams," her mother said one Thursday night at the end of March. The cold weather had packed away its snow and frost in its icy suitcases and left the city for good. Cautiously, as if begging for pennies from a haughty big shot, the sun appeared in the sky and people took off their winter coats.

"Yes," Di answered. "I do not have problems with my exams."

Her mother nodded her head; she had never had problems with Di. They had enough money for the electricity bill; they had turned off the central heating a long time ago and now mother and daughter opened all the windows of the one room flat welcoming the warm ray of all the suns in the universe to their home.

"I got an invitation from the University to participate in a scientific symposium at the Sorbonne, but I have to pay my travel expenses to Paris and back," Di said. "I turned it down."

The voice was hard like the pavement in a town square, but her mother knew that under the thick stones a wound festered, words that had been kept unsaid for so long that Arma avoided her daughter's eyes. She knew that the money for the travel expenses would be spent on bills, building materials, new wallpaper for their only room, where moisture and mould had crawled up the walls.

"It is not necessary to repair the flat, Di," Arma said gently. "I want you to go to Paris. I can borrow some money from Mrs. Aneva."

"No," Di answered and all the flights to Paris were cancelled, the young leaves of the trees were bitten by frost and Paris was a black unreachable dot on the geographic map.

"Mrs. Aneva called," Arma added with a guilty tone in her voice. "She needs another massage before 9:30 pm. She informed me she'd pay you double."

Di did not say anything. She stood up, went to the wardrobe and put on her black coarse sweater which she had bought from the second-hand shop.

"Do you know what," Arma started quietly, took a step to her daughter and looked into her eyes. "I noticed something... I didn't want to mention it, but..."

Di was scared of Arma's quiet face, of the pale cheeks and the wrinkles that had appeared around her eyes, of her smile that sank into a sad lake where her mother's days were stranded.

"Di, when you go to Mrs. Aneva's place you always... that happens very often... I mean that you put on that ugly black sweater. I think that..."

"It is nothing," Di said, but under the hard stones of the pavement Arma felt darkness that scared her.

"There's something wrong," Arma said. "You will accompany Mrs. Aneva to Germany and you don't have to pay for that. And you will not attend University."

Although the warm rays of the suns sparkled in their room, winter returned to Di and Arma.

"It is all right, mother."

"I am afraid it is not all right."

Silence in their room was the quiet blood that entered the veins of the two women and made them one being. Today silence was a closed door.

"I talked to Mr. Anev."

Her mother said her words, a handful of dead seeds thrown into the desert of silence between them.

"He thinks your massages do not have a favorable effect on his wife." Di was silent. She attempted to meet her mother's worried eyes and failed. She did not want to think of Mr. Anev now.

"Mother, I told you I am okay."

"Mr. Anev does not think so," Arma went on.

She was an obstinate woman, dangers and fears did not stop her.

"Mr. Anev asked me why you refused to give him relaxing massages. On the other hand he said you persevered in your efforts to work for his wife. Mr. Anev suspects that..."

Arma's voice broke and her scared eyes, rapid like a December wind, touched her daughter's dark face. "Mr. Anev suspects that there is an unnatural relationship between Mrs. Aneva and... you."

Di kept silent.

"Is that true, Di?"

Di did not say anything. She thought that she was going to cry, but hadn't Arma said it was a shame to snivel and show the world you were scared and desperate?

"Mr. Anev thinks you have a very peculiar influence on his wife."

"He is wrong," Di said.

"Peter is not interested in you anymore. Did he break up with you?"

"Peter is at some fashionable Turkish resort in Antalia," Di answered.

"It seems to me he stayed there too long."

"Yes, too long."

A WEEK AFTER DI PASSED HER EXAM in 19th century French literature, a stranger waited for her at the front door of the building where she lived. He did not introduce himself to her; he grabbed her hand and dragged her into the lift. Then he pressed her shoulders with his right arm and calmly, as if he intended to invite her to dinner, said, "Di, you, must sign some documents."

He produced a sheet of paper which read, "I, Di Kumova, holder of Identification Card N 1239865, issued on 12 June 2010 by the Ministry of Interior Sofia, Bulgaria, series A, Personal Citizenship Nr. 2004826564, declare that I received 1000 (one thousand) US dollars for the services I provided to Mr. Peter Petrov on 10 February, 2013. Signature..."

The young man's mouth touched Di's ear, then his marble cold voice hissed, "Di, be wise! Sign the declarations for the months of September, October, November, and December."

Di could not be anything but wise, for the young man opened his mouth and bit her ear. His right hand flattened her against the wall of the lift.

"Be wise," he mumbled as he bit her neck.

He paused, looked her in the eye and said,

"Sign here. If you don't..." he chewed her lower lip. Blood oozed slowly from the corner of Di's mouth.

Of course Di signed the documents.

She remembered the last day of February: it was very cold. Was the winter going to continue until the end of the summer? Di had already massaged Professor Metova's hands, arms, and shoulders with lavender spirits. The Professor had urged Di to have a bath before the procedure started and, being very practical in all her undertakings, the gynecologist deducted 5% from Di's fee for the hot water she had used. Doctor Metova insisted on Di's abstaining from using any deodorant or scent. The only smell that the Professor could stand was of the clean, healthy bodies of the personnel who took care of her. Di had started the regular pirouettes along her client's broad shoulders enveloped in a network of well-trained muscles. If Professor Metova was satisfied, her skin radiated happiness; it relaxed like a kitten that had feasted on the best cat food. This was clean and well-meaning skin. Di had to work on the legs, but she had to rub her arms, armpits, and elbows with lavender spirits; in Professor Metova's opinion the massage personnel had to clean their hands at least once every ten minutes. That was the requirement a masseuse had to meet to be honored to touch her skin.

Di's hands were laboring up Mrs. Metova's midriff as the door opened with an obvious lack of deference. That was an inadmissible act in Professor Metova's temple of massage. A divine miracle: Professor Metova's muscles suddenly sang, her skin gleamed, and Di was aware her client's epidermis experienced ultimate happiness. There is one possible explanation for that, Di thought, and was right. The enormous Peter, red-hot and sweating, rushed into the room, his face a sick mess of crimson confusion.

"My dear boy!" Di's client whispered in a blissful state of elation, but the dear boy did not pay any attention to her.

"You!" Peter shouted. "You!" His hands landed their enormous weight onto Di's shoulders. "You!"

Di didn't have to wrack her brains, she knew. She remembered the receipts for September, October, November, and December she had signed in the lift.

"You did it for money!"

"It is only natural," Professor Metova's clear voice rang like a church bell. "It is only natural she did it for money."

"It's not true!" Peter shouted. He was livid, and his face was about to disintegrate.

"It is not true," Di's voice sounded very calm.

She spoke quietly; she had developed an aversion to shouting, the stormy squabbles between her mother and her father a throbbing ache at the back of her mind. Arma went "to the radio" praying they wouldn't throw her out of the warm picture gallery; her father hid "in his studio," with his current girlfriend. Shouting meant isolation. Di had spent her entire life there.

"What your mother said is not true, Peter."

"So the signatures on the receipts are not yours?" Mrs. Metova asked, her eyes iridescent gems of sarcasm. "I told you, Peter, but you did not believe me. I'll share with you another fact you don't know anything about: Di has a boyfriend..."

Professor Metova's voice soared up to the sky and left a small beautiful pause in the air. Peter kept silent, tall, immense, red-hot, and miserable.

"I could convey the meaning behind this relationship in a much clearer fashion, but I am afraid this might be an insult to my masseuse's sensibilities. Di's boyfriend is in fact a lady."

Peter gasped.

Di's hands froze in their tracks, dark and numb on her client's muscular back.

"Go on," Professor Metova reminded her masseuse. "My massage has to go on forty-five minutes. I will not stand any interruption. I pay you, so I insist on having exactly the service I have paid for."

Di could endure anything — sarcasm, practical jokes, humiliation, and hunger under one simple condition: no shouting. The participants in the activities had to speak in a normal tone of voice. In this respect, Professor Metova was the ideal case; she never raised her voice.

"Can you pay me for the services I have provided for you so far and then let me go?" Di asked.

She felt as useless as an empty Coca-Cola bottle which had a meaning of its own only for the bums who collected empty bottles and exchanged them for cigarettes. Peter did not listen to her.

Professor Metova's voice waited, generating new layers of contempt for Di. Contempt left Di unimpressed. She'd been there for years. She wanted to take Peter to the best cinema in town. She wanted to be by his side, she had to soothe him; his heart was in his mouth now, she knew, as small as a hazelnut, a nest of despair.

"I talked to Mrs. Aneva's husband," Di's client went on to elaborate. "Mrs. Aneva's husband suspects you exert a disruptive influence over his wife. Di, you make the lady forget her household duties, you corrode the peace and quiet in their family, you destroy the deep affection Mrs. Aneva had striven to give her husband before she met you."

"This is not true."

Di had made up her mind to grab Peter's hand and take him to the best cinema in town or perhaps to the worst one. She had to drag him out of that room, haul him out right away.

"You are Mrs. Aneva's masseuse, aren't you?" her client asked, her muscles gleaming with satisfaction.

Her skin experienced another of its rare moments of insight and ultimate happiness.

"Do not stop. Go on."

"Yes, I am Mrs. Aneva's masseuse," Di answered.

"She will cover all your travel and accommodation expenses if you accompany her to Germany. It's most odd."

"Mother!" Peter shouted his voice splintering like a tree hit by lightning. His face burst into flame.

"I showed you photocopies of Di's airplane tickets, didn't I, Peter?" Professor Metova turned to her son. "Will you accompany Mrs. Aneva to Germany, Di?" She inquired.

Di did not answer.

"Will you go with her to Germany?" Peter whispered.

Di wrenched her hand from Mrs. Metova's strong elastic skin and took hold of Peter's arm.

"Come with me," she told him. "Come, I'll take you to the cinema."

Peter shook his head. He had long, curly hair.

"I like your hair," Di had told him a month ago. "I crop mine because I don't want to waste hot water on washing it often. But you can take baths as often as you like. Let it grow long, please."

Peter did not answer; he pushed her hand away, retreating a few steps backward.

"I will not pay you if I do not get the happy finish at the end of the massage," Mrs. Metova reiterated.

Di started for the door and did not turn back.

As a rule, she came to Professor Metova's office dressed in an Italian sweatshirt she'd bought from her favorite second-hand shop. She changed her clothes at home every time before she gave Professor Metova a massage. She was scared by her client's happy skin and was caught in the net of her elastic muscles.

"Peter, come with me," Di said, but he seemed scarcely to breathe as he stood immobile by the immaculately clean office desk. "I love you," said Di.

She didn't know why she said that; the door closed like a guillotine behind her back. Peter did not come with her.

D I'S MOTHER DID NOT KNOW anything about that; her intuition, stubborn like a river that bit desert sands to find the ocean, told her something had gone wrong.

"Peter left you," Arma said.

Di loved her for her matter-of fact voice.

"So what? Life goes on."

"Yes, life goes on," Di agreed. "Life goes on without Peter."

"But Mrs. Aneva..." Arma's words bent down and crawled on the floor ashamed. "Mrs. Aneva told me she'd cover all your expenses during your stay in Germany."

Di was afraid her face shone its guilt into the semidarkness of their flat.

"What Mrs. Aneva told you is not true," Di said.

"Mrs. Aneva is not a generous woman," Arma whispered. "It is strange...very strange. She wants you to go to her place right away. She said she needed additional work."

"What would you do if I really wanted to do something wrong?" Di's voice had lost its soft lilt. That was not like her daughter, the most brilliant student in French literature at the University of Sofia.

Arma kept silent. Her face broke down, her hands, like silver pieces of the moon, sank in the dark. Her lips froze. She remembered the evening, three years ago, when Di did not come home from school. Her daughter had entered the essay writing competition; the winner was to study philosophy at the Sorbonne. Di was an excellent graduate student in philosophy, at least Arma had always thought so. Her daughter's essay did not make it to the second round. Di did not go to Paris to study philosophy; she gave her father's girlfriend a massage instead. Then Arma said, "Shame."

"Do you think you could change anything, Mother?" Di asked, her face a frozen unexplored continent. Arma knew she could not change anything.

That night, her daughter did not come back home. She didn't come back on the following day as well. These were the blackest nights in Arma's life. She remembered the smell of death in all hospitals she had visited, the narrow reception room in the police station, the local psychic who burned a piece of Di's blouse in Arma's presence and whispered that her daughter had been raped brutally with a beer bottle. Arma was afraid of Di's stone eyes, of her face that was a path lost in the desert.

When Di was a little girl, Arma used to hold her and Di was not scared of anything.

"If... if you go to Mrs. Aneva for her money, I'll help you."

Suddenly her cheeks, the purple sunset on them, were wet with tears. Arma had not cried before her daughter. She did not mend her old clothes when Di was at home.

"I am okay. Just a little bit jittery," she added and wiped the tears with the back of her hand.

"It's all right, mother," Di's voice trailed off.

Arma thought it would have been better if her daughter had not said anything at all.

"Listen, girl," Arma took a deep breath. "I am sorry. You know what? I made up my mind. I'll marry Mr. Spiro and then... then we'll have money. Yes, Di. It won't be necessary for you to go to Mrs. Aneva."

Di's eyes said nothing. If Arma looked into them a moment more she'd be sick. Now she felt worse than during the black nights when Di had run away from home. She had stayed with a neighbor, she had said later, a diabetic, who sold flowers in front of the Opera Theater. She had tried to get drunk and wanted to have sex with him. It had been no good.

"I will marry Spiro," Arma's whisper was a small ray of hope. "I want you to stay at home today."

But Di was already at the door.

"Di... Listen, Professor Metova has called today. Di! Di!" Her daughter did not turn back. "Professor Metova wants you to give her a massage. She said you were the best..."

Di went out and closed the door behind her tiny, sad smile.

It was a yellow March afternoon in the street, a gray afternoon. Arma was afraid of March afternoons. She was afraid of the mornings, of the days and the nights. She would marry Spiro. God, please, God! Help Di! Look at Di, God. See how pretty she is.

*** *** ***

NORA

"LEAVE THE CLINIC IMMEDIATELY!" ordered the doctor in charge of Mr. Anev's health.

Then he took Nora by the hand and led the way to the door. His eyes cautiously touched the heap of dollars on the floor.

"Leave her alone," Mr. Anev commanded. "I want to talk to her."

"But you should rest, Sir," the doctor said, bowing courteously. "Please, sir. You can talk to her some other time."

"Some other time..." Mr. Anev repeated, as if he held a skein of wool in his teeth and knitted his words with it. "You heard that, Nora. Come again on Thursday. Five pm."

Nora nodded, opened the door, and went out before the doctor could throw her out like a used syringe.

"Thursday, five pm," the piece of thread produced a sentence as Anev pursed his lips. "I hope you won't forget."

Nora had to find one hundred levs by hook or by crook; if not one hundred, then at least seventy-five.

The heap of dollars lay on the floor of Mr. Anev's room. It was so wonderfully green, that heap of money, that it appeared blue under Nora's nose.

One of her brothers was ill. At the beginning, her mother said it was nothing, just snot and ticklish cough like every other year. Her two brothers habitually coughed all through the winter, day in day out. Their mother commuted by train from the town of Pernik to the capital; in the evenings she came home drained, swollen-eyed, and had no time to think of their coughs. Or perhaps she did. The skin of her face was brown like the beaten track to the bus stop, the chisels of the wrinkles cut her cheeks, and her eyes constantly stared at a road that led nowhere.

Nora knew the magical heap of dollars lay still on the floor of Mr. Anev's room.

"Boys," her mother said as she slumped down into her chair in front of the TV. Nora thought she became smaller every day. But her mother's voice remained the same: big, young although she spoke quietly, although her teeth were bad and hurt and her hands were dead in the morning. Her mother's voice was free like the wind. Soft and warm, that beautiful voice of her mother was strong even when the woman was crushed.

"Bring me some tea, boys."

Nora's brothers brought her a cup from the kitchen. That was their mother's cup, a brown one, cheap, very ordinary, but when the woman drank from it the thing became beautiful. Nora was a very little girl when her mother drank her tea from that cup. What a strange woman she was. She cared for all objects at home as if they were alive. The floor under her hands turned into a shining mirror and she fell ill when the glue under the wallpaper turned into dust with old age and the walls looked plain.

Nora's father lost his job years ago. She remembered he shrugged his shoulders and went to the town square. The natives called it "the tomb" for it was the place where in the evenings the men gathered together. They sat on the benches, on the grass, on the sidewalks; at the beginning of their career as unemployed men, they talked and smoked cigarettes, then they had no money, poured shag tobacco onto thin pieces of newspaper, rolled them and smoked. They didn't talk anymore. They gathered together, quiet, weather-beaten men without jobs thinking what the hell! They could shoulder a rucksack and take a bus to Spain, to Germany, to France. A neighbor from Building 51 went there and found a job. You couldn't believe how much money he earned within six months.

There were eleven recruitment agencies in town that promised you they could find you a good job, a cushy job in Germany, in the USA, Spain, and Portugal. You just had to give them fifty levs and wait for the agency to call you. But how could you give them fifty levs?

Nora's father counted the coins for the bread and gave seventy cents to each child to buy a roll in the morning. The kids' bellies have to be full while they attend classes at school, he said. Then he made up his mind seventy cents was too much. The children could buy a cheaper roll. In the evening, he came back home and he missed his shag tobacco. He told Nora's mother he'd been looking for a job all day long and he'd make a list of the people he owed money: Kiro — three levs, Ivan — five levs, Sabri the Turk — three levs.

He made that list. He made it very diligently, he tried not to forget anybody, and all the time he asked himself where he'd find the money. Then, his best friend Ivan dropped in, "Can you lend me three levs?" the man asked. His younger son had a birthday and Ivan hadn't bought anything for the kid.

"I don't have any money for your younger son," Nora's father muttered. It would be absurd to waste three levs on a toy, for a stupid birthday.

"It is not his stupid birthday, man, damn it. I don't ask for your money to buy a toy for the boy. I want to buy milk. Children have to drink milk, you know. My son's glands are swollen like hell, under his chin. You see now why I want to buy milk for him."

Nora's father, who was a calm, slow man, fumbled in his pocket. He knew there were only three levs and ninety-three cents there. He knew he had two sons, twins, at home. He did not think about his daughter. She was all right. She had a job at that sleazy café. She had a lot of dough and helped her brothers out. So Nora's father gave all his three levs and ninety-three cents to the boy with the swollen glands. The wallpaper at home was old and the glue under it had turned into powder. His wife was a clean woman, she made the floors shine like shop windows and wallpaper coming unglued made her sick. Her eyes were distant like the path to the deserted bus stop. And he felt like a dog. He felt like wailing. Years ago, he had held his woman's hand and the two of them had walked along that path. Her gums had bled recently. Thank God the tumor was benign. Thank God she did not leave him with the twins and the wallpaper coming unglued. He cared for that woman. God knew. He cared for that woman and he gave Ivan his three levs and ninety-three cents.

Well, one guy said bread was very cheap in Dubai, Arabia. There were seventeen types of bread in Dubai, the guy said, and everybody made money like mad in Dubai. Nora's father could not say boo to a goose, so maybe he wouldn't make money like mad in Dubai. Nora used to provide eight levs for milk per week, now she could not spare so much and gave her mother only six. One of the boys was ill and it was not an ordinary cold or snot and coughs as her mother thought.

The night stole half an inch from her mother's height; her eyes looked as if somebody had trampled them down on purpose to cram sand and dirt into them. But Nora knew: her mother's voice remained the same. How strange that people's voices did not get old. Nora slept in her mother's room.

It was pitch dark, and it felt good when her mother was awake and Nora asked, "How are you?"

"I'm okay", her mother said, and it was always so dark that the daughter could not see the night rob another inch of her mother. But her voice was strong, it struggled on, it didn't give in.

One of her brothers had viral pneumonia. The best medicine for this disease was a very expensiv"e medicine called Zinat. A very good medicine, you had to swallow one pill in the morning, one in the evening, and the nasty cough would go away leaving your lungs alone. You wouldn't probably become anemic, as usually happened.

That heap of dollars in Theo Anev's room looked so gorgeous, but Nora, stupid Nora, left it lying there on the floor. Jerks hated your guts when you ignored their gorgeous dollars on the terra-cotta tiles.

But if you didn't want to get anemic, you had to take in a lot of vitamins. Various effervescent multivitamins cost two months of your arms buried in the fat avalanche of minced meat, two months of cooking stinky chicken broth. Two months under the shadow of Gozo's fists that could gouge your eyes or hit your belly where a small desperate embryo had dug a hole for itself. Nora had to get rid of that embryo as soon as possible. What sort of a man would grow out of that trick of genetics, nervous tissue conceived from Gozo's or Anev's sperm? It felt good when the stone hit Anev's skull and made it creak. That was the loveliest sound Nora had heard, sweeter than sausages sizzling in hot sunflower oil; and she didn't have in mind these cheap horse meat sausages, she thought of the ones in the Metro Store. Oh, the stone cracked Mr. Anev's skull like thunder... Now she had to destroy the small curly worm of the embryo and she didn't have enough money for a good doctor. She didn't have enough even for a bad one.

She had to find one hundred levs, had to borrow them; if not one hundred, then at least seventy for her brother's medicine, for effervescent vitamins and milk. And she had to concentrate on the embryo. Who could she borrow money from?

In the family of their neighbors, the ones who lived in apartment 6, the wife, Maria, had a job. She sold children's clothes for some company of unknown origin and evolution and earned enough to buy food for her son, Rossen. Rossen's father had stopped smoking; he was ashamed he had found no job and rarely went out of their apartment. At times, Nora saw his face glued to the window watching the passers-by. Even though his eyes were still young they had already turned into a beaten track to a non-existent bus stop. Very rarely, at the time when Nora's father didn't speak about Dubai and the seventeen types of bread there, their neighbor knocked at their front door. He carried a bottle in his hand; this was the cheapest brandy one could imagine, which he bought from The Greasy Café.

It was he, an old and loyal friend and ex-patron of The Greasy Café who said, "Nora, why don't you ask? They might need a new waitress at Greasy."

Of late, this man clutched the same bottle in his hand, but it was empty and hung to the ground like a dead bell. Rossen, his son, turned sixteen a week ago. He was a student at the local high school, once in a blue moon had a coffee at Greasy Café and smiled at Nora. She left a bag of french fries on his table or thrust a Coca-Cola bottle into his hand. In the evening, Nora saw Rossen's father; for a moment, his eyes left the road that led nowhere and gleamed gratefully to her. He waved the empty bottle and the mysterious white fire of the cheapest brandy sneaked no more in his gaze.

Maria, the wife, sold children's clothes in a small shop as if she sold her blood; her face thawed and became smaller, like a tiny snowdrift behind the block of flats in the last days of March. Nora could not borrow money for the medicine from this family.

She thought again of the dollars on the floor in Mr. Anev's hospital room. They were magnificent, damn it.

The neighbors downstairs, the Petevs, kept a stiff upper lip; Mrs. Peteva, nicknamed "the Broom", sold socks in Sofia, in the towns of Pernik, Sliven, Varna, and in virtually all settlements of the country she had enough money to buy railway tickets for. Her husband did odd jobs working for a couple of weeks as a baker or as a bricklayer or as a porter, although he was a chemical engineer. His dream was to join Nora's father in Dubai and work with him, so he saved money for courses in Arabic and soothing massage. He had read that masseurs made easy money in Dubai and earned handsome salaries.

His daughter Irene was a slender, small thing and the neighbors said she had cobweb instead of bones in her body. The girl was a ballerina. Nora had seen her on TV several times. Irene was a quiet, unobtrusive kid that stole ballet steps to build an insurmountable wall around her life. Nora wanted to talk to her, but the girl blushed and said she had no time, she had to rush and she was all right. Perhaps she lived in the castle of her ballet where hunger did not exist. Was it possible for a girl with cobweb bones to be hungry like the rest of us?

Yes, it was possible, and Irene's father became a baker, a bricklayer, a porter and low-priced cosmetics salesmen, and her mother sold socks. The woman tried hard to convince her customers that the socks she offered them were simply wonderful: not only you, but your children's children could well wear them if only you bought a pair. Nora liked the ballerina very much. Once she asked, "How are things with you, Irene?" The girl's cheeks turned scarlet and Nora was suddenly ill at ease. She knew words embarrassed the girl, took her away from the beautiful ballet steps.

"I can find a job for you..." Nora had said.

Then she felt she was all wrong. The Greasy Café was not a place for ballet dancing. She saw the cobweb of the girl's bones and Gozo's thick, short fingers; the kid's slender back on the battered concrete floor in the kitchen. Nora did not worry about her own back, she was healthy, she was strong, and she feared no one. But now she was scared. She cared for that girl. The wall of ballet steps could not save the kid from Gozo.

"A job?" the girl had asked, but Nora shook her head.

She could not borrow money from the Petevs either.

It made no sense even to think of Grandma Anna. She was seventy-seven years old. The old woman had already saved money for her funeral, she said, and had kept it intact four long months. When the technician from the municipal company declared he'd cut off her electricity supply, she took out the black kerchief she had hidden under the sideboard and paid the bill. That day, Nora brought a small greasy package of french fries to Grandma Anna's apartment.

Grandma Anna took it and her cheeks that looked like an unfinished grave, for a moment, were an endless smile with a hundred sunsets in it. Grandma Anna's eyes were not a beaten track; they were ordinary, old happy eyes that looked at the greasy package as if it was pure gold.

"Girl, come and count my money, please," Grandma Anna had asked Nora.

As Nora took a step forward, the old woman unclasped her fingers and a little pile of coins glittered on her wrinkled palm. It was small change, beautiful coins wet with her sweat.

"I've been collecting these for three weeks," her toothless mouth said. "I am ready now," she stood up, sunsets and sunrises shining on her cheeks. "I am going to buy some rice. I'll cook it with leeks. I'll boil the rice and it will become *very* soft. My teeth have almost all fallen out, you know, but it's all right."

Grandma Anna went to the grocery. At that time, Nora hung her clothes to dry on the clothesline. She had a very cunning way of hanging them: she hung out the best clothes on the first line that people could see from the street — the new T-shirts of her twin brothers, her three white blouses she put on in the evenings at The Greasy Café. She took pride in her clean clothes and walked with her head up to the customers who, at least in the beginning, were still sober. Her father's faded jeans inevitably took the last two lines. Her mother had only one nice pullover, which Nora hung out proudly on the first line and felt like shouting: "See? She's alive and kicking. She'll be stronger tomorrow!" Then Nora hung the other clothes: her mother's green mended blouse, the old cardigan, the sweater, and she saw all the long days in her mother's life, the train in the morning, her chair in front of the TV, her brown cup. The woman who had such a young voice was tougher than these black days, bigger than the old mended blouse and dark cardigan, higher than the last clothesline.

As Nora hung the wet clothes, she noticed Grandma Anna plod back from the grocery store clutching her walking stick in one hand and a big bag of rice in the other. Her smile had driven away the unfinished grave from her face. Perhaps the old lady was thinking about the meal with the very soft rice, a delicious plentiful stew she would cook at home. She deserved it and the beautiful pennies she'd saved deserved it. She'd have plenty of rice, five or six days she'd have delicious dinners. An old woman didn't need much food; she'd eat well in the evening and sleep until dawn.

Grandma Anna reached the entrance of the building and lifted her walking stick, searching for support on the concrete steps. Suddenly, her rubber shoe slid forward; she reeled and her back hit the glass door. The old woman let the bag of rice slip through her wrinkled fingers. Nora saw it fall onto the ground. The plastic package was too weak or maybe the floor was too battered and dented: the bag burst open and the rice flew all over the place. The grains rolled over and over on the cracked tiles of the sidewalk and disappeared down the stairs to the dank cellar. A small, white heap of rice remained at the old lady's feet. She dropped her walking stick, bent down slowly, laboriously. Her warped fingers touched the grains of rice, snatched at them, as she tried to collect her little fortune. The old woman buried her hands in the small heap of rice and her face was an empty crumbling house.

"I spent all the money for my funeral," the old woman muttered to herself.

From that day on, Nora brought her a little food in small paper bags. She chose the softest french fries for her, like the ones she brought her twin brothers at home. It was absurd to think about borrowing money from Grandma Anna.

Perhaps the heap of dollars was still on the floor of Anev's hospital room. Nora had not bent down to pick the bills.

She made up her mind: the safe harbor of The Greasy Café. Gozo.

The safe harbor of The Greasy Café had been hit by a hurricane. It was 3:28 pm. The cold wind did its best to tear up the paving stones from the street, thick snowflakes hit the road, and she saw two nests roll in the frozen grass, wrenched from the naked boughs of the poplar trees. The Greasy Café jutted out like a crow's broken wing in the cold.

"Stop it! Clear out!" Gozo was shouting at the top of his lungs. The new waitress, the brand image and meatball maker of the eatery, stood by the front door, her head drooping, her face both guilty and defiant like a sheet of cooling lava in the afternoon. The collar of her white blouse was wet, tears rolled down her face. The imposing café owner sported an apron, which a century ago was probably white or orange, and hurled a chair at the weeping waitress.

"You animal!" the meatball maker sniveled. Then, suddenly, she wiped away tears and snot with the sleeve of her blouse. "I'll kill you!"

Nora watched as the young woman tried to implement her threat. She looked very strong and brawny. Her hands were big and calloused, with broken fingernails and scars. The girl gripped a loose chunk of the cement floor at the very entrance of the café, wrenched it free, and the small of her back first cracked then creaked. Knotty muscles jumped in her jaw, her shoulders charged forward as blind as an avalanche. The mass of concrete flew in the air dripping mud and pebbles in its wake.

"Moron!" Gozo shouted as he dodged the blow.

The brand image and meatball maker, inspired by her first triumph and very much enraged, snatched one of the plastic chairs and rushed to him.

"Okay, here's the money," Gozo grumbled.

His paw, like a soft parachute of fear, sank under the apron. The man produced a dazzling bundle and tossed it on the floor. The bills flew and fell at the waitress's angry feet.

"I don't give a damn about your money! I don't want it, you animal! I don't want it!"

Suddenly the voice drowned in the torrent of tears and became slippery as if it spouted from the top of a fountain.

"Well, if you don't want it..." Gozo's voice was no volcano anymore. It was quiet and tame as it crawled towards the banknotes scattered on the floor.

The young woman's enormous square jaw fell like a guillotine, the sturdy pillars of her legs trampled on the bundle of bills, and the desert in her eyes glared deadlier than the Sahara. The dangerous weight of the plastic chair collapsed on the floor failing to touch Gozo's apron.

"I love you," the waitress whispered amidst the chaos of tears and sobs.

Nora watched, holding her breath. Suddenly, she felt sorry for the enormous jaw of that plain girl, for the ugly slush of make-up on her face, for the deceitful roulette of love that had spat her out on the barren shore of Gozo's café.

"Cow!" was the brief comment Gozo passed as he kicked the concrete slab she had hurled at him. "Scram!"

Then his thickset body bent down to the money and the vacuum cleaner of his big hand sucked the bills into the pocket of the apron.

"Dirty cow!"

The girl's rage had subsided. There were again tears in her eyes. Suddenly, she jumped and hurled herself against Nora.

"He threw me out because of you!" the young woman roared as her mighty fingers squeezed Nora's throat. "Bitch! Bitch! It's your fault. Bitch! Now I'll show you!"

"Look at her, then look at yourself," erupted the volcano in the dirty apron. "I'm giving you the sack because I don't care a fig about you. Haven't you got a mirror in your room? Huh? Scram!'

More tears drenched the girl's already sodden face. Her powerful leg, that a minute ago was ready to crush Nora's head, changed its dangerous trajectory and settled down on the concrete floor.

"Why is he doing this to me? Why...?"

The girl's sad words mixed with her slushy make-up and Nora again felt sorry for her.

"Why was he lying to me? Why...?"

Her questions hovered in the air like the disconsolate crows perching on the branches of the poplars. No one was interested in birds or tears. Yet Nora made an important inference: the only thing Gozo reacted to was the big clump of concrete which a minute ago was about to hit him on the head. The weight of that clump was more convincing than love and loyalty. It turned out Gozo spoke only the language of iron bars which could squash his ribs.

"What do you want?" he turned to Nora.

Nora stopped paying attention to the waitress' plain face. She was not afraid of Gozo. She did not fear anybody now and that was a wonderful moment in her life. She hated him and she could scoff at him. Wasn't that a moment worth living for?

"I want one thousand levs," she answered calmly.

It was miraculous not to fear anybody, absolutely anybody.

Gozo was too flabbergasted to speak. His gaping mouth formed a tunnel through which Nora could see his lungs if she cared to. After a minute, the owner of the café realized it was high time he spat on the floor to calm down. He clenched his fists and fell upon his impudent visitor ready to kill. Nora, who usually bent her head hoping to dodge the blow, this time did not recoil. Gozo stared, his mouth wide open, the tunnel to his lungs looming black and threatening. The shock was too much for him.

"Are you crazy?" he spat out his words, gawking at Nora, unbelieving. "Don't you understand I'll beat you up?"

Nora did not deign to answer him. She passed by Gozo ignoring his purple face and the spluttering sounds he produced. She slowly walked to the drawer where he kept the money, cracked it open as casually as if she opened a porno magazine, then very calmly took out one thousand levs from its dark recesses.

"Don't touch my money!" Gozo wheezed, gasping for air.

Nora had the feeling blood fumed and boiled in his cheeks. His flat face looked like the place where the sun had just set.

She opened the drawer once again and extracted several bills more, another hundred levs. Speechless, Gozo coughed and choked. His powerful body plunged tornado-like towards Nora. He clasped his fists so tightly that blood could drip from his nails any minute now.

"Leave the money, bitch!" the volcano in his throat roared, but instead of lava spittle and a series of amorphous gasps gushed forth.

"I speak on behalf of Mr. Anev," Nora said quietly. "You know Mr. Anev was beaten almost to death not far from your café, don't you?"

"So what?" Gozo's teeth fiercely smashed the words. "Who gives a shit?"

"His guys think you organized the attack against him," Nora said. "They saw you talk to somebody on your cell. The police think you called some of your killers."

"Bullshit," this time Gozo did spit on the floor.

Nora neither confirmed nor denied the assertion about who attacked the illustrious businessman. She simply put the money in her pocket. Now she could buy Zinat for her brother who suffered from pneumonia. She could give him the most expensive multivitamins in the drugstore, and she would still have money to fill the old refrigerator to the brim with choicest food from the supermarket. However, Gozo did not think so.

"Give me that money!" he shrilled.

Nora knew that if he kicked her, the human embryo would ooze out of her womb and she was almost sure to die immediately after that. Yet she was not afraid. She didn't give a damn about Gozo.

"Give me the money!"

"I work for Mr. Anev," Nora said.

Although these words were the most brazen lie she had told anyone in the past few years, Mr. Anev's very name — the surname of the local potentate sprawling like a layer of mud in his expensive bed in the clinic — the very name of the layer of mud protected Nora better than a steel shield. Gozo unclenched his fists and his bones seemed to rust through with fear. His boot that was ready to splinter her skull remained hanging in the air. Evidently, the owner of the greasy harbor had not made up his mind if he was going to kick her or strangle her. Nora approached the shelf with the bottles, studied them, and chose the most expensive whiskey — the autumn brown magic of Chivas Regal. Gozo bought Chivas Regal after Mr. Anev paid an unexpected visit to The Greasy Café, and now the golden miracle wetted the most high-ranking throats in the run-down neighborhood.

"Bitch!" Instead of lava, there was only mud in Gozo's voice now.

Nora knew there was a glass made of silver on the shelf. Gozo boasted he had inherited it from a deceased priest. The truth was he had bought it at an auction organized by the local craftsmen's league. It was his treasure and he polished it every single day. As Nora took the heirloom from its prominent place, Gozo wheezed and coughed. This "masterwork" was used on exceptional occasions. It was an honor for the guests invited personally by Gozo to touch "that great thing" and get drunk gazing smugly at it.

Nora poured herself some whiskey, sat at the table and said, "Easy, my friend. You can make me some tomato salad now. I'll have a beefsteak, too, a pan fried one."

Gozo did not move.

"I said a pan fried one," Nora repeated slowly. "Mr. Anev will get very angry if he finds out that his personal assistant has not been waited on in the appropriate way."

"Personal assistant..." Gozo's eyes burrowed deep into the floor trying to find a hiding place for their owner. "You are his personal assistant? You?"

"He's recovering from his wounds in a private health center. You are responsible for my good mood and well-being until he starts kicking around the country again. Is that clear?" Nora was murmuring now. "My well being, if you know what I mean."

Gozo hesitated. His eyes brushed her blouse and didn't know what to do next. He just stood there goggle-eyed, his lips dumb.

"Take your clothes off," Nora ordered.

Gozo did not move. She tiptoed to him, then her lips sucked in his, her hand slowly and very gently removed the thick leather belt that held the faded jeans below his beer belly. The café owner's body responded to hers. It trembled violently. It wanted her.

Nora lifted the belt high in the air, very high indeed, almost touched the sky with its buckle. Unexpectedly, the belt whizzed and cut the space in The Greasy Café into two unequal parts; the iron buckle hit Gozo's forehead and the leather seared his cheeks. Gozo roared with pain, but the belt sawed the space into smithereens, hissed and howled, poured its painful singeing weight onto Gozo's face, chest and butt, which was as round as an anthill.

Nora was not afraid. She didn't care a fig about anybody. The thought of Anev did not terrify her and she felt happy. Gozo took the blows and did not dare to budge.

*** *** ***

Moni

THE STUDIO APARTMENT with the beat-up walls and a lathe and plaster ceiling which, in my opinion, could come down onto my head any minute, looked like a ship sailing stormy waters. I glanced through the window. Dilapidated blocks of flats, balconies and faded clothing left to dry stretched as far as the eye could see. The black coats, the evening and the buildings appeared dirtily gray. The window overlooked the back of another shabby block of flats. Children's washed pants and panties hung on the clotheslines like sails torn in a storm. The radiator in my flat was precariously fixed to one of the naked walls and its ribs were covered with rust. The tenants living in the flats of my building had unanimously turned off the central heating. Perhaps they were right to curse the price of the natural gas as the basic source of melancholy and empty purses in the neighborhood. In winter, the city folks in these parts switched on the electric heaters only in the rooms with very young babies, two or three hours during the night. In the evenings, they plastered their beds with blankets, quilts, covers, comforters, and old clothes, transforming them into hideouts where they spent as many hours as they could in the daytime. It was so cold in the rooms that one could see the frozen wisps and puffs of one's breath dissolving slowly in the air.

Now, the last days of April dragged out of the calendar like weak, frightened worms. It was warm outside; the unemployed men basked in the sun in their old clothes. They couldn't care less that their coats had shriveled and lost color, blending all hues in a steady shade of gray. The benches in front of the buildings had all been broken and burned in the cooking stoves in the flats. The men collected plastic bags thrown on the ground, spread them on the asphalt, and sat silent and happy, getting the warmth of the sun free of charge.

Before I entered my sleazy studio apartment, I underwent a metamorphosis. First, I stopped my Grand Cherokee in a derelict shed in the stone quarry. The shed used to be some sort of an office building or a warehouse made of concrete panels and its windows were boarded up by rusty iron bars. My father had bought the jeep three weeks before he met his maker. Well, he was never happy with cars or with anything that had wheels, so he dreamt of buying his own ocean liner. Alas, one could not moor a ship to a dock in a stone quarry. This place was deserted, no one worked there. I believed my father had used it as a base from which he distributed the stolen cars or even drugs, but I was not interested in that. I did not steal cars nor did I sell drugs, at least not at present.

I had an old skirt that looked horribly cheap, the only one I kept in the office. I put it on and chose a pair of torn old shoes that were a sorry sight: their heels threatened to fall off any minute. It was only natural that I did not get into the Grand Cherokee. The cops would think right away that I had stolen it, God bless their remarkable brains. I walked from that quarry to the studio apartment. There, dressed up in my dirty clothes, I waited for Simo.

If Gallantine and the town elite could see me making love to the gypsy they would howl with indignation. Simo came again without underpants, his frayed jeans thickly packed with marble dust. He had put on his T-shirt which used to be mauve or purple, but now it had no color at all and was torn at the back. I asked him to go to the washroom where I had heated some water for him to wash himself.

"You heat this for me, Moni? You are crazy, I tell you."

Simo didn't even look at the pail I had prepared for him; he turned on the tap and showered with freezing cold water instead. His swarthy body glistened like a giant piece of rich coal. A thought crossed my mind: if Gallantine wetted his heavenly head like this, his days would be numbered for he was sure to die of meningitis. Simo snorted and filled his mouth with tap water, a liquid that Gallantine never tasted for fear of contracting dysentery, cholera or jaundice. His personal secretary procured imported mineral water from France for him. Twice a day, Gallantine took interesting combinations of vitamins compounded by the local medical institute especially for this renowned lawyer.

Simo drank the water from the shower and admired it.

"Your water's so good, Moni. I know now why you're so pretty."

Well, could a woman let such a man freeze in the cold? Could she let him go hungry if she was in her right mind? I had made a bean soup for him, the first thing I'd ever cooked in my life, and I even bought a cake of soap. It cost ninety-two cents and was the cheapest item in the supermarket.

"You squandered your money on soap for me!" the gypsy choked with gratitude, his face opened and beamed, his exceptionally good white teeth shone to me with the most radiant smile in the world.

"You are crazy, baby. Today you gave money for the soap and tomorrow you won't have a penny to buy bread with."

I had arrived twenty minutes late in the seedy studio apartment. This time the weather was good and I didn't mind the empty plastic mayonnaise boxes and ketchup bottles strewn all over the place.

I hated every minute I spent in the tomb of the single room of my bachelor apartment. I tried to imagine the way people lived all their lives in these funeral blocks of flats. They had no water beds, no swimming pools in the backyards of their houses, in fact they had neither backyards nor houses and lived in the cold rooms with all their clothes on to keep them warm.

That particular day, Simo pressed the doorbell as if he intended to dig a hole in it with his thumb. The sound the thing produced was remarkably piercing and hoarse. It scolded me for having made a mess and used all the power of its electricity to warn me that Simo had entered my property. Although I told the guy time and again not to take off his shoes, he kicked off his torn sneakers and came up to me barefoot.

"You've got a nice home," he sighed as he gulped for air with such thirst as if he wanted his heels to breathe together with his lungs. "It's so warm in here."

Every time I objected that the nice home was a ramshackle hole, he interrupted me and declared I was rich. He knew some other rich sluts and they were no good. Their souls, he said, smelled of rot and poison.

"Sometimes I'm afraid you'll become spiteful and greedy like the rich farts," he said once. "Why don't you give this apartment to some sister of yours?"

"I don't have sisters, Simo," I answered.

"Then give it to you your brother."

"I don't have brothers either."

"Then things with you are really very bad." He thought about it a minute and advised me, "Sell it. You'll be wallowing in money!"

I could object, "Who will I sell it to, man?" To the guys who basked in the sun because they did not have money to heat their living rooms in the winter? To the woman who rummaged through the trash cans for the remains of her neighbor's lunch? To the men who produced brandy from birch barks because they could not afford to buy beer from the shops in the cellars of the blocks of flats? People like my mother and people like Gallantine would never drive their jeeps through this neighborhood. They were afraid of flea infestation on stray dogs, they detested the gray balconies and they regarded the washing as not washed well enough. Soap was expensive and you could not eat soap, but you could put on clothes which weren't washed well enough, couldn't you?

Although the only window of my apartment looked to the north and it was constantly cold in the room, the place was overrun with cockroaches. They crawled energetically in the empty kitchenette,which was at the same time a living room and a bedroom. Simo and I had lunch there and crumbs of bread fell onto the floor. But what were the bugs looking for on the walls? There was nothing to eat there.

Today I had only an hour for my date with Simo. I had planned to invite quite a crowd to a reception I had organized for the evening in the house, which my mother left a few days ago at my express request. It was only natural to invite her, hoping she would impart aristocratic and academic brilliance to the event. My mother had majestically thrown her arms in the air as she declared that there was not a crumb of gratitude in me and she was happy I looked so fat. She proclaimed that fact had convinced her that God and retribution really existed. Doctor Xanov had said he thought I suffered from grave hormonal dysfunction, which had transformed me into a freak. After these revealing statements, I doubted my illustrious mother would agree to illuminate my reception with her amicable smiles.

It would be a manifestation of gross impropriety if I were late for the party I was throwing. What the hell! No matter what, the elite would accept me as a backwater keg of lard smelling of the rabble and garlic. They would understand very soon how much that opinion of theirs would cost them.

"Why were you late?" I asked Simo.

This time his ancient jeans were very clean. His tattered T-shirt was clean as well and shone like a lighthouse on his dark slim body.

"What's up, Simo?"

He was smiling, and that was the normal state of his face, his eyes glittering, enormous and black, like the big letters in the newspaper headlines, his smile stretching from the North to the South Pole.

"What is it, tell me."

"I'll tell you later," the man grinned and did something absurd. He held me in his thin arms, which were dirty from shoulder to wrist, and lifted me up. A reasonable human being wouldn't bet that a lamppost could heft up a tub of lard like me that high in the air. He did it and, staggering under my weight, carried me to the mattress by the window that looked to the north. I had to admit that the strenuous efforts he made left him breathless as a result of which he collapsed in my arms. It would not be very hard to describe what Simo did next: he simply sank deep into me, and I wanted him to remain there forever.

His smile hanging between the poles of my thighs was endless and I thought the universe was smiling at him. I saw his face above each square inch of my body. It felt so good that I doubted if any other woman could endure that without fainting with happiness. It was my vast mass that saved me from dying on the spot. Finally Simo buried his head between my breasts and went to sleep. I had already left him several times like this, spread-eagled on the mattress, clutching my best bargain blouse to his heart, his breathing deep and steady, his mouth a happy thin curve. When I came back an hour and a half later, he still slept, his face the quietest and loveliest thing I'd seen.

Sometimes the noise of my steps woke him. He jumped as tight as a trigger of a gun and loved me again. I could buy a freight train of food, I could bury him in delicacies, but I wouldn't do such a thing. I had a chunk of bread with me, not the fine white bread that melted in your mouth; it was one single bakery in Sofia that produced bread like this for me. They had unearthed some secret recipe from Macedonia, the baker told me, and charged me double on account of the Macedonian mystery. His loaves were very good, I granted him that. The grub I brought to my studio apartment was the best bread bargain I'd ever struck. I bought discounted bread dirt cheap because no one wanted it. I wonder who on earth thought of calling "food" that clump of underdone dough in a town where every three guys out of ten were unemployed.

Even the unemployed did not want that discounted bread and rightly so, for if you bit into it your teeth were caught in a quagmire of mud-like substance. The shop assistants regularly tried to foist a loaf or two on me pointing out, "That's the ideal thing for your pet, Ma'am."

I didn't have a pet, but mother had a Labrador retriever, Mozart by name. If Mozart had a bite of that three-day-old discounted bread, his stomach would develop colic and the noble beast might acquire severe cardiac problems. Every time Simo hungrily jumped at the big chunk, I couldn't but kiss him, which made him of course love me one more time. Now I let him eat peacefully and watched the bread, much darker than his skin, disappear in his mouth as if it was caviar, smoked salmon and expensive French red wine all rolled into one. These were the delicacies my mother adored. She had hired an artist who pretended he was in love with her and dutifully painted the culinary subtleties in a dozen pictures. She was the Sun Goddess in all his masterpieces.

"It's good you brought something to eat here," Simo remarked. What made my heart soft and sunny was the absurd fact he left the best part of the quagmire bread for me. "It's wonderful, eat it quick!" he urged me.

I refused to taste this highly nutritious product, of course. I was positive I would not be able to sink my teeth into the underdone dough, but after Simo implored me to, I flexed my muscles and bit off a microscopic piece of the discounted miracle.

I could not describe its taste. The only thing I'd say was I felt like throwing up. The smell of mold and rot prevailed, and I had to wipe the tears from my eyes.

"It's delicious, isn't it?" Simo exclaimed. This almost killed me, too. I went to the open window and spat out the piece of bread.

Today, Simo did not fall asleep in the valley of my blubber, although his eyelids looked heavy and were about to go to bed.

"Moni," he said. "I've brought you something to eat."

He scrambled to his feet, staggered and stumbled, and finally reached the plastic bag he had left at the threshold when he arrived in my studio apartment. He opened the bag proudly and produced a smoked sausage out of it. It is very hard for me to describe the thing: big lakes of yellow fat glistened in its pith, amazing red veins were clearly visible and a suspicious smell of dead animals reached my nose. Then Simo produced a loaf of bread. I wondered how many times a discount had been applied to this particular article of trade.

"Eat, Moni," he urged impatiently, as if the sausage was an ancient treasure he had extracted from the ocean floor. "Yesterday, I unloaded marble blocks at the railway station and now I have money to burn!"

His hand sank in his pocket and fished out two five lev bills from it. "

"I'll take you to a restaurant, Moni. I want the whole world to see my pretty girl."

I tried to eat a piece of the sausage which smelled of old stables, but as it touched my lips I felt dizzy. At the same time, Simo drifted off to sleep. He had no underpants and lay peacefully, spreading his legs and arms as wide as they would go. His clean, colorless T-shirt had got stuck to his ribs. His penis was not very long. Prostrate like this, Simo resembled large seaweed having numerous thin outgrowths.

I sat lost in thought for a while. Even my mother, by no means a fond admirer of my accomplishments, pointed out I had lost weight. I asked myself the same question all the time: why was I losing weight? The answer was clear and simple: sex. Perhaps it made my lard thaw? Perhaps if I came to the studio apartment more often I could achieve even more remarkable results?

Watching Simo's body sprawled like an old rag on the thin mattress, I suddenly felt sorry for him. This scraggy man, the only one who told me I was a pretty girl, who unloaded marble, scrap iron, and tons of rusty metal at the Dawn Railway Station, got home in the evening dog tired. This man had ten levs in the world, and said he wallowed in money, and slept with me. After sex he was totally drained. I did not give him money any more. After the second time he made love to me, sinking into my cushions of fat, he said, "Listen, Moni. Forget about levs and cents. Do you want to be my girlfriend?"

What could I say to such a guy?

"I have no girlfriend," he went on. "And if you want to know, I've never seen a prettier woman than you. Honest. You know how much I earn every day at the station? Eight to ten levs! You can fuck ten women on that. But I want you. Do you understand? Tell me if you understand."

Simo wanted to introduce me to his cousins and asked me to accompany him to the wedding party of one of his elder sisters.

"I can't come," I answered. "I have to go to work."

"Where do you work?" Simo asked. "Tell me where and I'll come every evening to see you. You know what, Moni? A friend of mine has an old Moskvich, a broken Russian car. He sold his cooking stove and bought the boneshaker. I can buy it for you if you want. I'll take you to the Struma River in the old Moskvich, okay? The grass there is ve-e-ery soft. Sorrel grows along the banks. I know the place. I'll pluck sorrel for you, Moni, I promise. I have saved money and I'll buy you some goulash to eat, too."

"Maybe another time," I said.

"Why another time? Why not now? Listen! There is an old abandoned cottage near Dawn Station. Give your mother and your father the slip and come live with me. I tell you, give them the slip. The roof tiles of the cottage were stolen a long time ago, and one of the walls just fell in. I know the guys who stole the tiles. They are stealing the bricks now. But I'll beat them up. Okay? They'll stop stealing. You and I can move in together there; I'll build the bad wall. Okay? In the beginning we'll live in that cottage, but after we get rich..."

"Are you sure the wall's fallen in?" I asked, and my heart was soft, soft, soft, as it swam in Simo's smile. "Why should we move in together in that shack?"

"Because we'll get married," he answered. "You'll be my wife. Listen. I know a priest. His name is Savo. I get drunk with him from time to time. He has a grocery store, too, and I regularly load and unload vegetable crates for him. Savo will marry us and we won't have to pay him for that. He's my friend. He's promised me a Monday or a Thursday for our wedding day because the church is very busy during the weekends."

My God, I said to myself. Here you are: a run-down cottage and a church wedding on a weekday.

"Listen, Moni. I've saved money, don't be afraid. I'll buy you the best white dress. The whole town will be out of their mind when they see you. You'll be so pretty! Honest."

Then I was again thinking I lost weight on account of sex. That was an indisputable fact. Perhaps I could have sex with somebody else, some guy tougher and burlier than Simo. I could well afford that. I'd be committing a crime if I slept with Simo so often. I felt guilty I had been taking advantage of him. I thought about him very often, so very often, and I even didn't know what to make of my thoughts. Should I select a heavier, sturdier man who would dedicate his sustained efforts to a rich heiress, a girl who paid well and wanted to lose a dozen pounds of her blubber?

Could I make a job offer to Dancho, the chauffeur with the busted right hand, or should I ask Debra for assistance, Gallantine's personal secretary? No, this one was no good. The universe would know every detail about my plans within an hour. I had no friends. I trusted no one and at the same time I desperately wanted to get rid of my excessive weight. But if I hired Dancho the chauffeur what would happen to Simo?

An utterly unexpected and very embarrassing thought crossed my mind. Never in my life had I seen a handsome guy like Simo. Except my father, nobody had said I was a beautiful girl. Simo gave me so much happiness that I felt giddy with excitement.

"You want to marry me for my apartment," I said.

"Nonsense, Moni. Don't you know me, girl? I hate apartments. You know what I love? To be with you by the river! There is sorrel there and the grass is two miles deep. I can build a house for you. It's child play! I'll steal some marble from the station. I am good at it, yes, I can steal you blind! I don't want your flat. Give it to your mother or to your father. I want you. Do you understand?"

What could you say to such a guy?

I WAS STILL CLUTCHING THE HORRIBLE SAUSAGE and the loaf of bread as I wondered where I could throw them. I didn't know why I hadn't tossed these abominations into the garbage can. Maybe it was because Simo unloaded marble and scrap iron from dawn to dusk to make money and buy bread for me. He could give the food to his four sisters, actually to the youngest, because the three elder ones had already married. I could not bring myself to chuck the sausage through the window to the stray dogs. I had never felt this way before. He curled up on the bumpy mattress and I thought that perhaps he was cold. What could I cover him with? There was a ragged tarpaulin, not particularly clean, in the studio apartment. It belonged to Dancho the chauffeur with the busted right hand, the guy who got shot at for my father's sake. He was handsome, brawny and I'd probably never fire him, but I had to admit he was a sloppy fellow. The tarpaulin had evidently never been washed. There were mascara smudges, oily spots and streaks all over it so I guessed he had enjoyed his breakfasts and lunches, as well as his women, on the waterproof material leaving marks of soup, love and goulash in his wake.

I reckoned it would be necessary to often leave Simo all by himself asleep in my tiny apartment. On the one hand, he had boasted he could steal anybody blind; on the other I somehow could not believe that the skinny gypsy guy would rob me of my possessions even if I forgot my wallet full of fifty lev bills on the floor by his feet. One had to be careful all the same. My father used to say, "Money, my girl, turns your guardian angel into a Satan if you don't pay him well." I got up quietly, took a step to sleeping Simo and covered him with the dirty tarpaulin. Then I decided to leave the key next to his pillow so he could lock the front door when he wanted to go home, but the sound of my steps startled him. He was a queer fish, that guy. I suspected he had an additional ear in his stomach for he heard everything. I was just reaching my hand to the door knob as he opened his eyes wide.

"Moni! Was the food enough for you?"

"Yes," I lied to him as I tried to hide the hideous sausage behind my back. Well, it was impossible to trick Simo, I knew it.

"You haven't had a bite, gal. Why? You don't have to leave the bread for me and my sisters. It is for you, do you understand? Hey, do you understand?"

This time he didn't say much although he had the gift of the gab. He enjoyed speaking. His words gushed like a hailstorm from his mouth, dazzling and snappy, brisk and sharp.

"I'll be under you now. Come on! Quickly!" he told me.

But this would threaten his life! If I plummeted to his poor chest, a pool of broken ribs would be the only trace left of him.

"Don't be afraid, gal. Five guys kicked me in the ribs, two of them trampled on my neck and I was still alive and kicking," he said evidently reading my thoughts. "Don't be afraid."

After half an hour, I left him sound asleep, exhausted, face down under the oily tarpaulin. This time he did not notice I covered him. The key to the studio apartment lay by his head.

I was shamefully late for my own party and I couldn't care less. It was high time I found a big, husky man to remove my padding of lard and stomach flab. I was willing to pay him a fortune in grateful fees. But I cared about Simo and didn't want anybody else.

*** *** ***

BECKY ANEVA

IT WAS THURSDAY AGAIN, in April, and a hot atmospheric front had declared war on the city. Pedestrians hurried along the streets mad at everything surrounding them; the sun, the spring and the trees in bloom that exacerbated their allergies. The townsmen were angry with the insufficient water supply that had turned numerous neighborhoods into nests of peculiar smells exuding from the waste bins, the carpets in the apartments, even from the patches of grass between the blocks of flats. The sparse spring vegetation looked gray in the dim light of the morning. Plastic cups, like remnants of ancient ruins, lay by multicolored empty cigarette boxes and roadside litter strewn on the ground. The town, baked dry in the drought, was a paradise of parking lots, thriving places heavy with rusty skeletons of buses and second-hand cars bought dirt cheap from Belgium and Germany. In the morning, their half-dead engines coughed, gurgled, and stalled, swathing the town in fetid mist and black spawn of sputter from the exhaust pipes. A peculiar mixture of smells besieged the buildings and there was no free space for the spring breeze in the streets. The city dwellers swam amidst vapors and odors like insects, lifting their umbrellas against each other, adapting themselves to everything under the sun including the ear piercing sounds of the parking lots.

I could say I am a happy woman, Mrs. Aneva thought bitterly. I live in a respectable neighborhood, lilacs are blossoming in my backyard, I'm far from the stench of the garbage bins, and the hysteric roar of the cars cannot reach me. Yes, it is Thursday again, but it is not as bad as it used to be.

Her husband, Mr. Theo Anev, was in the private clinic and the wound on his head did not pose an immediate threat to his life. Ironically, his complexion, reminiscent of a greasy mixture spilled onto soft asphalt, had appealed to her. His hands, covered with thick hairs like an inexpertly tanned hide, had appealed to her as well.

As Mrs. Aneva entered the clinic, the head doctor of the ward, searching insistently for her eyes, assured her that, "Your husband is out of danger, Ma'am. His body is exceptionally healthy."

Mrs. Aneva reached out to her purse; she tipped people who did her dry cleaning and never looked them full in the face. Her tips were small and well balanced: tiny, excellent marks on the scale of her conscience. This time however she stopped short, it was improper to tip Doctor Ivanov, so she simply nodded her head at him and said, "Thank you, Doctor."

The moment she entered the room, her husband's gray lukewarm eyes bit her skin. Mrs. Aneva sensed something disagreeable was going to happen. Her husband's eyes were moist and she almost felt dank mucus on her cheeks.

"This time, you'll be on top of me," her husband said calmly, pouring gray slime from his eyes into hers.

"No," Mrs. Aneva said as calmly as him. "I am not prepared to do it now."

"Take your clothes off."

His words glided towards her, injections of poison meant to destroy all resisting cells in her brain. Mrs. Aneva was not scared. Nothing in that man with a livid bruise below his left eye thrilled or frightened her. He slowly took off his pajamas, his scraggy legs triggering the old mechanism of repugnance in her head. She felt she was going to be sick.

"I did not expect this today."

She uttered all the words distinctly and took a deep breath at the end of the sentence. This trick sometimes drove the wave of loathing away from her and the sensation of nausea vanished. Other times, the sticky mass of disgust clawed at her stomach; Mrs. Aneva went to the bathroom and vomited, purifying her body from the memory of those scraggy legs overgrown with colorless hairs, kicking and jerking between hers. Sometimes it gave her pleasure to think that her husband's arms were two worm-eaten stumps which she threw in the fire of her imagination, and watched them burn, sizzling with all their sinews and cells, the ocean of his brazen hemoglobin disintegrating, spattering venom all over the place. But the stumps burned down rapidly at the stake in her thoughts; she was deluged again with the oily mudslide of repugnance and all flames went out quickly.

Loud and obnoxious, his naked body jutted out in the middle of the pink hospital room. A tumor that devours everything surrounding him, Mrs. Aneva thought, but she was not scared. Nothing in this man could frighten her. Suddenly, she loved the bandage wrapped tightly around his head. She was deeply impressed by the sight of his blood with a lot of hemoglobin seeping through the bandage. It somehow cheered her up. Theo was badly wounded.

"Lie on the floor," he said.

The tile floor covering was slip resistant, and the terra-cotta tiles, as a special notice board installed on the wall said, were imported from the region of Venice. At least that was what the medical head of the ward, the doctor she'd been about to tip, had explained to her in great details.

"It is cold," Mrs. Aneva answered evenly.

"If you do not take off your clothes by yourself, I'll send for the attendants to do that for you," her husband's gray voice added as his colorless vocal cords tightened the noose of the imperative mood around her neck. "Lie on the floor!"

"No," Mrs. Aneva responded.

He grabbed her by the hair and threw her on the floor. Then slowly and rhythmically, as if sawing the thick trunk of an old tree, he directed his usual movements above and into her. The pink terra-cotta from Venice chilled her to the bone as it stuck to her back, although she had not taken off her dress. His naked body slumped over, slid up and down her breasts, making her feel colder. She tried to visualize him as a big log she could toss into the incinerator of her mind. For a split second she could see one of his hands burn down, then the head, the torso, the penis, the legs burst into flames, and the pain he inflicted on her became bearable. Suddenly, Anev stopped slithering up and down and nailed her body hard against the pink terra-cotta.

Her head hit the rose-colored metal frame of the bed. Both his head and the blood drenched bandage slid down her breasts, carving a bloody path along the silky surface of her stomach, pausing for a long while at her Mons Veneris.

"As you see, I can do it exactly like Bakalov," her husband's vocal chords explained offhandedly. Mrs. Aneva froze. "The only orgasm you've ever experienced with me," the man remarked. "But it was an orgasm of fear, not of pleasure."

Mrs. Aneva felt her fingers go numb. She stared at her husband in consternation. He knew everything. Of course! Theo found out everything in the long run. Although she made great efforts, she failed to see her husband's body turn into a piece of worm-eaten wood which she could hurl into the blaze raging in her imagination. He pushed her onto his Italian hospital bed and moved laboriously to and fro, up and down above her, like a truck skidding off a narrow muddy road. Dry throbbing, thick and bitter like death, tore her body apart.

"You don't like it at all," Mr. Anev remarked.

"No. I don't," his wife answered, ignoring the arid thrusts of pain.

"I'm not going to daub my hands with gloss paint the way Bakalov did," Mr. Anev said, as he savored the suffering he gave her. "It was very interesting for me to watch the tapes," he remarked idly. "They turned me on."

Mrs. Aneva felt the strain slowly leave her limbs. The hot spring of fear that spouted frightened beads of perspiration on her skin ran dry. For a moment, she ordered herself to think about that swarthy girl. It was enough to imagine the masseuse's silhouette, and a cloud of craze and beauty enveloped her body. The pain inside her began to wear off, the frigid fabric of repulsion thawed. For a second, Mrs. Aneva imagined that the man's hands that groped her, that shook and shoved her body onto the floor, were actually Di's, and a storm of electricity cruised through her muscles. She felt tantalizing hunger for that girl, so beautiful and unattainable now, that even her husband's flat body was a category existing beyond time, beyond the rosy hospital that belonged to death.

Mrs. Aneva realized she wanted to see Di now. She would brook no delay. There was no doubt: she allowed that absurd fool Bakalov to meddle in her life only because he had such a high forehead like Di's. His breasts protruded a little too, big breasts of a man which, to a certain extent, reminded her of the girl's small hard hillocks. The thought of them turned her breath into a cloud of bitterness.

Finally, Mr. Anev collapsed on her, the blood on his bandage appallingly russet-brown. Probably his hemoglobin had disintegrated with his efforts to harass her. His hands let her shoulders go. The gray bats in his voice perched on her throat ready to peck at her.

"Do you know what the husbands of cheating wives do?" Mr. Anev asked.

Mrs. Aneva got up slowly. Her nice blue dress she bought a month ago in Bonn was dirtied by his semen, and that suddenly made her angry. But wrath was a feeling one should not give vent to in the presence of a guy like Mr. Anev.

"That's what men do to their cheating wives," he said.

The sleeping wound in his voice did not alert her that his hand would do a nasty thing. It stole away from her naked neck, drew a parabola and slapped her in the face. His left hand hit hard her beautiful mouth. Methodically and consistently like a conveyer belt, Mr. Anev delivered a series of identical blows to different parts of his wife's body. Her nose bleeding, he took a towel from the edge of the bed, wiped the blood, then landed a precise, even knock on her face.

Careful not to crash her head against the frame of the rosy hospital bed, he pressed her stomach against the floor and tore the hem of the blue dress she had bought one autumn day in Bonn.

"I was a little surprised you did it with Bakalov," Mr. Anev murmured under his breath as he lay down naked on the bed. "I have always thought that girl, your masseuse, would be a better choice for you."

Mrs. Aneva stood up. She was a woman who was not afraid of anything. Nothing could defeat her. He looked at her: his wife was so attractive, so unbearably beautiful. At that moment, painful with sharp rosy vibrations, he made a decision that Bakalov would have to pay or perhaps die. It depended on his performance in the near future.

Mrs. Aneva went to the sink, turned on the tap and carefully removed the spots of semen from her dress. Her nose still bled and she washed it with cold water. Her pantyhose were torn and she examined them, taking her time, then she looked at her reflection in the mirror, ran her fingers through her hair and said evenly, "I am leaving you, Theo."

Mr. Anev did not answer. Naked, except for the bloody bandage on his head, he opened the drawer of the bedside table, rummaged in it for a while, then, after a minute, took a step to his wife.

"Will this serve to excuse the just punishment you received?" he asked.

A bundle of dollars shone in his hand like a bunch of snowdrops just plucked out of the snowdrift, green like emerald fronds of a palm tree in the desert, like the enticing eyes of his wife.

"Twenty thousand dollars," the man declared. "Well, what do you think?"

His gray eyes crawled under her blue dress. Mrs. Aneva did not respond. Then Mr. Anev raised his left hand. Another bundle shimmered in it. The money looked fresh like a spring day, like the lawn in front of the Building of the Presidency, like a girl in love.

"Six thousand more," the gray voice declared. "The hookers take three hundred dollars if you add a few spanks to the regular service they provide. You can take twenty-six thousand. Think about it."

"Can I stay six months in Germany with my masseuse?"

"You'd like to know if I'll pay for your stay in Kassel with that disagreeable slut. No, I will not. You can stay one month with her in Kassel, dear. I cannot live without you longer than that, you know."

"Nonsense," Mrs. Aneva said calmly. "You don't need me."

The pink curtains on the windows flirted with the pink breeze, which edged its way towards the hospital room. Perhaps death arrived that way, dressed all in pink, or naked and flat like Mr. Anev. The fruits in the pictures on the wall sweated blood.

"Lie on the bed," Mr. Anev said languidly.

His wife did not react, but it was evident he was not angered by her demeanor.

"You will stay two months in Germany with your masseuse. We'll make it like Mr. Bakalov now."

Mrs. Aneva was an unbearably beautiful woman. Her body glimmered like a pearl in the shell of the rosy room, in perfect shape after the complex series of massages. The bloody bandage on her husband's head swooped down from her neck to the silver plane of her stomach.

"If you do it once again with Bakalov... if you do it with anybody... anybody, I will kill you," Mr. Anev said smoothly and languidly. After the hemoglobin of his blood had evaporated between her thighs, and he had no energy left to keep bothering her, he reiterated, "I will kill you. I will kill you."

Mrs. Aneva knew she could easily neutralize her husband's threats — it was enough to visualize Di's silhouette. She did that repeatedly and unexpectedly discerned different details in it. This was one of her rare moments of happiness. Before she left, she collected the two bundles of banknotes which brought to mind the memory of the expensive spring flowers Bakalov strewed on the floor for her two days ago. The money smelled beautiful, the presidents' portraits on them looked magnificent, and her nose had stopped bleeding.

Mrs. Aneva made her way to the door. Her clothes were stinking dirty and no one except the doctor, mute as an eel, saw she was drenched to the bone. What a pity it was inappropriate to tip him. Well, why not? Mrs. Aneva liked men who made her think of eels. She appreciated their ability to get out of her way and watch respectfully at a stone's throw from the mainstream of her life. She had no desire to turn back to the pink hospital bed, in which her husband lay like a log.

"A girl said she was pregnant by me," he mentioned casually. "Our son will have a brother or a sister."

"Yes," Mrs. Aneva responded indifferently as she felt the pleasant coolness of the dollars in her hand. She had no wish to speak to Mr. Anev.

"I love you," he said morosely, as if he had been soaked to the skin by a cold, passionless rain all his life.

All the same his voice made a little jump to the sky, or perhaps bowed low to the pink terra-cotta from Venice. Spatters of thick blood from Mrs. Aneva's nose were all over the tiles.

"Wait for me at home on Thursday. I'll leave the clinic and I will come back home to you."

"But there are only three more days until Thursday," Mrs. Aneva objected.

"You want to go to Germany with your masseuse," his gray voice attacked again, this time aiming at her heart. "Wait for me on Thursday at seven pm. Remember, I enjoy watching you.

IT WAS THURSDAY, 6:55 PM. The engine of Mr. Anev's car purred along the drive to the house. It snarled quietly, like a well groomed, pedigreed pet. There were no empty cigarette boxes or beer cans dumped along the roadside in the neighborhood. Soccer hooligans did not set the garbage bins on fire, and there were no beggars in the street. There wasn't even a neighborhood here: just her beautiful marble house with statues in precious metals and an enormous wrought iron gate. There were no neighbors here either, just maintenance staff, and the air smelled of lilac blossoms and blue skies. But it was Thursday, God damn it, and the punctual engine of the automobile had just stopped growling like a perfectly trained watchdog. Mrs. Aneva saw her husband climb the stairs; although he was two hundred feet away, she could discern the enormous curly hairs on his arms and legs, so hard and long that she could see them under his socks.

Mrs. Aneva wanted to go to Bonn and to Kassel. But more than Germany, more than Bonn, more than the air redolent of birds and lilac blossoms, more than Vivaldi's *Spring*, more than the discreet aroma of the banknotes, she longed for the massage of the dark girl.

It was Thursday, 6:55 pm, Goddamn it.

Well, Becky Aneva was a strong woman. Thursday would be over and Friday would come. She went on a date with Bakalov on alternate Fridays, but this was of absolutely no consequence. The important thing was that Friday would be over as well and then Saturday would come, the day of the week with the longest and most beautiful evenings, the day when at eight pm her massage began.

*** *** ***

ARMA

IT WAS APRIL 9TH and it had rained all through the night. The rain-drops were so heavy that the lights of the cars drowned in them, the blocks of flats dug the mud, and their TV antennas scrawled dark sentences on the blackboard of the sky. Arma was asleep in a chair and snoring gently. She had been watching TV since midnight: first a mystery thriller movie on Program One, followed by a horror film on Program Three, then a maudlin love story on Program Two. She had turned down the volume, of course; her daughter had come back very late that night after a series of massage sessions and went to bed without dinner.

Arma had stared at the screen, but sleep did not come. Earlier that evening, the telecommunications tycoon took her to a posh restaurant. He had asked her there to commemorate a historic event — the restitution of his property at the Black Sea coast, which had transformed him overnight into a proud proprietor of 18,000 acres of fertile land, three fisheries, plus a small winery. This event, planned as a major milestone in his ascent up the social ladder, left Arma unimpressed; actually, it brought about a drastic decrease in the shabby reserve of ten lev bills in her purse. She had to buy a modest gift for him.

"We'll be drinking famous red wines, dear. We have to celebrate another historic episode: the beginning of our relationship," the tycoon said, his eyes digging for buried treasure under her old-fashioned skirt.

Arma had changed its lining several times and had it dry cleaned so often that the employees of Ivan's Dry Cleaners warned her that one more try would positively destroy the fabric.

"Your clothes are quite shabby, my dear," Mr. Spiro said, making no attempt to conceal his dissatisfaction. "The restitution of my property was an act of tremendous importance for me, so we have to celebrate it in the most fascinating way possible."

His hands that touched the cuffs and lapels of her old coat did not care a fig about the special occasion. His fingers squeezed and despised the collar that had lost color on account of its frequent visits to Ivan's Dry Cleaning workshop.

At first Arma had suspected he'd be itching to demonstrate his unsurpassed masculinity on the fur of the polar bear, which, as the man told her time and again, he had killed in his youth. Spiro was very open with her: he readily shared with Arma what sort of vitamins he took in order to increase his virile potency and enhance his sexual desire as he subtly alluded to the amount of money he had paid. He liked to add that so much energy should be harnessed and invested in her if she were kind enough to allow him to do so. Arma was blessed with outstanding beauty, Mr. Spiro remarked every now and then, but that day he really astonished her.

"Put this on, my dear," the telecommunications lion said as he pointed at two clothes hangers, his gesture as flamboyant as if he were opening the tunnel under the English Channel, or at least a new station of the underground in Sofia. A dark blue coat and skirt and a blue blouse of a visibly expensive fabric radiated their magnificence from the clothes hangers. Under them, unattainable in their immaculate glory, a pair of shoes of unmistakably natural leather waited for her. Arma gasped for breath.

"Everything is for you, my dear. I want you to put it on. I can assure you I know very well your dress size and I hope this surprise is a pleasant addition to your life."

Mr. Spiro very chivalrously took the famous product of the Bulgarian dry cleaning genius off Arma's shoulders. He had attained the stature of a man performing a miracle, so he contentedly nuzzled Arma's ear. She cowered. Her neck was wrinkled; she waited, ashamed of herself, as the tycoon whispered, "I want you to be pretty, little Arma. I invested money in you, my dear, do not forget that."

Such behavior was not typical of him. Mr. Spiro wouldn't give a beggar a piece of cheese for free, so Arma assumed he had rented the expensive clothes for the evening celebration and she would have to return them to him after it was over.

"My son will come to dinner as well, and I want you to meet him."

The voice of the retired communications expert did not shiver with anticipation as usual. Rather, a trigger of a gun snapped in his throat, or perhaps it was his teeth that snapped, and Arma was again on high alert.

"My son will make an assessment whether you are suitable to become my wife, my dear."

Arma swallowed with difficulty and felt an overwhelming desire to bolt out of the room. She had always detested tests, examinations and checkpoints.

"Don't be afraid," Spiro cut in, his voice grand with the knowledge of how generous he was. "My ex-wife is his mother. He's a very civilized boy and works in Germany. Unfortunately, he is not a married man. Well, maybe I should say fortunately. So I'd like to know what he thinks of you, my dear."

At that point Arma's strength was completely drained, but Spiro's voice reverberated like a tolling bell in her mind.

"Invite your daughter as well, dear. I would like my son to meet another beautiful creature besides you and me."

Arma tried to turn down the kind invitation.

"Di should be at the university at that time."

She tried to conceal the fact her daughter was massaging elite backs to make ends meet, but Spiro didn't care either way.

He asked as he winked broadly at her, "Has she got an intimate friend?" to which Arma gave a negative answer. Suddenly, Spiro insisted on personally dressing Arma. He admired her drooping skin, the quality of the skirt and the jacket he had bought her, and emphasized the fact that he had reached an agreement with the shop assistant to bring the clothes back if they were too loose or too tight. The skirt was very becoming, the shoes pinched Arma severely but her feet looked ten years younger after she put them on. Spiro kissed her ankles, a move that threw her into a fit of wild confusion.

"Please, recite something by Lermontov for my son, dear. His mother was an exceptionally dull-witted person and, by the way, that was why we separated. Well, my son is a brilliant economist and a lawyer, a supporter of restrictive social policy. I am sure he has read the world's best literature on these issues; he has written a lot of it himself and he is an extraordinarily knowledgeable person,

I grant him that. He likes his orange juice fresh and will appreciate the fact if you make it for him or if you pour some freshly squeezed juice into his glass from time to time. But you must not under any circumstances fill the glass to the brim, my dear. Fill it four millimeters below the brim. That's a must with him. In that respect, the boy is an esthete like me. He adores well educated people and he *can* be grateful, believe me."

Arma felt lonely, a little monkey tethered to an invisible pole by an animal trainer who was preparing her to ride a bicycle in front of a fault finding audience.

IT TURNED OUT it was totally unnecessary to open her mouth during the dinner and the recitation of Lermontov's poems seemed redundant. Mr. Spiro Jr. stared at Di explaining all the time the positive aspects of restrictive social policy. At the very beginning of his brilliant monologue, Di nodded her head, then simply did not budge as Mr. Spiro Jr. hoisted his sails in the fair wind of self-confidence. He had won the Young Alumnus of the Year Award of Köln University after all, as he proudly declared. The young man talked glibly on and on about economy, reforms and legislation. He was accustomed to the fact that the aboriginal Bulgarian populace should by all means get acquainted with his insightful ideas for their own good. He was trying to convince Di how colossal the significance of restrictive social policy was — which was not particularly difficult for Di couldn't care less and had no desire to contradict anything he said. In the meantime, Spiro Sr. held Arma's hand and kissed it every now and then, lavishing sparkling compliments on her new coat, her shoes, eyes, legs, arms, and her extraordinary mind. Arma kept silent, her heart small as a hazelnut as she stealthily watched her daughter and the German alumnus float into the dangerous whirlpool of the tango, their discussion focused on restrictive social policy. She knew Di was dog-tired and was probably making efforts to swallow her yawns. In fact, Di yawned only when the German alumnus was not looking at her, but such moments were extremely rare. Di yawned to her heart's content at the end of each dance, as she tried in a civilized manner to stuff the noise of the exhaled air back into her lungs. At the end of the celebration, Spiro Jr. kissed her daughter's hand, then he kissed Arma's hand as well.

"I know you are in charge of the upbringing of Mr. Anev's child, and I congratulate you on that," he said.

Arma nodded civilly and produced a smile for him. That was the only manifestation of her presence at the historic dinner.

Mr. Spiro Jr. went on confidently, "Mr. Anev is one of the most influential Bulgarian partners of the firm I am honored to provide legal advice for. I am convinced that you really possess the necessary qualities for that highly responsible job, otherwise he wouldn't have hired you."

Then the award winning German alumnus navigated again through the gulf of restrictive social policy, as he at times turned the knowledge of his eyes to Di. Di ate in silence, wielding the fork diligently throughout the dinner as if she were conducting a laboratory analysis of the stuffed pheasant sauté Spiro Jr. had ordered.

"She knows all Lermontov by heart," Mr. Spiro Sr. said, waving the banner of Arma's literacy. His son said he was enchanted with Lermontov, and continued elaborating on his favorite restrictive social policy as he looked into Di's eyes.

At the end of the evening the retired communications expert

held Arma's hand, hailed a taxi which drove them to the spacious living room with the bear fur Arma knew too well. There, the expert demonstrated to her all the advantages of the multivitamins he had taken.

The success of the evening was crowned by Mr. Spiro's confession that, "He approved of you with all his heart, dear! He's crazy about you." Then the trigger in his voice squeaked again, "I think your daughter impressed him very much, too. I am afraid he can break her heart. Vitaly is a kind and generous person, that's why lots of girls love him so much, and they feel upset, miserable and used as he abandons them, poor pretty darlings..."

Arma shivered on the bear fur. "Do not worry, my dear, do not worry! Simply tell your daughter not to pin all her hopes on Vitaly, if you understand what I mean. He is a handsome young man. He has a heart of gold and enjoys harmonious relationships with beautiful women. Furthermore, I should point out the fact that he is of a marriageable age. Suffice it to say he is a brilliant match, his inheritance amounts to..."

From that phrase on Spiro described in minute details all the acres of land, the fisheries, and the wineries his son would inherit one day.

Mr. Spiro's Mercedes remained with his son who promised to drive Di to her one-room flat. On the following day, in the morning, Arma asked her daughter what had happened during the dark evening after the pheasant sauté and the magnificent red wine. Di responded with her regular "Nothing special." Sometimes Arma thought that ugly things lurked behind "nothing special." Her daughter had become secretive and Arma failed in her efforts to change this. Di's only reaction to the world was a colorless silence, a deep reserve that permeated her eyes, her shadow, and her steps.

Spiro Jr. often telephoned Arma after dinner, regularly squeezing into the conversation his favorite terms in the field of the restrictive social policy. After that amicable prelude he wanted to know where Di was, he would like to inform her of significant development in his work, he explained. She usually was not at home and the expert promised he'd ring up again at eleven pm since they had been working on a joint project.

Di did not reveal what that project was; she had remarked it was "nothing special," and Arma was worried. At eleven pm her daughter answered the phone call.

"Yes, Vitaly, it's me," she said, and then she listened for half an hour to what the wire poured into her ear. At the end of the chat she inserted, "I love you too." Once, after the interminable tête-à-tête, Di told her mother, "I'm okay. Don't worry. I'll come back tomorrow in the evening."

She saw her daughter in the evening on the following day.

*** *** ***

Di

LIFE HAD GONE ON, drab and uneventful, until April 9th, when Arma and her daughter were together in their one room flat. Arma snored softly and Di, covered with many blankets, slept on her stomach. She had turned her back on the night and on the world. It was midnight. The rain poured its cold revenge on the blocks of flats, the buses had given up running to and from the central station, a lonely window in the building opposite theirs glittered hesitantly, and Arma thought, folks in this neighborhood switch on the lamps after midnight if something bad has happened. After midnight the old telephone on the night table cut the night with its electric shrieking. Arma jumped out of bed. She was afraid of its stinging sound.

Perfectly composed, as if friends regularly rang her up at two am, Di lifted the receiver off its hook. The telephone had landed by a miracle in their apartment after one of her father's drunken sprees when the man was seized by untypical generosity. Although the thing was quite old, it still worked — unlike other pieces of electrical equipment in Arma's home.

"Yes?" Di's voice sounded calm as usual, a trained voice of a person accustomed to being polite in all situations, one expecting anything from smart big money guys.

"Dilina," the telephone shot at her. "Professor Alexandra Metova is speaking!"

"Yes, Mrs. Met..." but the electric current did not allow Di to complete the sentence.

"I have explicitly told you not to address me as 'Mrs. Metova.'" The receiver was suddenly mad, then it evidently made up its mind that it was not the appropriate time for squabbles and spats. "Dilina, Peter is sick. Come to my home immediately."

"Peter?" Di gasped. "What's the matter with him?"

"You have the nerve to ask me!" the electricity in the air snapped and the cracked bedside table shook. "You have no right to act like this, Dilina! You know what happened yesterday, don't you?"

Fuming silence waited for Di to reply, but Di had no idea what had happened the day before.

"Yesterday Peter met you. You were with some...vagabond."

The Professor's voice despised Di after midnight on April 10th, and at the same time it was fed up with the pouring rain.

"Come immediately, Di. Peter...Peter...I feel ashamed to tell you. I am in a very difficult position... Peter must have taken sleeping pills after his painful encounter with you. Fortunately, I never let him drift far from my eyes. The experts at Pirogov pumped his stomach."

"Mrs. Metova..."

"Do not address me as Mrs. Metova," the voice attacked, but then calmed down quickly and continued along the meek route of request. "Please, Dilina, come. Peter threatened he'd take more sleeping pills again and then perhaps I wouldn't be nearby."

"I'm coming," said Di quietly.

She never took the liberty of raising her voice, and was sure she had fallen out of habit of shouting. Her responses circled within the radius of "No, Ma'am" to the reverential "Yes, really, Ma'am." Outside this range the words she pronounced disintegrated into silences and nerves.

"Dilina," Professor Metova had taken hold of the situation and controlled it with the iron will of a born leader. "An hour ago, I sent a car to bring you to my place. My chauffeur is waiting for you in front of your block of flats."

"Yes, Professor Metova."

The rain beat against the window of the one-room flat intent on drilling it then drenching Arma's bed.

"What is it?" Arma turned to her daughter.

"A taxi is waiting for me in front of the building," Di answered. After that conversation about Mrs. Aneva something between them had broken. Di avoided looking at her mother when Arma left the food in the fridge and the fridge became the object through which they communicated. It was something else, too. The fridge was the only place where the cockroaches could not reach the bread. This device, too, faithful so far, betrayed Arma: the bottom compartment could not freeze the cheap sausages she had left there. The cockroaches seemed to have gotten wind of this peculiarity and at times Di found several of them in the plate with the cheese. The freezing insects lay on their backs wriggling their tiny legs, their bellies full. After her mother had spent several weekends with Mr. Spiro, she resembled more and more these obstinate hardy bugs that crept at the risk of their life into the refrigerator: her stomach full and almost dead with cold.

Arma's dark, intelligent face shone in the dusk and the bitterness of her expression made Di feel like a rat. Her mother's loneliness was intense and frightening. Di could see in her eyes the shadow of the ugly fights which would explode in the future on the bear rug in Spiro's brilliantly clean living room, in the kitchen with the expensive appliances, in his bedroom where the furniture was Dutch and Flemish and the mattresses were made in France. Her mother had to keep quiet; in fact, that would not be difficult for her. Her mother had always been unobtrusive and discreet, but somehow Di could not imagine her sitting on the bed in her pajamas in Spiro's apartment — the man of property who owned fifty thousand acres of land — with the big refrigerator full of expensive foods, and now with Arma.... Arma...a little frozen cockroach that had dragged itself to the plate with the cheese to have a bite and die.

It was weird Di thought about her mother now when Peter needed her. Her mother and Peter were her whole world. Even this cold April rain that brought the winter back to town, even the black sky and the air that smelled of parking lots: everything mattered only if Peter and her mother were around. Only if her mother and Peter were okay.

"Don't go," Arma said from her bed. "Will you go to Spiro's son?" she asked.

"To Peter," Di answered.

Her calm voice left a neat trace like a champion skier who did not fear the heaps of ice in his way. "If he is all right, I will come back home. If not, I'll see you tomorrow in the evening."

"What's the matter with Peter?" Arma asked. "You broke with him, didn't you?"

"He is all right," Di answered as she put on the inevitable pair of black jeans she had bought from Chic Store, second-hand clothes from Germany and the Netherlands.

"There's not a living soul left in the streets," Arma muttered. "You could get killed."

Di did not hear that somebody could bump her off. She was already climbing down the stairs.

I can do nothing for her, Arma thought, absolutely nothing. If I had been stronger, if only I had not divorced then maybe...If she had not been so reserved, if I... If I marry Spiro, perhaps I'll be able to help her. Of late, Spiro's son, this paragon of economics, preferential shares and imperturbable self-confidence, showed up regularly in front of their cracked and crumbling block of flats, looking very grand behind the wheel of his Mercedes. After the cold winter months the one room flat seemed even narrower. Arma's admiration for the prosperous consultant had evaporated. His eyes, razor blades that cut all they touched, seemed to do a rapid calculation when her daughter spoke to him. A smell of success exuded from that man and engulfed Di in its self-confident cloud. Perhaps Spiro was right; the son should go back to his thriving Germany and leave her daughter alone.

Arma thought about the bear rug in front of the fireplace and imagined Spiro's perfectly kept hands on her shoulders, then on her breasts and haunches. Then her evil eye, buried deep in her brain tissue, the eye of imagination, saw the well groomed, extraordinarily fine hands of Spiro Jr. on her daughter's shoulders. The hands slid further downwards. She felt sick. Cold April drizzle regularly accompanied this eminent man. The rain at least leaves green grass in its wake, Arma thought. Dirty dishes marked the visits of Mr.

Spiro's son to their town. The empty plates on the restaurant tables were the only tangible insignia of his genius, but Arma and her daughter enjoyed the meals. Every time the food was good and perhaps cost much more than what Arma needed in order to keep their one-room flat going for several months.

It's cold, and Di did not take her coat, Arma thought. She hated it when her daughter went out in the dead of night like this. But one had to get accustomed to things, otherwise... Her daughter was the best student in contemporary French literature. She wanted to study at the Sorbonne. Arma didn't have money and Arma could not help her. Her daughter did not sleep at home at night. Where did she go? To Mrs. Aneva? That woman was dangerous; Arma sensed the threatening impenetrable depth in her eyes. To Peter? Perhaps Di had lied to her they had split. Or did Di visit Spiro's son? Lies appalled Arma. Her thoughts about her daughter had been free of doubts and fibs, but now she was not sure.

Well, one had to close one's eyes and use earplugs in order to survive. Otherwise one disappeared, vanished like wastewater in the sink. But then life made no sense. Arma did not know what was better: to think Di had lied, or to close the earth behind her.

"Mother," Di had said quietly as if her voice was wrapped in a gauze pad.

Di was in her old black sweater, but in spite of that, and in spite the cold, rainy night she looked beautiful.

"What happened to that man from the cheap café? The one you went to book parties with. He brought us eggs last night, but you were with Spiro. He left some money for you to buy vitamins." Arma didn't answer.

"What happened to him?" Di asked again.

"Nothing."

The vacuum behind this word was an important part of Arma's life. If she shouted her blood would turn into a cloud of dead atoms.

"You sleep with Spiro. Do you sleep with the other old man as well?" her daughter's voice pushed on. Arma wanted to scream, but she did nothing. She made no reply. Arma had to get out of the old crumbling building. She dreamt of running away from her room. She didn't want to set foot in this place again. But she could not live without Di.

*** *** ***

NORA

IT WAS ABOUT NINE PM, and in April at that time the dusk was thick and clammy. The sky split into angry clouds and rain swept the streets. At that moment, God was perhaps plowing a celestial cornfield, so he was too busy to keep an eye on the town by the Struma River. The rain was coming down in torrents. Her mother had forgotten to take her umbrella. She came back from work at 11 pm and Nora kept the potato soup hot on the plate for her. Her brothers were not at home, but she did not worry about them. They sat on the bench in front of the block of flats and either gambled or sold scrap iron which they stole from the villas in the nearby villages. They walked off with barbed wire, iron fences and iron pails from the backyards, plundered all sorts of metal objects and later peddled them to dealers for a handful of small change. Her twin brothers were fifteen years old and both drank a lot. Sometimes Nora saw them on her way home from The Greasy Café, two shadows with arms around each other's shoulders, staggering, stumbling, one of them roaring a dirty word in English or shouting a ditty. The other one sang an entirely different song or rather he snarled or howled it, so ugly and unintelligible that no man alive could recognize the tune.

Nora showed them the way home. The smaller one, Geno, was very good at mathematics in school and when his math teacher met him in the street very drunk, cursing at the top of his voice, she sent for Nora's mother. Nora's mother could not go to the schoolmaster's office because she worked in a bakery owned by a wealthy Arab. The Arab was a decent guy, although the minute he saw Nora he said he was in love with her and asked how much it would cost him to take her to a famous seaside resort of her choice for a week.

"I don't like you," Nora answered him bluntly, and the conversation died.

The Arab said he would fire her mother if she didn't show up on time and added he was not interested in teachers, young or old. It was Nora who met Geno's math teacher.

"Geno is a very clever boy," the woman started. "It will be a great loss not only to your family but...but to the whole town if he quits school. I mean it. I've been working here for twenty-two years now, and I've had only one more student like him. She became a professor at the University of Sofia then went... was it to the USA, or to Germany? I can't say for sure. Geno has natural talent for mathematics. Exceptional talent! It is in his blood. Please, ask him not to drink. My sons are in Germany. They work there. I know Geno's twin brother, and I know you and your mother. So if you want I'll pay for the subscription to the *Mathematics and Programming Journal*. Geno will love it, I'm sure."

"Thank you," Nora had answered.

"It's a crime if he loses interest in mathematics," the teacher had said. She was tall and dark, a thin woman with long beautiful fingers.

She gave Nora money to pay the subscription price. That evening Geno came home early. He looked guilty when he and his twin brother Gero went out, the money for the subscription to *Mathematics and Programming Journal* burning a hole in his pocket. That evening, the twins frittered away all they had on booze.

Now and again, Nora gave them money she had saved for a rainy day when she worked in The Greasy Café. She was happy this time that it was only bronchitis. Her brother Gero had not contracted pneumonia as she had feared. Although he coughed badly and was still weak, he went to school. He was an industrious boy, cleaned the garbage bins in the cafés on Main Street, swept floors, sold the scrap iron he had stolen, and always had money. Geno was no good at stealing; guards often caught him and beat him up. Once, he had to stay in the hospital because his collarbone was broken in one of his frequent fights. His math teacher went to visit him; she lived near City Hospital and her sons lived in Germany so she had a lot of spare time. Nora and her mother wondered what they should do to thank her.

"Enroll him in the specialized high school for mathematics and science," Mrs. Getova said.

"But..." Nora's mother, with the most beautiful voice as free as the wind, could say nothing more.

"There is a good course for advanced students of mathematics in our school. It will be free for him because he earned the top score in the mathematics contest of the region. I...I feel embarrassed, but...there are some good pairs of slacks and shoes at home. They were my son's. Now are too small for him. Perhaps, Ma'am, you could take them for your boys. I'd very much like

Geno to represent our school at the national mathematics competition in Varna."

"All right," Nora's mother had said.

Nora knew very well that they had no money to buy a round-trip ticket to Varna. But perhaps they could sell the small old TV set and Geno would go to the competition.

Well, the boy did not travel to Varna. He and Gero sold the pants and the shoes that the math teacher had given them. In the evening, they came home drunk, reeling and stumbling up the stairs.

Nora saw them and muttered under her breath, "This is not honest. This is not right, God."

In the morning, she asked Gozo to let the twins sweep the floor of his café for eight pounds of minced beef a month. Nora had to do something for Geno. That sickly boy had to study! He could make a great scientist one day.

In the evening, after her mother came home from work worn-out, her sons and Nora sat at the kitchen table to have dinner together, all four of them.

"Will you take part in the math course?" Nora's mother asked as she looked Geno in the eye.

"What for?" the boy answered. "Does mathematics fill our stomachs? Dad should have taken me and my brother with him to Dubai. We'd clean hotel rooms and we'd send you money."

"Your math teacher said you were doing very well, son. She wants you to enter the competition in Varna."

"She's crazy," Geno snapped.

SOMEBODY WAS POUNDING at the door of the flat. The bell did not work for any reason at all. It seemed the person banging at the door outside had lost patience, for the door opened and wet shoes splayed muddied water onto the concrete floor in the corridor. There was no linoleum on the floor behind the threshold. Her brothers had sold the flooring months ago. The newcomer walked in as freely as if he was in his own home.

"Hello. Is somebody in here?" a man's thick voice cried out.

Nora was silent and scared. She grabbed the chopper hidden behind the door of the kitchen.

"Hey! Are there people in here?"

What Nora saw in the corridor made her drop the chopper on the floor. A big man dressed in a pair of denim overalls stood in her flat shouldering the warped and ragged figure of a boy. Blood dripped onto the cement floor. The stranger's trouser legs were blood-soaked up to the knee.

"So, you're here," the man said. "Where should I leave this one? The second one's outside."

Nora pointed at the plank bed in the kitchen where she sometimes slept. It was covered with an old, shabby rug.

"He'll mess up the bed," the man said in a non-committal voice. "I see it's not very clean though, so don't worry. Wait here. I'll go and bring in the other one."

The second one was Gero. His face resembled a sunflower without its seeds, the skin was covered everywhere with small sores as if pierced with a gimlet.

"Nora," the boy groaned, a stream of blood trickling down his mouth.

"Don't panic," the man said. "There's nothing busted. His ribs are okay. He's bleeding at the mouth. Bit his tongue. The other one's not okay — that's a fact. Show me a place where I can leave him."

Nora entered the living room. When her father still had a job, he'd partitioned the room with lacquered, smoked boards on which her mother laid various flowerpots. When her brothers were younger, her mother used to arrange textbooks on them too. These days the boys threw dirty socks and smelly T-shirts all over the place. Her parents' broad bed was in the darkest part of the room. Nora wondered where she had met the stranger before and what he'd say about the mess. There were two bunks by the wall, one above the other, in the better half of the room where the twins slept, but the shirts and shorts on the floor looked knee deep. When the man in the blue overalls came back, carrying Gero on his shoulders, Nora took him to the half of the room behind the varnished smoked boards.

"I'm sorry to bring you in here. It's a little untidy," she mumbled.

"It's piggish," the man said. "Hey, be careful. Maybe he has some ribs busted. They beat him with iron bars."

"Who were they?"

"Who do you think? Mr. Anev's guards. They caught the kids stealing scrap iron from his warehouse."

"Who are you?" Nora asked.

"Why? Why do you want to know?"

"I'm curious," Nora said.

"I'm one of Anev's guys."

"Then you beat him too?"

The man did not look embarrassed. He peeked into her eyes — his were as round and brown as a dog's — and answered flatly, "Yes, I beat both of them."

Nora saw that he was tall and thin, with a volcano of bushy black tousled hair that even dirty looked beautiful. A thought crossed her mind: if she had to push him out of the room, perhaps she'd have to hit the back of his head with the chopper and then drag him down the flight of stairs. This would be a very tough task indeed.

"So why did you bring the kids here?" she asked.

The man showed no embarrassment, explaining curtly, "I'm waiting for you to pay me a lev or two for my kindness. If I had left them in the yard outside by the scrap iron, the stray dogs would have pissed on them. It was raining. And there's flu in town. They might have died."

"How much do you want?" Nora asked.

"A fiver," the man answered. "Two point five levs a boy."

Nora eyed him carefully: yes, he was quite tall, but looked weak. She could thrash him with the chopper all right, but well, would those thugs from his gang come searching him out? Hardly possible. Hardly indeed. After they had squashed her brothers' backs they most probably drank beer in a sleazy pub, maybe even at The Greasy Café.

"There's something else," the man went on. "Gozo from Greasy thought you were Anev's assistant, so he went and checked on you. Anev said it was a pack of lies. It turned out you were nobody. If you ask me, you should beat it. The sooner the better! Gozo will rip you open if he gets his hands on you."

Nora was silent. The gloomy allergic rain went on knitting its cold straightjacket for the town. The windows of the other small blocks of flats irradiated their faint-hearted light; in the distance the Struma River glided under the iron, fleeing to Greece as fast as possible. The potted and rifted asphalt glittered at the places where the street lamps were not busted, silver seas of asphalt-paved rain flooding the cheap neighborhood.

"Will you help me wash them?" Nora asked. "I'm by myself. They're heavy and I can't lift them."

The man looked at her, flabbergasted.

"Are you crazy?" he shouted. "It's a pigsty here and you're a woman. Aren't you ashamed to live in such a hole?"

"Don't you live in a similar hole?" Nora asked him. "I'm positive your mother washes your pants. Your socks, too. If you don't want to help, go away."

"Listen, bimbo. I carried these wretches to your hole. They could have died. Is that clear? Give me a fiver. Now."

"I have no money," Nora declared, looking him straight in the eye. "Even if I had some, I wouldn't give you any."

The tall, thin man bent over Gero who lay prostrate on the bunk, pulled at him roughly as if he were wrenching a post out of a fence, then shouldered him.

"If you have no money, I'll bring him back to the yard of the storehouse," the stranger said. "Is that clear? Let the dogs piss on him again."

"Take something from the apartment instead of money." Nora pointed to the only flowerpot — the single remaining proof of her mother's efforts to refresh the atmosphere of the flat.

"Are you crazy or what?" the tall man glared at her. "What the fuck would I do with that? Is it true you were Gozo's lover?"

"Yes, it is," Nora snapped at him.

"Is it true he got you pregnant then kicked you out of The Greasy?"

"Yes, it is," Nora bit the words to shreds.

"You're in a fine pickle," the stranger said sounding unconcerned. "Come on, give me a fiver."

He still had not taken down Gero's shabby body from his shoulders. Droplets of blood dripped from the kid's face onto the front of his overalls.

"Help me wash them," Nora repeated.

"You are an insolent bitch."

Nonetheless, the man obeyed: he left the bigger twin on the bottom bunk and his head overgrown with the volcano hair crashed into the planks of the upper bunk.

"Fuck, it's as narrow here as in a rabbit warren." His enormous shoe kicked a pile of creased clothes.

"Calm down," Nora said. "If you kick around like that the house will collapse." She worked her way into the man's brown eyes, asking, "What's your name?"

"Why are you so interested?"

"Because whenever I fall in love with somebody, I write down his name," Nora answered not looking at him. "I never saw you at The Greasy Café when I worked there. Take this," she said, pushing a rag into his hand.

In fact, it was not a rag but an old T-shirt that she tore into three pieces before the dog-brown eyes of the stranger.

"Wipe his face."

"My name is Petko," the man muttered. "I'm not going to wipe the face of this scum bag."

"If you call him scum bag once again, I'll cut your belly with the chopper."

Nora stood up pointing at the small hatchet by means of which her mother and she cut the meat in happier days. The blade was rusty — no member of the family had resorted to it on account of the constant lack of meat.

Then she went to the bathroom; of course it was dry. There was a schedule according to which different neighborhoods in town had the water turned on. Now the drinking tap was dry. She grabbed the

20-liter canister, and after a tedious trudge across the corridor, dragged it to the plank bed in the kitchen on which her brother lay, a kid good at math, wearing a torn wet jacket and trousers soiled with blood.

"It hurts, Nora," the boy cried out.

She began washing his face, then tried to take off his trousers and froze in her tracks. His left knee was swollen — black and hideous. The boy groaned quietly. "It hurts. It hurts a lot. A lot."

"His leg is broken," Nora said.

"It's not," the man shouted.

He'd already started wiping the blood on the face and chest of the second twin.

"The other one's leg is broken. The one in the kitchen," Nora shouted back. "Get up. Carry him to the bus stop then help me get him into the bus to the hospital."

"You're crazy!" the man yelled. "Why should I carry him?"

"You are a human being, aren't you?" Nora asked quietly. "His leg is broken."

"If you go on babbling, I'll break your leg too," the man said. "And I'll take the small TV set."

Spiders jumped out of his eyes catching the two halves of the room in their cobwebs. The only thing of any value they had was the puny black-and-white TV set Nora's mother wanted to hock in order to pay the ticket to Varna and send one of her sons to a math competition.

"I'll take the TV set and after that I'll carry this wretch to the bus stop. I can carry the other one as well, but I'll take the alarm clock, this one, on the table. I'll take..." He did not like anything and trying to make the best of the bad bargain, added, "I'll take the cushion in the corner. The embroidered one."

At that moment the smaller twin, who was absolutely no good at any subject at school, swollen and black after the beating, said spitting blood with his words, "Nora, I am okay. Bring Geno to the hospital."

Nora saw a shadow in his sly green eyes. All his cunning had evaporated and it was a sad thing, but she did not say anything.

"This is our grandpa's alarm clock," the boy said, spitting blood directly on the carpet that once was a Persian rug and now was so worn it had no nationality whatsoever.

After a while Nora and the stranger walked in a single file to the front of the block, under the rain in the tight screw-press of April, the tall man in the blue overalls carrying on his back the boy with the limp squashed leg. Nora padded after him trying to protect her brother from the downpour with an umbrella.

"Guys say you are pregnant by Gozo, the owner of The Greasy Café?" the stranger muttered to the rain. "Listen," he went on. "Give me the key to the front door of your flat. Leave the brat in the hospital. Then I'll take the TV set."

Nora did not answer.

"Give me the key!" the stranger repeated, bending like a woman in childbirth.

The boy's groans dissolved in the rain and mixed with the wet noise of their steps. When she did not respond again, the tall man left the kid on the ground. Nora bent down, clutching at her brother's coat to lift him. Geno was heavy. Although his body was small she could hardly carry it along the sidewalk.

"It hurts! It hurts!" the boy moaned. "Nora, give him the key. Let him take the TV. Please!"

The stranger's overalls were dripping, his trouser legs too short. Sodden, they stuck to his skin.

"You didn't give me a fiver," he reminded.

Nora lifted the boy on her shoulders and tried to make the first step. Her foot slid; she staggered, but managed to keep her balance then took another step.

The kid's leg hit the curb, his sick voice pleaded, "Nora, please, give him the TV. Give it to him! Give it to him!"

Nora straightened up. Very slowly, step by step, she walked on to the bus stop that had thawed in the rain, its silhouette resembling a mysterious, unattainable galaxy. Suddenly the man caught up with her, grabbed the boy and without saying a word shouldered him as easily as is if he were shoveling sand into a ditch.

"You are a beast," the man said.

"I won't give you the TV set," Nora snarled. "I won't give you a fiver. Remember. I'll meet you somewhere and I'll beat you black and blue by the end of the week. Today is Wednesday. By Sunday you won't be happy and kicking."

The tall man didn't say anything. He spat, but the rain quickly brushed his spittle from the sidewalk. Then he held the boy with one hand, ordered him to shut up and spat again. His right hand sank into the pocket of his overalls, wet like a soldier's shoe in the deluge, rummaged around in it for a while, found nothing then tried another pocket. Finally, he extracted a five lev bill folded four times over and waved it in the dark.

"I'll give you a fiver if you sleep with me," he said lifting the money to Nora's nose. 'I won't take your TV and I'm giving you a fiver at that. I must be crazy."

"You aren't crazy," Nora said. "I am pretty and you're not blind."

"Give him the TV, Nora. Please. Tell him to walk faster," Geno moaned. "It hurts a lot. It hurts."

"You'll help me to clean my place," Nora said pushing his shoulder. "We'll clean my place and you'll get laid."

A car passed by, its tires cutting the moist lane of the highway, throwing waterfalls of chilling rain over the three of them. But Nora was not scared. She was sopping wet. She knew that at 10:30 pm her mother would come back home from work. Perhaps she already had. Then she must have seen the other twin on the plank-bed, the blood on the colorless Persian rug, the dirty marks of the stranger's enormous shoes.

This evening Nora had not left warm food on the hot plate. This evening her mother would have to eat the rolls she had thrust into a plastic bag and hidden under her shirt. The Arab was a decent man, but he did not tolerate thieves. He'd fire her mother if he caught her. Sometimes at dinner, Nora's mother put in a good word for that man, blessed him, then distributed the rolls among her children and very quietly, sitting on the plank-bed covered with the shabby blanket, watched them eat.

"Where do you live?"

Nora turned to the man who had already reached the bus-stop. "You can't come to my place after the doctor examines Geno in the hospital. My mother will be home from Sofia."

"I thought we would do it at your place," the man said looking at her.

"You are no good at thinking," Nora said.

"Oh, Nora, Nora, please!" her brother shouted, deafening the thunderbolt that the black pack of the clouds dumped on them.

"I haven't touched a woman for two months," the tall man mumbled. His right hand let go of the boy reaching out to Nora's wet turtle neck sweater.

"No," she cut him short. "You still haven't brought him to the hospital. Give me the fiver," she said, hiding the wet bill in her coat pocket. At that moment she had forgotten the embryo that fed on her blood and breathed her air. Now it surely resembled a tadpole and was not a human being at all.

*** *** ***

MONI

IT WAS ABSURD! Imagine me tiptoeing out of my own house smiling guiltily at my own bodyguards, who on all occasions froze in their tracks when I was in sight, their perfectly shaved faces beaming devotedly like Christmas trees. I relieved them of their duties by a clumsy twist of my plump hand and the two of them stared at me shocked, uncomprehending.

"But Ma'am," the most intelligent among them started as he timidly pushed the sounds of the word up the slope of panic. The mountain of fear he felt for me shook under his feet. "You yourself instructed us...not...not...to allow you to undertake any ac... activities in town without your bodyguards, Ma'am."

His voice broke up into scared and obedient consonants. Well, a young heiress like me should not permit her employees to take the liberty of going against her will; otherwise one day she might find herself in a difficult situation: a little bullet in her clever head.

"Mr. Stoyanov...."

I always addressed my subordinates by their family names which, I believed, infused them with dubiousness and insecurity, as a result of which my statements fully suppressed their aspiration to reason in my presence.

"Mr. Stoyanov, have I asked you to make a comment on my professional conduct?"

"But, Ma'am..."

"I'd like my car ready for me in three minutes. Park it in front of the main entrance. And I'd like to add something else..."

At that point I allowed my voice to trail off in the air as I watched the most intelligent bodyguard's face take on the shape of a broken limb that had not recuperated after a severe accident.

"If you, Mr. Stoyanov, do not want to work for me, you can hand in your resignation now. I will accept it."

"But Ma'am..."

"I want my car in three minutes," I repeated.

My old Citroen, as small as a Coca-Cola bottle, showed up in front of the main entrance seventeen seconds after I had offered the intelligent young man to hand in his resignation. His intelligent face expressed most passionate devotion and huge admiration for me, his eyes spilling out lakes of sincerity at my feet.

"Madame," the young man's vocal chords tiptoed around a subject I was not interested in. "Madame, I would like to apologize..."

My deceased father used to advise me to mercifully leave a man alone until he "familiarized himself with the situation." If his nervous system was stable enough he'd make a clean breast of it.

"Would you like to tell me something, Mr. Styanov?"

I asked him. He, of course, was still not fully aware of the situation, but I was in a hurry.

"I am sorry about the remark which... about the remark that..." He got fatally mixed up. I had heard that he had enjoyed my mother's unwavering protection. She was impressed with his capacity to be a perfect bodyguard; in the past she used to share her admiration for his heavenly intellect with me. She took him to opera performances, making desperate efforts to make him look academic. That was a long-term goal she struggled to achieve, so she bought him an expensive suit plus a matching pairs of shoes on my father's money. Their good working relationship flourished and that was only natural. My mother's standard of a man's intellect was his height of six feet two inches, no less, no more. She treated shorter men as amorphous mass, lacking high morale, devotion, loyalty, and totally unworthy of protecting her. So this bodyguard had a heavenly intellect, and my mother bought him a new car, a Citroen, exactly like mine. When father was still alive she shared with him her admiration for Citroen cars and a week after her idle chat the heavenly intellect drove a car exactly like mine.

"I will never again discuss your preferences, Ma'am," the bright bodyguard declared. "I would like…"

I had not made a sign he could go on, so his jaw hung before he had time to finish the sentence. He had to know I differed from my mother with respect to understanding human intellect. He was permitted to talk to me only when I felt like talking to him.

"Ma'am…" his vocal chords started again their precarious climb along the mountain range of fear. "I would not like to hand in my resignation."

"Therefore you desire to work for me in the future?" I asked.

"Yes, I do desire to work for you in the future, Ma'am."

"I'm not married yet," I put in casually. "Does that fact make any difference to you?"

"I think that…I am convinced that…" Obviously his mental

power was exhausted, so I presumed he thought nothing at all about my marital status.

"My mother sent for you on Wednesdays, at 7 pm sharp," I said watching his face closely. "I am a civilized person so I will not ask what she and you did during those long Wednesday evenings."

"We...we...we went to the opera...to theatrical performances..." Although his voice was strong and booming it swam with difficulty through the rapids of the complicated explanation, so at places its melodious quality was almost entirely lost. Oh, my clever, beautiful mother! She was really very good at establishing stable contacts with people. As a result of which this intelligent bodyguard not only attended opera performances, but also drove a car exactly like mine. Of course, now I could buy a limousine, I could buy a helicopter, even a submarine, but I liked my antiquated Coca-Cola bottle Citroen. Let me add that I intended to buy a rattletrap car for 500-800 euros so nobody in town could recognize it.

"What operas have you seen?" I asked.

"Well...well...well..."

That was the answer the young man could elicit from the boundless world of opera.

"Would you like to continue the Wednesday opera tradition at 7 pm with me?" I asked politely.

His face turned into a heap of twisted muscles. Was it sudden onset of toothache, or perhaps he thought he was a victim of blackmail? We'd never know. He was so upset that the skin of his face seemed to peel off, the epidermis first, then the other layers whose scientific names I didn't care about. If the process went on his naked skull would soon emerge before my enchanted eyes. To be honest, I was not excited by this prospect. I did not like the guy.

"But…but I am engaged to be married, Ma'am," the bodyguard said, avoiding my eyes.

"I am engaged to be married as well," I informed him. "You know Mr. Gallantine, don't you? He is my fiancé."

"Yes, Ma'am," the hunk's vocal chords bowed down before me.

"What do you mean by 'yes'?" I intercepted him as he tried to back out. "Do you say 'yes' to my invitation to come over to my place on Wednesday at 7pm, or 'yes', you do know Mr. Gallantine?"

"Yes, I will come over to your place on Wednesday at 7 pm, Ma'am," he answered, his eyes carefully examining the floor. I asked him to repeat his statement once again.

"I will come on Wednesday, 7 pm," he declared emphatically. "Yes, Ma'am, I will positively come."

"Do you know Gallantine?" I went on.

"Yes, Ma'am, I know him."

"Do you think he will be a good husband to me, or is he marrying me for my money? Look me full in the face," I said, and he lifted his head.

His eyes were glistening, and there was a peculiar mixture of arrogance and uncontrollable curiosity bound together by their dark blue color, eyes that immediately reminded me of clams that closed quickly as they felt a dangerous sea creature's shadow flit near them.

"Well, what do you think?"

"I think…I was thinking…" was his very intelligent reply.

His eyelids hid the mixture of impudence and nosiness of his eyes in their shells.

"You think he's marrying me for my money?" I whispered.

"No, Ma'am," he mumbled unconvincingly.

"Why? Perhaps you think I look attractive?"

There was a pause in our dialogue that paved the way for a long silence.

"Yes, Ma'am," the bodyguard answered. "I do think you look attractive."

"In this case we'll have a lot to do on Wednesdays after 7 pm," I said.

The bodyguard nodded his head. I had never accepted the body language as a sufficiently understandable means of communication, especially when I talked to a man who received his remuneration from me.

"Stoyanov," I started gently, "I hope that in our future dialogues you will use articulate speech to convey the meaning of your ideas. Please, make no signs with your hands, head, or other parts of your body. These are inadmissible in a normal conversation with your employer."

"Yes, Ma'am," he answered me in the spirit of diplomatic protocol. Perhaps he still grieved for the time when he and my father used to get drunk together. I had vague memories of the days when my father used to appoint an employee whose sole task was to drive Dad's blind drunk friends to their homes after triumphant inebriation. Dad gave his guests the best free whiskey in the district, and they guzzled down as much as they could hold. But thugs shot my father; perhaps if his bodyguards had minded their business, he would be alive and kicking now, complaining occasionally of his weak stomach. I took the precaution of eliminating hazards of this type.

I went out of the house, one of my father's many buildings imitating Alpine architecture, the most modest among them all, with the smallest swimming pool in the backyard. It was a place my father let to one of his friends and never bothered to make him pay rent. This friend used to throw stunning parties seven nights a week, so not only the spacious dark cellars, but the laundry room, plus two rooms on the first floor, were full almost to the ceiling of empty bottles. Of course, I threw that friend out of the house ten hours after my father's funeral. Now he showered me with poisonous threats whenever he saw me driving my Pajero Jeep and made indecent gestures in the wake of my powerful car. The situation in town was further inflamed by his promises to break my fat head, after which he intended to melt my lard in a rusty iron tub. I had to admit that his malice was great fun. I sent him a letter in which I made it known that I allowed him to berate and rail against me until April 26th: that was the date when William Shakespeare was baptized in 1564. After April 26th, my loyal employees would bring in a claim against him and he would certainly do time in some cozy Bulgarian punitive institution. It was on the 19th of April that he could make his rude gestures at my Pajero Jeep for one more week.

I took the comfortable seat behind the wheel of my Citroen, sinking into my bodyguards' silent horror, enveloped by the squeaking sounds of the leather upholstery. Four of my bodyguards bowed down before me as the most obsequious one hurried to fasten my seat belt, an exercise in the course of which he almost lay on my breasts.

"I am sorry, madam," he made an attempt at a lame excuse.

"It was a pleasure," I said arrogantly.

I didn't know who did it; perhaps it was my mother and her as yet loving husband Doctor Xanov who spread legends of me in town. According to the myths, I was a profligate monster whose only pleasure was to sexually abuse my subordinates in a most humiliating manner. I was rumored to buy apartments for my numerous lovers from desperate people whom I cast out in the street. Although my father was disgusting, illiterate, and saucy, he was by far more compassionate and honest than I was; people thought I was a freak. The combination of millions plus an inferiority complex I suffered from on account of my body was the most dangerous evil under the sun for our town. Well, I did my best to rise to the occasion and met the expectations of the general public.

The truth was I abused nobody as far as sex was concerned. And who wanted to buy real estate in a town where coal existed only in the memories of the old colliers who could hardly buy enough bread on their meager pensions? One tenth of the blocks of flats jutted out empty into the fields, their windowpanes broken, their doors wrenched from their fixtures, heaps of sunflower husks like black snowdrifts piled in front of the gaping entrances. The arid earth yielded potatoes the size of beer bottle caps. Why should I buy houses in this town? Nobody bought anything here. In these parts, everybody sold whatever they possessed and fled to Spain, Israel, Canada, France, and Italy looking for jobs. Dozens of families had already settled in Hong Kong.

I drove the Citroen to a small garage in the stone quarry where I kept my old beaten Trabant; its engine started with remarkable enthusiasm despite the depressing appearance of the car. I always went to meet Simo driving my Trabant. One of the windows of the rattle-trap was knocked out; four different names of men and women were written in black ink on the hood of the ancient car and each name was surrounded by a big heart painted red and pierced by the arrow of love. I suspected it was the broken heart of the previous owner of the bone-shaker. It was evident one of the doors had previously belonged to another wretched transport vehicle: how could a normal person even begin to imagine that the wealthiest heiress in western Bulgaria, the daughter of the richest and filthiest gangster in town, Bloody Rayo — God save his soul — would drive such a crate of a car? It was unthinkable that the heiress should be seeing some man in his right mind. She was so fat, although she sat in a special chair that hid the blubber around what one would with utmost difficulty call "the small of her back." Well, her man was a ratty tatterdemalion that didn't have underpants and wore an old pair of jeans to hide his bare ass. Simo didn't possess a checkbook, had no laptop, used toothpaste once a week, had no medical insurance, and no hospital in Bulgaria would give him medical treatment. In short, he was a guy who lived with his two married sisters, two young women who had nine children altogether. Well, Simo bought food for his sisters' kids, frittering away his last pennies on cheap second-hand toys for them. In the evenings, his boss paid him the wage for the day after Simo had unloaded wagons and wagons of marble at the railway station in Pernik. He went home worn out and brought two big bags full to the brim of loaves of bread, crackers, buns, cheap sausages, dumping everything on a rickety bed. I was sure he did not eat, he just watched the kids wolf down the delicacies, his smile reaching from the horizon to the highest peak of Vitosha Mountain; a quiet smile on his tanned, handsome face.

THE STRUMA RIVER FLOWED by the metallurgical plant that had been closed down, an old, inactive chimney was the only sign that here, some years ago, people earned their livings. The roof tiles of the old workshops were all plundered and the wooden boards underneath were shattered. Inventive people had started stealing the bricks as well: five or six bricks in a rucksack on your back every day, and you could make a hen coop or even a small garage for the automobile you had bought dirt cheap at the second-hand car graveyard in the nearby village. All plundering stopped after my father's death. My employees put a full stop to that looting odyssey. I thought it was a very lucrative business to buy the dead combine. I simply had to wait a little until I married Gallantine; then I would be ready to discuss emergency resuscitation of the dinosaur that in the past fed the town, killing it at the same time with its pungent lavender smoke that left the Struma River without fish, frogs or reeds. Years ago when my family was not rich, my father and I took long walks in the woods and we saw enormous mushrooms of the same yellowish suspicious color. My father said these mushrooms made the cow's milk taste bitter. He drank it all the same and was not scared he'd die of cancer, while mother bought her milk from Greece. In the long run, my father had not contracted cancer; his friends or his competitors simply shot him dead.

There was a deserted, decrepit building nearby the bend in the Struma River, at a stone's throw from the dead combine. Perhaps it used to be a small power station, guards' headquarters, or a warehouse at the time when the plant produced expensive steel using methods of the 19th century. It might have been a chemical department or a lab because from time to time, Simo showed me test tubes and flasks that he had found in the building. I saw him rinsing them in the doubtfully clean waters of the river and after that he filled them with cheap brandy. I did not know what the original purpose of the building was, but I now slept with Simo in it.

All the roof tiles, without exception, had been looted: there were neither windowpanes nor window sashes. Some clever guys had evidently attempted to wrench the concrete panels from the cement base as well, but had sadly failed because the walls, reinforced with thick iron rods, proved to be too much trouble.

Everything that could be plundered had already been plundered, but Simo, proud of the building, which he treated as his own property, assured me, "Moni, you and I will live here like an emperor and his empress. You can take my word for it."

One enormous cement panel served as a roof to one of the rooms. There was a little window looking north towards the Struma River and several veteran willow trees whose twigs pushed their way into the tiny place. The rain could not reach me there. One day, Simo did not bring cheap sausages to his sisters' children; he bought an old rusty second-hand iron bed instead. There was no mattress on it; there was virtually nothing but a heap of willow twigs. Every time I came into "our cottage," I expected that Simo would throw some old clothes or an old blanket onto the rusty metal bed-spring, but he had no spare T-shirt. So he brought more sprigs, and after sex I smelled of willow leaves for a whole week. It was wonderful.

Sometimes Simo took my big face in his dark hands and whispered, "Moni, come to the window."

"Why?" I asked.

He hugged me close, stuck to my skin, his body one thousand degrees warm, his cheeks touching the thin willow twigs as he looked at my face.

"I can see you better near the window," he said. "You are very pretty, Moni," he whispered. "Let me watch you a little bit more. You are the white marble that I unload at the station, the whitest marble, Moni! I tell you the truth! O, boy, forget the white marble. It's not worth the beetles crawling in your shadow!"

We made love on the bedstead that had no mattress, on the willow twigs, then on the floor without willow twigs. Simo had not had time to steal canvas or tarpaulin.

Before he fell asleep, he murmured, "I'm afraid someone will steal you from me, Moni. My folks can't believe I've got a girlfriend like you. And I'm not crazy to show you to the other guys. If the milk stays hidden, no cat laps it, don't you know that? Well, I'll have to show you to them someday soon. They want to meet you, you know."

That day it had looked like rain which came and flooded the valley. It was Easter Sunday, in April, and the heavy rain turned into snow, so I had driven my Trabant to the bend in the Struma River, shivering with cold. Simo saw the car and said, "Listen, Moni, let's throw this rattle-trap into the water. I'm afraid you'll have an accident. I'll push it into the whirlpool for you if you want. We'll buy a second-hand Moskvich, a sturdy car, in a couple of months. You can find one for five hundred euros in my neighborhood."

The heat soon thawed the snow and this time I drove my pitiful Trabant to the roofless concrete panel building. I arrived there earlier than I had intended, but I loved the Struma River and its silence, and I loved the water that hurried below the willow trees and did not grow old. I liked the rain galloping onto the concrete panel, which served as a roof to the room. It was cold, so I built a fire between two stones that Simo had dragged in and enjoyed the heated race of the flames under my hands. My parents had never taken me out to the river. Mother and I used to spend months at expensive resorts and there always was a shoal of admirers thronging our apartment, itching to see her new dress or shoes; she talked to them, worshipped, desired, caressed by their enchanted eyes as I tractably watched TV till I fell asleep. The other children played with dolls or motley balloons, but I was too heavy for that, so I sat on a bench under the shadow of my enormous hat, asking every five minutes what time it was. I hoped some cartoon series would start on the TV or one of my mother's adorers would be good enough to read a fairy tale to me.

Now I was waiting in this derelict concrete building near the Struma River in the company of the twigs that had squeezed their way through the narrow window, the smell of wet willow trees and cold rusty bed spring all over the place.

This time Simo came with an umbrella in his hand — an old black one, a little tattered, too, as one might expect. Although it was raining hard again, he was in a T-shirt, but oh, my, what a T-shirt! It was yellow, big and clean, sparkling with joy, like a gold nugget on his skinny back, and he was not wearing his jeans cut to the knees, he was dressed up in a pair of black corduroys, a brand-new one, although spattered with mud from his buttocks down to his heels. I began to take off the cheap dress I wore whenever I came to "our cottage": the cheapest rag I hid in the chest where my mother kept empty bottles and old shoes.

"We're pressed for time, Moni," Simo muttered. "My folks are waiting for us."

"For us?"

"We're pressed for time," he repeated as he unbuckled his black belt. "No time...what a pity...Well, they'll wait for us half an hour more."

Suddenly I thought of the golden T-shirt. The rust of the bed-spring would positively soil it. I thought of the new and already quite muddy pair of corduroys which lay on the floor, I thought of the rain outside, of the Struma River and of my waterbed, which I liked very much. Then I stopped thinking because it was raining and Simo was by my side together with the Struma, the sky, the rusty bedstead, the missing mattress and the willow twigs.

"Hey, they are waiting for us," Simo said. "But we can be late one hour more."

"Who exactly is waiting for us?"

"My sisters, their husbands, my cousins and their wives and all their kids... They want to see you, Moni."

The air suddenly froze. I had to get out of this somehow.

"Don't be afraid, girl," Simo went on. "There is nothing to be scared of," then his big smile turned his face into a sunrise, into a generous rain with a lot of white clouds and sun in it.

I flowed with the river like a small silver raindrop. "Listen, girl, they all have already seen you — in your nasty Trabant, at the end of the town."

Suddenly I remembered: the stone quarry where my father used to dig for marble, the place where I always hid the glorious rattle-trap, was a gaping wound on the mountain face. I parked my jeep in that maze of fallen crags, then I hopped into my old Trabant and drove to Simo. I remembered a whole flock of little Gypsy kids as thick as swarm of bees, running after my rattle-trap; I was afraid I might run over one or two of them so I always took a handful of coins. One of my father's leading principles was "Always have pennies for the beggars, my girl. Beggars are people, too, although they are dressed worse than us and will live shorter then you and me." So I tossed the coins to the Gypsy kids and they would stop running like mad after me.

"The kids love you," Simo grinned. "They just love you! You can take my word for it. They promised they'd wash the Trabant for you if you let them drive it along the dirt roads. Even if you don't let them, they'll wash your rattle-trap for you if you'll become my wife."

He was smiling happily, his chin sinking between my breasts and I presumed he intended to stay there for a couple of centuries more.

"'Moni's so beautiful,'" the kids said. "She's as soft as Easter bread, and her eyes are as green as the willow trees by the river.' Don't you understand, Moni, you are the most beautiful girl among all my kinfolk?"

"I..." I had to tell him I could not come over to the party, I couldn't meet his sisters and their husbands, his cousins, their wives, his mother and father, but I wanted to be with them so much. I enjoyed the feeling of being the most beautiful girl among all his kinfolk.

"Do you know I helped Fatma a lot... you remember who Fatma is? She's Natasha, the woman who brought you to me. I built a whole floor of her house for free...because she introduced me to you. She'll be the guest of honor at our wedding. I bought ten gallons of brandy, ten gallons of vodka and seventeen crates of beer cans. I spent all my salary on the beer, Moni, and I don't regret it a bit. I want to give the guys enough beer to swim in, do you understand? You are worth it! I bought the kids many things: each little girl got a hairpin, but a good one, not the ones that costs thirty cents apiece. I paid two levs for every single one! Each boy got a penknife. See? And now everybody is waiting for you!"

His face shone like a gold nugget in the rain, the most precious chunk of gold the Struma River had unearthed in Vitosha Mountain. His teeth shone white, his heart beamed, a heart full of joy, the jolliest heart of a man I wanted to be happy. I really wanted him to be happy.

In the evening, Gallantine and I had to attend a reception, an important event at which my fiancé was expected to introduce me to his business partner. As far as I knew, this important man desperately needed my assistance; his goal was to make the entire population of western Bulgaria dead drunk on the cheap alcohol he intended to produce jointly with me. The alcohol business used to be my father's first and foremost love; my opinion was it could become mine as well. I enjoyed disciplining proud, eminent, guys like Gallantine and his business partners. I observed with pleasure men's eyes growing soft like a cheap pair of shoes in a seedy second-hand shop when I talked to these powerful businessmen. At times I visualized Gallantine's great partner as tattered merchandise in that second-hand shop, and felt happy. My father used to remark, "Nothing compares to your enemy's obedience, my girl. It is the most delicious thing in the world."

"You are driving me crazy, Moni," Simo whispered.

I did not want to see him obedient and tractable. I could not imagine his dark beautiful face obedient. I'd rather die.

"I love you," I muttered.

It was the first time I had said these words in my life. I knew very well love was men's invention, a procedure designed by guys who longed for rich heiresses' checkbooks, but there was no money between Simo and me. He lay naked on the battered concrete floor in the dank, sleazy building and I was scared stiff he would catch pneumonia. I had never cared before if a man caught pneumonia or not. "I love you," I repeated out loud.

"I know, girl. I can see it from twenty-two miles away," he grinned. "Let's go. My folks will be fed up with me if I make them wait half a minute more."

His smile loved me, his skin loved me, his heart that shone with joy in the rainiest afternoon, the most old-fashioned heart of gold the Struma had stolen from its springs in Vitosha Mountain loved me, and could not live a second without me. It was clear. I wanted to stay in this miserable shack of concrete panels for a century. I wanted Simo.

But I said, "I can't come and meet your relatives, Simo."

*** *** ***

Di

"Perhaps Mrs. Aneva has already told you that you are very pretty?" Di did not wince; she broke that habit a long time ago, her face remained inscrutable and her dark eyes were calm as she nodded her head. "I know she has told you so."

The man's voice probed deeper, its indifference allowing a feeble rivulet of curiosity to stream into the last sentence. Di made no comment. The blond man's voice sounded apathetic again; it was evident he couldn't care less. Guys like him could be intrigued if only you shot a bullet through their brains. He looked like an ancient Viking: cold bluish-gray eyes that at times appeared colorless. There were no secrets for such eyes; they knew everything that was worth knowing. The meaning and contempt they conveyed was of the highest quality. The man would not waste his time looking at unsubstantial items. Everything he touched was noble, clean and pure. Di's mouth was not noble at all. She had just swallowed the piece of the eel in special Burgundy gravy that the Viking had ordered after a long consideration for and against Burgundy. Di had eaten a roll before she came to her date with the Viking at the restaurant. She did not want to demonstrate her voracious appetite and attack the dishes he had ordered, succumbing to their delicious aroma.

"In fact," the man went on, "my father will ask your mother to move in with him. He has selected her as his life partner, and I approve of that scenario."

Di nodded her head, but Mr. Spiro Jr. didn't say anything more on the issue of holy matrimony. The restaurant was an expensive place and a sense of harmony was reflected in the gilded edges of the tables. The flowers were not artificial. A waiter stood at attention not far from their table, following with utmost devotion every gesture of the couple, but the Viking dismissed him and he flew away, a friendly black-headed gull holding the tray to his heart like a shield.

"I was much intrigued," Mr. Spiro Jr. murmured slowly, as if his words were loaded in wagons that he, the famous financial consultant in Bulgaria, had to push out of his throat single-handed. "Mrs. Aneva seldom approves of anybody; she has never liked any man or woman so far. You are the only exception."

"She is a refined lady," Di responded in the standard manner concentrating on the dish. The eel on the plate watched her carefully with its broiled eyes.

"Oh, come off it. Your mother is a refined lady, too, although Becky does not like her at all," the man remarked.

The fact he consulted powerful commercial and industrial firms had taught him to separate the conversation into two branches, leaving his interlocutor on a desert island in between. Spiro Jr. was convinced that every single word he pronounced conveyed enormous meaning. Di had already met similar approaches; she got accustomed to everything very quickly and ignored the issues she could not get accustomed to. Her face remained a doused lamp one would not notice in the dark of a posh restaurant.

"Mrs. Aneva said she intended to take you with her to Germany for two months. She wants you to visit Hanover, Bonn, Frankfurt..."

Then the Viking's non-committal voice provided detailed information about all these cities, putting a particular emphasis on the powerful firms for which he had worked in a brilliant manner.

"But..." an underwater reef unexpectedly cut the ocean of the geographical-statistical information, "Mr. Anev thinks you exert an unsavory influence over his wife."

The Viking again resorted to the two branches of the conversation. Di was abandoned on the desert island between them, accompanied only by the broiled eel that could hardly assist her. Her life had always been a desert island anyway.

"I am quite intrigued. How did you use your influence with Mrs. Aneva? I know she is enchanted with the massages you give her. Did you do anything else apart from massaging her?"

"No," Di answered calmly.

"I don't believe you," the Viking answered, putting no passion in his voice.

Di did not try to convince him, so his bluish-gray eyes waited patiently.

"You know what, Di, this evening I will bring you to my villa in Draga valley. I have a mansion in Boyana as well, but I usually bring Elizabeth there. You know who Elizabeth is, don't you?"

"I do," Di answered. Elizabeth was Mr. Spiro Jr.'s fiancée; the lady consulted famous commercial and industrial firms as well. She was a big, plump Austrian and the Viking always carried her photograph in his wallet. He had made a dozen copies of it and always had Elizabeth's smile at his disposal whenever he felt lonely or had to make an important decision.

"Now we will go to my Draga villa," the consultant reiterated.

He brought his Bulgarian girls there.

"So what wine would you prefer for the evening, red or white?"

"Unfortunately I am busy this evening," Di answered.

"Busy?" the apathetic voice repeated more indifferently than ever.

The Viking's voice was so sure of its great value that it had no desire to subside at the end of the sentence where the full stop should be. It simply moved on along its star orbit of grandeur and power where no bus stops for common mortals were built.

"I'll go to Pirogov Hospital," Di said. "One of my friends is ill."

"Mrs. Aneva mentioned you did not have friends," Spiro Jr. remarked directing his colorless eyes to her face. The effort exhausted him so he spoke directly, "I invested a lot of patience in this evening. Golden Club is not accessible to the general public. It is very expensive and to be honest with you...your dress is no good..."

Di was not scared; she had rented the dress for that evening, in fact she had paid to keep it till 11 am on the following day. Spiro Jr.'s monologue left her exhausted and pleasantly drowsy in the taxi on the way to the university where she had to attend lectures in French phonetics.

"Your mother also told me you had no friends," his voice shone from its star orbit.

"No, I don't," Di said. "There is a guy in Pirogov Hospital I would like to stay with during the night."

"I hoped we'd spend the night together," the Viking declared, his face revealing none of his hope. "In fact, as I have already hinted, I invested a lot of time and money in this evening."

Di was not impressed by his remarks on the issue of money; they were as permanent and unflinching as the North Star, and since she felt uninterested in his ideas about investments, she paid as much attention to them as she did to the North Star.

"Actually, I asked you to my Draga villa because Mr. Anev mentioned you attracted his wife. He said there was an unnatural contact between the two of you. I am in love with the adjective 'unnatural'. Personally, I am strongly in favor of all sorts of unnatural things. My relationship with Elizabeth is so banal that... What would Elizabeth say if she saw me bringing you to my Draga villa? I admit the Draga neighborhood is not as select and smart as the Boyana neighborhood however... The Boyana neighborhood is the place where Bulgarian men of genius live and you should understand what I mean."

"Do you know what? Your relationship with Elizabeth is surely important for you," Di said. "But it is hardly of any interest to me in spite of the investments you made in the evening today."

"I know who is in Pirogov Hospital." A categorical smile crowned the Viking's blond beard. "A man who was unfortunate to see us kissing. Then the wretch made a decision to commit suicide. That's his right after all."

"We were not kissing," Di interrupted him. "What would Elizabeth say if she saw us kiss? We stood pressing against each other. Everybody does that, don't they?"

"I know and respect Professor Metova. Professor Metova is Mr. Anev's family doctor. Anev Jr. was born in her hands. Maybe you didn't know that."

"Good hands," Di remarked quietly.

"Doctor Metova pays you a monthly fee to take sexual care of her son. That is a stroke of genius on her part, if you ask me. I have to attend to a small legal-financial operation in Paris," the Viking said. "Elizabeth cannot accompany me to France, so why don't you come with me? My French is not that brilliant and it will be a pleasure to pay you for your translation services...in addition to... you know what."

"I'll think about it. This evening, however, I'll go to Pirogov Hospital," Di said.

"Okay," the star orbit and the voice sounded willing to agree. "We'll do it in the car. Then I'll give you a lift to Pirogov."

Spiro Jr. beckoned to the waiter, who immediately flew over carrying the tray exquisitely; an employee whose white shirt gleamed like a lighthouse in the restaurant amidst an ocean of confidence and reliability.

"What can you offer us for dessert?"

After the waiter wrote down most diligently the gentleman's order and went away, Spiro Jr. added, "Di, if you come with me, you won't go to Germany with Mrs. Aneva. An unpleasant alternative, but I am positive you'll make the right choice. What's your decision?"

"What would Elizabeth say if she could hear my answer?" Di murmured.

In the beginning Spiro Jr.'s voice reminded her of a big chunk of meat in a freezer, but it suddenly sounded human: the voice of a man who wanted to sleep with her, Elizabeth and her smile watching him closely from a color photograph all the while. His fiancée Elizabeth, who had visited Sofia several times, and Spiro

Jr., the prosperous consultant, had built the "manor" in Boyana neighborhood especially for his beloved Liz. Yes, Spiro Jr. loved all untraditional approaches, cars and women, and for that reason he invested so much energy and time in talking to her.

"You have to buy an apartment to which you will take only me," Di said quietly.

On principle, she never spoke loudly. Her words, however, made Spiro Jr. choke on his own tongue.

"An apartment for you?" his voice collapsed from the star orbit drowning in the expensive red wine. "For you!"

"Mrs. Aneva sends a driver to take me to her massage sessions," Di said. "If the driver is not smooth shaven I do not go with him."

"Are you trying to hint I'm not smooth shaven? Or that I am as cheap as Aneva's lousy driver?" He smiled behind his Viking's well-trimmed beard.

"We'll do it in the car," Di said calmly.

He was not her client and she did not have to give massages to his white back redolent of first class deodorant, balm, and musk: evidence of his superior position in the consulting firm. She did not have to be too careful what she said to him.

"Then you will give me a lift to the hospital."

"What will you do for the guy there?"

The Viking was suddenly lost in thought. "He is a man that did not act too cleverly. He was downright stupid if you ask me. Maybe Professor Metova will give you a studio where you'll take care of her son."

"I care about him," Di said.

"Do you care about me?"

Di looked at him. It was not necessary to lie to him.

"You are a clever and ambitious person," Di said.

All her clients received such standard responses. That was the most neutral statement she could produce. It resulted in higher fees for her services. She was a good masseuse and her clients knew that very well.

"I prefer young women like you," Spiro Jr. smiled. "Women capable of appreciating all good things a man does for them."

Then he took her hand and most unexpectedly kissed it; his lips were slightly wet with the wine. It seemed to her that he had disinfected them with a small cotton-ball soaked in lavender spirits to meet Professor Metova's requirements.

"Sometimes I wish Elizabeth were like you, at least a little bit. One can be silent and comfortable with you."

Then he carefully wiped his hand with the white silk napkin, cautiously inserted the spoon in the saucer with the fruit salad, and his hand vanished under the expensive brocade tablecloth and perched on Di's knee. It was an unnecessary activity if one considered the fact they were going to do it in the car.

"Am I embarrassing you?" he asked her.

"You don't need to do this," Di answered, unperturbed.

"The last time when Elizabeth came to Boyana I thought about you all the while I was with her," Spiro Jr. said unexpectedly, and Di thought he was drunk. This, of course, was impossible for he was very temperate even with respect to the number of times he kissed her. He was of the opinion that the more he kissed Di the greater the number of wrinkles around his mouth. His lips were always wet enough; he took the precaution of preventing them from getting dry. A pleasant aftertaste of a mouth freshener remained in Di's mouth after the Viking kissed her, and she was sure that he had included its price in his investments for the evening. His hand groped her knee very temperately, a move which could pass for a gentlemanly gesture, then his fingers slid up her thigh and that was nothing gentlemanly anymore.

Suddenly Spiro Jr. bent towards her and whispered, "I wish Elizabeth's legs were like yours."

It was rainy and very cold outside so Spiro Jr. hailed a taxi. They did not go to his Draga villa with which Di was vaguely familiar: a very strange building of abstract architecture surrounded by a big stone wall. He ordered the taxi to stop in front of the first elegant hotel that came their way.

"You have a particular effect on me," he whispered hoarsely. His whisper also flowed along the star orbit. "You are driving me mad."

"It's the wine," Di said. "You drank a lot."

"I didn't."

The orbit of the voice and the cosmos around it engulfed Di, but she was not afraid of the cosmos.

"I wish Elizabeth had the same effect on me. Listen…listen, why don't you come with me to Austria? You'll stay there a year, what do you think about that? I'll see Elizabeth and her father on Mondays, all the other weekdays I'll be with you. You'll have everything, absolutely everything."

The aromatic antiseptic mouth deodorant mixed with the trailing fragrance of the wine as he kissed her.

"I understand what Mrs. Aneva wants…You've driven her mad. She's a bitch. Give her the slip."

The rain beat the windowpane of the beautiful hotel room; the wind hurtled between the buildings as if trying to play an ancient pipe organ put much out of tune by the spring. The wail of the cars in the main street floated in the air, which was yellow with neon light. Spiro Jr. said he loved rain, the roar of the cars, and the nasty June weather because he didn't have to go back to Austria to Elizabeth. He wondered why he felt like that. After a moment, however, he admitted he felt magnificent: all of Elizabeth's photographs were arranged in a row on the hotel table facing Di.

"Let her learn," he remarked.

Moreover, Spiro Jr. was convinced that he wasn't concealing anything from his fiancée and he could have her forgiveness very easily after that.

"I'll give you a lift to Pirogov Hospital," he told Di.

"Thank you," she answered.

"Listen, this dress is abominable," Spiro whispered. "Perhaps you rented it for the night, I'm right, aren't I?"

"You are right," Di answered.

"I'll give you a lift to Pirogov hospital and we'll do it again in the car."

Spiro Jr. coughed and the other branch of the conversation took on an unexpected turn.

"Buy a new dress. Here, take this," his white well-groomed hand opened the wallet negligently taking out a banknote. "Five hundred dollars. No, that won't be enough. You are so pretty, buy a nice dress. What would Elizabeth say if she saw me squandering the money for our future wedding ceremony?"

There were not many cars on the way to Pirogov. The rain became more persistent, the pavement more slippery, and the windshield wipers did not function too perfectly.

"You're crazy. Don't waste your time in that foul-smelling hospital," Spiro Jr. said, his hand searching for her knee.

He had drunk a whole bottle of wine in the hotel.

"I can pay somebody else to take care of that guy in Pirogov."

Di did not answer.

"I can give anybody money to see to him."

Di was silent.

"You don't insist on my going to meet him, do you?"

"No, I don't."

SHE RAN TO THE LIFT. The corridor was packed with people: young and old, bandaged heads, broken limbs, frightened eyes. Di saw a middle-aged couple and a seventeen- or eighteen-year old boy. The boy's face was sallow and horrible. Pain had distorted his lips, which were hardly visible, muttering something, chopping the words; his parents' scared eyes, hopeless, stared at him. Di saw a child, very small, a baby as big as a doll, crying, left on its own in an old baby carriage. She bumped into people in white coats. She ran by patients hunched over bags on the benches in the corridors. She caught a glimpse of a very ill man sitting in a wheelchair, and the eyes of the woman that pushed him towards the end of the passageway paused on Di's face. Professor Metova waited by the window, a tall strong woman; however, Di did not notice her. She entered the narrow cramped room that could hardly hold two beds and saw there were four gurneys inside. Peter lay on one of them, his face colorless and horrible, so pale that she shuddered with fright and pain. His hands, big and pink like a little child's, lay limp on the blanket. His shoulder-length hair was tousled, thick and curly. Di told him once, "Don't cut it. Look at you, what beautiful hair you've got. You can wash it as much as you like. Well, we don't have hot water at home."

His beautiful hair looked greasy on the pillow. Scared, Di bent over his sallow face and looked at him. At that moment Peter opened his eyes. They swam in mist, he could not see her, could not recognize her. Then suddenly his face lit up.

"Di!" he whispered. "Is that you? Di…"

She did not answer. Her black dress with the deep neckline was ugly in the hospital room with the colorless faces and the gurneys pushed tightly one against the other. She did not think of her high heels, of her naked shoulders, of her thighs that could be seen through the black rented dress. She didn't care if she was pretty in the hospital room. She looked at Peter's ashy face. The eyes that had recognized her were so dear, so happy she could not breathe.

She bent down, her cheek gently touching his.

"I love you," Di whispered. "Can you hear me? No, no! I won't go away. I'll stay with you. I love you."

The rain beat the windowpanes; it was gloomy and cold, and Di smelled of expensive cigarette smoke and alcohol. But death was no longer in the hospital room. Death ran away far from that place. Peter's eyelids trembled, his hand, as pink as a baby's, tried to reach hers, and could not move. The corners of his lips twitched. A tiny, almost invisible twitch, but it was clear he was smiling. It was a very small thing, hardly a smile at all.

"Who let you in here?"

Professor Metova rushed into the cramped space between the four gurneys. Her mouth, open and ready to shout something about Di's indecent dress, did not produce a sound. Maybe the Professor intended to summon the bodyguards and make them throw Di out in the corridor with the sallow faces and the doctors' white coats. Then Professor Metova saw her son's lips. His lips budged one-hundredth fraction of an inch, or even less. The corners of his mouth had hardly twitched at all, but his face was smiling and it looked very beautiful, that pallid face, around which death had tied its icy knot a minute ago.

"Peter," Professor Metova whispered. "Peter... she... she is..." But her son was smiling, such a tiny smile that one could notice it if only one had known the boy since the day he was born. She was his mother and she knew he was smiling. Di had noticed the smile too. Maybe Professor Metova wanted to say something else, something harsh and insulting, but she only muttered, "She is... she's not... oh, Peter..."

*** *** ***

NORA

THE TWINS HAD LEFT a hand-written message on the kitchen table, but Nora did not read it. The sheet of paper had been torn from a notebook. Nora was suddenly angry — they had surely written that they had taken money from her mother's old purse. That was the family's savings for a rainy day, a ten lev banknote folded in two, hidden in the small pocket with the broken zipper. That was the money for medicines in case someone ran a temperature or one of her brothers came home with a broken head or limb. The twins should not poke their noses in that purse no matter what. Nora thought they had gambled and lost.

In the morning the two of them had been unnaturally quiet, had just looked at her, two identical pairs of eyes: Geno, the one who was so good at mathematics that Mrs. Getova, his geometry teacher, still phoned their home offering them her son's math texts. Gero, with the shrewd glitter in his eyes in the morning, had looked at her and was strangely quiet — meaning, no sly tricks, like the little brother whom she had given water in a tiny cup at night. The two of them were awful; Nora did not even care to look at the sheet of paper and rushed to the chest of drawers in the living room where her mother's old purse was hidden and all their money for the rainiest day. Nora thrust her hand almost to the elbow into the pocket with the broken zipper; her fingers grabbed a banknote, then one banknote more. That was strange.

She took out the first one, a ten-lev bill, then another one, a big, almost brand new, fifty lev note. Instead of feeling happy, Nora was suddenly scared. Her mother had not told her she'd left more money at home. Had she fallen ill again? She had mentioned something about pain in her left breast. Nora panicked. Was it possible her mother had given up hope and, feeling the end was near had prepared money for medicines? Nonsense, Nora snapped. Rubbish.

She rushed to the table; perhaps her brothers had stolen something and it would be clear where the money came from. She darted a glance at the message and the very first word written in big block letters made her freeze in her tracks: "MOTHER, NORA, I and Geno will go to Spain with two other guys. Everything will be OK. In the beginning, we will work at a bar. Mother, we are sorry we did not tell you earlier. You wouldn't let us go. We'll send you money. Don't worry. Everything will be OK. GERO and GENO."

Nora could not move. She stopped breathing. She ran to the living room; it was so clean and tidy, so awfully clean, no clothes on the floor, no heaps of socks, no blankets fallen onto the colorless Persian rug that at present had no native land. The two beds were made; the sheets were folded so carefully that Nora sobbed. They had wiped the dust from the chests of drawers; the windows had been taken care of, too. The windowpanes that had not been touched by a human hand for ages, so that the sun had looked like a rusty blotch, were now immaculately clean. A fearful empty space gaped above the old wardrobe which was bought a month after the twins were born. Two old suitcases used to be there, battered things that Nora's father didn't want to take along when he started his trip to Dubai.

"They are so weather beaten," he had said, "that I'd be ashamed to show them to my employers."

The twins had taken them — the two old suitcases which many years ago Nora took on an excursion to a seaside resort with her classmates and their teacher. A boy in Nora's class, Misho by name, a thin guy with black hair, silent and unobtrusive, had scribbled on Nora's suitcase, "I love you." Then everybody mocked Misho and in the evening he got drunk. No one knew where he bought the booze from. The teacher found him by accident. He was sleeping naked behind the hotel, a broken brandy bottle lying by his side.

Now the old suitcases were gone, the old alarm clock was also gone. Nora's grandfather had brought it from some obscure village by the Oder River in Germany during World War II. At that time, he served as a platoon commander in the First Bulgarian Army. This clock was Gero's favorite; he wiped it with a woolen cloth and wound it up every day.

Even the old unfortunate flowers had been watered. The floor in the kitchen was clean, the dishes were washed, and there were cheese, sausages, butter and olives in the refrigerator, something that didn't happen too often in their home. Gero's old training suit and Geno's ancient, almost entirely torn jacket hung on the coatrack in the corridor like old battle banners. Nora took them, examining the apartment: it was so clean, tidy and unbearable that she felt sick. Nora pressed her brother's jacket to her chest. She was not crying, she was a very strong and tough girl, so strong and tough that she even thought of starting to sing. Songs always helped her along; she sang very often in her mind for it is not appropriate to walk in the street shouting a song. She forgot to close the door of the clean and tidy apartment; it didn't make sense to. There was the old TV set in the corner of the living room, which her mother wanted to sell so that Geno could attend the math competition in Varna. Gero had wanted to pawn it and then go to gamble in the Lucky Bar. The twins didn't pawn the TV set and it remained in the living room, but Nora was not thinking about it. She squeezed the sheet of paper, her fingers starting to ache. It was a yellowish sheet of paper torn from the only notebook the twins had and took turns going to school with. Geno could not forget mathematics and was not able to run away from it so easily.

Nora walked quietly. She didn't know when she had passed by the street with the cafés, nor by the newspaper stand nor by the store selling American washing machines that no one could afford to buy. She had passed even by the unpleasant black hump of The Greasy Café. She tripped over a stone in front of a bridge across the Struma River, a small hunchbacked bridge under which there was a whirlpool. Heaps of stranded empty plastic bottles bobbed up and down churning the oily foam, but now they did not appear ugly.

Nora remembered: her mother and her father used to go on picnics here, the twins were little and her mother was afraid to buy them ice cream, her father muttering all the time he could never relax on account of these naughty kids.

The twins had run away to Spain, to Germany, or to Portugal. She didn't want to think about the place where they'd go hungry looking for the clean well-lit bar they would work at in the beginning. She did not think of the construction sites where they could probably find work; they were too weak for that. Geno's broken leg had not yet healed and ached whenever it rained. Gero caught colds so easily; he smoked heavily and coughed as if there was a muddy well in his chest he wanted to shovel out.

Nora did not cry and did not think of her mother. She could not imagine how she would show her that message on the rumpled sheet of paper. Nora passed the bridge across the Struma River and walked along the road between the willow-trees — old willow trees, thick with ravens' nests like black commas on the desolate notebook of the sky. The whole town seemed deserted without the twins.

Nora did not cry at all; she was a strong girl who hummed different tunes in her mind. The songs were her only way out. She crooned them in her mind, then started singing them out loud. She sang the songs without words, telling about the desolate sky with the black commas of the ravens and about her brothers. When the twins were little babies she didn't want to sing to them in the evenings. They were jumpy and fretful and her mother often asked her to lull them to sleep.

Somebody could hear her snarl, but she didn't give a damn about that. She could not see the road in front of her but loved it; she loved that road which remembered the small heels of her brothers and her father's steps, though the man was now in Dubai. She loved the dark, quiet river; she loved that absurd neighborhood with the old blocks of flats, the black cramped windows, all people who had run away to Canada, Germany and Belgium. She loved all folks who had remained in the narrow apartments with the rickety beds and white sheets, the people with decayed aching teeth who did not have money for dentists. She loved the town where her mother returned in the evening and feared the moment when she'd have to read the message on the yellow sheet of paper. Her mother would not cry. In spite of her aching hands that went dead at night and in spite of her aching teeth she never cried. She would start singing in her mind as Nora did, then perhaps the two of them would sing out loud. What else was left to a woman when she was down and squashed, what was left to her mother but these songs that would never end, the songs that went to Spain with her sons? Perhaps the boys were humming them in their minds, for could one sing out loud in a rotten train which left Bulgaria and took them away from the dark warm river, from the blocks of flats with the black windows? From the people they had grown up with, from their math teacher who gave them her sons' textbooks.

A tear gleamed in her eye, but Nora wiped it off with her fist. She was a tough girl. Exactly at that moment a song crossed her mind, such a beautiful song that it would be a shame if she cried.

SHE HAD REACHED ONE OF THE BUILDINGS with the black windows, the place where Petko lived. Petko was the man that had carried Geno with his broken leg to the hospital. He worked for Mr. Anev, but Nora didn't give a damn. The man showed up at the front door of the small ugly apartment, tall, scraggy, his hair shaggy, tousled, three days' stubble on his cheeks.

"Nora!" he exclaimed.

She had never come to his place before. Petko's mother cleaned several blocks of flats making ends meet and his father traveled to different cities searching for odd jobs.

"Nora, what's the matter with you?"

She looked at him: a thin lamppost of a man, his eyes as black as midnight staring anxiously at her.

"Is Anev after you, Nora? Come in, quickly. His thugs might see you here."

Nora didn't say anything.

"Is Gozo chasing you? Has something happened to your baby? Are you sick?"

The flat was clean; the floor was covered with linoleum with a strange flower pattern on it. There was a beautiful coat rack in the corner of the corridor — as beautiful as an object of cheap plastic could be.

"My brothers ran away to Spain," Nora muttered. "They are not at home anymore."

NORA WAS BACK AT THE PRIVATE CLINIC. A dazzling car had pulled up as she walked to her building. An enormous man in black suit sat behind the wheel.

"Mr. Avnev would like to speak to you, Madame. He is waiting for you in his hospital room," the black suit had said. "Get into the car."

This time there were neither doctors nor nurses in the corridors of the health institution. The mammoth in black took Nora to the second floor, opened a grand upholstered door, bowed, and said, "I brought her here Sir," then pushed Nora inside a spacious room.

There was an antique, elongated table and a dozen expensive looking straight back chairs arranged around it. A big man sat bolt upright at the far end, a respectable gentleman with hazel hair, wearing a large bandage on his head. A lady seated on a chair by the man was staring out of the window. She was as stunningly beautiful as a malachite statuette of a Russian empress. It was only natural Nora recognized the man: he was Mr. Anev, the man who strewed dollars in his wake, the owner of the whole town. Nora had not hit his skull hard enough. Now, she was not scared. The instinct of self-preservation had utterly abandoned her; she looked at the flock of bodyguards without curiosity or trepidation. Just for the sport of it, she tried to imagine absurd tattoos on funny parts of their bodies, taking off their shirts, visualizing their cheap and not too clean linen, making up her mind to give Mr. Anev a prize for the most absurd tattoo she could invent.

Of late, she had gone to a number of cafés taking generous sums from the cash desks, declaring she was Mr. Anev's right hand, which of course she was not.

Unexpectedly two sturdy bodyguards ushered Gozo into the spacious room. This time he was not in his faded pair of jeans, the soiled kitchen apron was gone as well, so he reminded Nora of an old lady, very big and disconsolate indeed. He had shaved his trademark beard, and his suit was so tight fitting that Nora felt sorry for him.

"This man has complained to me," Mr. Anev announced. "He said that you went to his café several times. You took considerable sums of money from him, you refused to pay him and you lied to him that you worked as my assistant."

"She had thirty-two meals and did not give me a cent," Gozo said.

"I confirm this is true," Nora declared. "That is exactly what I did."

The man that wore the impressive bandage on his head waved his hand. He produced no sounds, simply lifted his pinkie from the table and Gozo, silent and perfectly well-mannered, padded for the door taking his tight fitting suit out of the room.

"Becky," Mr. Anev turned to the incredibly beautiful woman

who sniffed at the air showing no sign of curiosity about the man that had just spoken to her. "This is Nora, the girl who's expecting a baby with me."

Then Mr. Anev turned to Nora, "Nora, this is my wife, Becky. I have lived happily with her for several years now."

Nora studied his wife's expensive dress, her slender figure, the pale skin of her cheeks and hands, the hair flowing down her shoulders in a well organized waterfall. For a moment, Becky's eyes were interested in Nora, too. They touched her face lightly, unobtrusively, examined her shoulders like a child peering at a fish in an aquarium, not giving a hoot if the beast had been fed.

"She is very pretty," Mr. Anev's wife remarked indifferently. "I hope her baby will have her green eyes."

"Is that all you have to say?" Anev said, not bothering to glance at Nora.

It was evident he couldn't care less about her beautiful green eyes. Her presence in this spacious room was of no consequence.

The lovely wife stretched against the back of her chair, saying nothing, oblivious of Nora. There was a bottle of mineral water on the table in front of her that attracted her attention.

"This young woman has used my name in an illegal manner so I am entitled to punish her. I can order my subordinates to break her arms and legs," Mr. Anev said evenly.

Nora imagined the great man's nameless "subordinates," and for a split second felt sorry she hadn't chosen a sharper and heavier stone to crush his head with. Then she remembered the squeaking sounds his skull had produced and felt happy. She was not afraid of him. It was absurd. She thought of her mother's tidy empty apartment, of the cheap, disintegrating furniture. Now her brothers toiled and moiled in Spain. What would happen to the boys in Spain? Maybe they'd land in bed with rich gay gentlemen. The twins were handsome and gay men noticed that first.

"I can beat her up myself," Mr. Anev went on, unable to take his eyes off his magnificent wife.

It was evident he cared about her. The man watched the expensive dress the way the shabby drunks at The Greasy Café ogled Nora, admired Nora and wanted her. Nora thought of her father's eyes staring at her mother in the evening when she came home from the bakery. Her father used to worry himself sick that he had no money for the twins and he couldn't buy books for Geno who was so bright. All the drunks at The Greasy Café cared about Nora and once in a blue moon even Gozo looked at her that way. The big shot who wore a bandage on his important head gazed at his wonderful wife, his eyes doting as if he was not all there.

"I can crush her myself, Becky."

"You'd better kill me," Nora said evenly. "If I survive, I'll kill you."

"Are you sure?" Mr. Anev asked, his eyes shining.

"You won't be breathing after I'm done beating you," Nora said. Now she was singing that crazy song in her mind and didn't give a damn about the haughty woman who sat in front of her.

She said, "Your wife is pretty enough. Why did you make a pass at me?"

"Do you really care to know?" Mr. Anev asked.

"She must be frigid," Nora said. "Well, that is her problem. My brothers are in Spain. My mother is alone at home. Let me go."

"Will a thousand dollars be enough for her to have an abortion?" the beautiful woman asked, her eyes forgetting Nora right away.

"Have you ever had an abortion, madam?" Nora asked.

The fair lady glanced at Nora, her face serene, evincing no interest in gynecological surgery or intervention whatsoever.

"We can give you money and you can marry Gozo if you want." The woman rubbed her chin adding after long silence, "He will not mind."

"He's a nice little chap," Mr. Anev said, his smile revealing half his teeth. "I talked things over with Gozo. Actually my bodyguards have had a word with him."

The man's teeth snapped so hard that Nora thought he was ready for an appointment with his dentist. She cared neither about Gozo nor about the gentleman's teeth.

"Well?" the man's teeth spoke out.

Nora smiled.

"I am prepared to take the money that your wife has offered me, Mr. Anev," she said.

The lady slithered her nimble hand into the purse producing a bundle of banknotes in subdued green color, the most eloquent color of all currencies in the world, that of American dollars.

"I don't like you," the beautiful woman said thoughtfully, her eyes cold.

They neither noticed nor cared about Nora's presence. "This is for you. I do not want to know what you will do with the child or with my husband. It is up to you."

Nora studied her closely. Mrs. Aneva's dress was of a warm melodious green color that made her skin sing.

"I do not like you either, Mrs. Aneva," Nora said calmly, shouting in her mind the crazy song that transformed her fears into a universe of suns.

Their rays could wipe out that woman. Yes, they certainly could.

Mr. Anev's wife did not say anything; her hand reached out and took away half of the dollars from the bundle.

"I dislike you much more than that," Nora remarked.

There was no sense in acting like that, but it gave her great pleasure just the same. She felt like a million dollars.

At that moment, Mr. Anev's hand sank into one of his pockets or perhaps into one of the many drawers of the table; his well-groomed fingers were out of Nora's sight and she felt none the less happy about that. Finally, Anev's hand extracted another, much bigger bundle of banknotes and left it negligently on the table.

"I appreciate witty retorts," he said. "Take this and get out of here."

Nora took the money, looked him in the eye, and remarked, "I wouldn't care about Mrs. Aneva if I were her husband."

She thought about Petko and his tidy little flat near the river; he had been so gentle with her.

"One day I will have more money than you. Remember that."

*** *** ***

Di

"I WOULD LIKE a fifty-minute full body massage."

Di studied the young woman lying on the mattress and swallowed hard. Her new client was plump, even fat, quite fat, and not very tall. She had immaculate white skin and green eyes that didn't bother to look at the masseuse.

"Yes, Ma'am," Di said.

"Mrs. Aneva enthusiastically recommended you," Di's client said confidently. "I trust her tastes. I would like you to work for me with the same diligence, competence, and loyalty as you work for her."

Di glanced at her startled, expecting her new client's white hand to perch on her fingers. She thought she would have to bend low to the perfect skin of the plump back, the lady insisting on having her massage procedures repeated till kingdom come. Di hated it when she had to make her client's legs glow like a sunrise. She was positive she'd have to listen to long-winded explanations like, "I hate being told I look pale. Mrs. Aneva personally recommended you so we can start. As I said, I strongly hope you'll work as devotedly for me as you do for her. Oh, before I forget... Di, you can use my shampoo and my body lotion. Please, do not put on the thick black sweater. I think it smells."

"Please call me Miss Doneva," the plump young woman said from her mattress. "Mrs. Aneva informed me your massages have the refreshing effect I need. If I approve of your work, I will hire you on a long-term basis. I intend to send my chauffeur to take you from the University of Sofia and bring you to my place."

"Yes, Miss Doneva," Di offered the client her standard reply. "I'll need a minute to prepare myself."

She wiped her palms carefully, disinfected them with a small cotton ball saturated with an antiseptic aromatic solution, spread lavender oil on them, then asked,

"Would you like my palms heated to a particular temperature while I give you your massage, Ma'am?"

"I insist your fingers be clean. I would appreciate it if you would concentrate entirely on the task at hand. I don't like my massage interrupted. One more thing, Di, I enjoy Wagner's music and I truly like the *Siegfried Idyll*. I'll listen to it while you work. Do you mind that?"

"Not at all, Ma'am."

The plump lady's skin was soft and warm. She did not speak or look at Di, just waited silent and relaxed, her eyes closed. It would be a miracle if she's not a pack of fads and vagaries, Di thought.

"Do you drink?" the new client asked.

"No, Madam."

"Are you a smoker?"

"No, I am not, Madam."

"Do you have a boyfriend?"

"No, Madam."

"You study French literature and, as far as I know, you are an excellent student," her client remarked, and after Di's usual "Yes, madam," she stopped paying attention to her masseuse.

One of the beautiful and exceptionally rare moments in Di's life finally came. It was precious and magnificent: the moment of silence when her client did not ask questions, did not want anything, did not complain and was as good as sound asleep. Di was alone with her thoughts. The air in the room was clean and pleasantly warm; the plump woman lay flat on her stomach as Di worked efficiently on her legs, feeling her flesh soft and relaxed under her fingers.

"I'm sorry that you have to constantly look at a fat body," the client said. "It's not the best of sights in the world."

"It looks all right to me, Miss Doneva." Di said. "I will do my best to make you feel good."

"I would like you to come to my place every Thursday, at 8 pm. As I said, my chauffeur will take you to my place. I don't like lavender oil. Can you use something else?"

Di did what she was told, then another exceptional scrap of time came her way. Her client kept silent and Di concentrated on her back. The woman had small fragile bones and too much flesh. Well, men often liked plump round girls like this one that looked so meek and vulnerable. However, her client sounded neither meek nor vulnerable. She had the voice of a person accustomed at a very early age to have her orders instantly obeyed. Di imagined scared people tiptoeing as the plump female commander spoke, and did not dare to ask how much Miss Doneva would pay her. She could only surmise that her client would pay her after the massage or perhaps after a long series of visits to her place. The thought of remuneration sank in the cold, fearful recesses of Di's consciousness as she remembered her mother who had lost her job as Anev Junior's governess. Mrs. Aneva had fired her two weeks ago.

ON THURSDAY, AFTER THE MASSAGE, as Di was about to leave, Mrs. Aneva held Di's palms in her own to check their temperature and asked Di to wait a minute, then she said she wanted her shoulders and thighs massaged once again, promising to double Di's fee.

"As far as I know, Mr. Spiro Jr. asked you to live with him in Austria," Mrs. Aneva had said.

"Yes, Ma'am."

"Did you accept?"

"No, Ma'am."

"But you were with him at Ambassador Hotel, weren't you?" Mrs. Aneva asked.

"He is engaged to be married to Miss Elizabeth Fabien, Ma'am."

"Well, this fact didn't prevent you from staying at the hotel with him. Did it feel good?"

Di was silent but Madam's insistent eyes went on searching for information.

"No, Ma'am. It did not feel good."

"I am married to Mr. Anev and it does not feel good either," her client said.

Di hoped this would be the end of their dialogue this evening, but it wasn't.

"I think it is disgusting that you were with Spiro Jr. at Ambassador Hotel."

Usually when Mrs. Aneva gave Di money after the massage, her fingers touched Di's, trying to drink the dark luster of Di's skin.

That evening, Mrs. Aneva dropped the banknotes on the table saying, "Come earlier next Thursday. You will, won't you?"

In the evening, Di's mother told her what had happened. Mrs. Aneva had said, "Arma, my son has grown up a clever boy due, to a certain extent, to your efforts. Thank you. I would like to inform you that I will not need your services anymore." Then she left the money she owed Arma and was gone.

At midnight, or maybe half an hour later, the old telephone rang and Di, half-awake, saw her mother pad over to it. She could not hear what Arma said but when she caught a glimpse of her mother's face in the light of the reading lamp she felt stone cold.

"What's wrong, mom?"

Arma looked at her. Her mother's life had become an island in a lake of uncertainty a long time ago; now the waters had finally got the better of Arma. The eyes of the middle-aged woman were so deep and empty that Di rushed to her.

"What's wrong?"

On Sunday, her mother was fixing the kitchen sink that that had leaked for years when Spiro Senior's chauffeur called explaining that Elizabeth was in Boyana with his son, the prosperous financial consultant, and Spiro was mightily proud of this fact. The chauffeur's instructions were to take Arma to Spiro Senior's place, since the telecommunications tycoon intended to share something very important with her. Arma refused to go. After an hour, the chauffeur came again with an enormous bouquet of red roses in hand: an interesting investment that her mother probably had to pay for on top of the bear fur.

A gray boring day passed. After the telephone rang at midnight, Arma's face became gray and distorted. Di shivered.

"His son...his son thinks you are a lewd bitch," Arma whispered. "Spiro Jr. said you want to ruin his relationship with Elizabeth. His father is disgusted."

Di did not flinch. She had gotten rid of that useless habit a long time ago, and she had not cried, sobbed or shouted for a year now.

"Is there something else he said?" Di asked.

"Spiro Sr. does not want me to move in with him. He insists I give him back the suit he bought for me."

Di sighed with relief.

"Don't you think the suit isn't worth your while?" she asked.

"But his son thinks you are..."

"A lewd bitch," Di finished the sentence for her.

Arma's eyes were so empty that her daughter got scared.

TWILIGHT HAD DESCENDED on the only room of their apartment; the new wallpaper which mother and daughter had bought recently was barely visible, the two of them even had a new kitchen appliance: Spiro Senior bought a second-hand fridge at an unthinking moment of generosity.

"He wants his fridge back," Arma said.

They had new second-hand curtains: her mother bought them from a "Chic-Chic" store. That happened again at a moment of generosity, this time on the part of the book launch party man that courted Arma at the Municipal library. There was a new carpet on the floor, a gift from Spiro Jr. Two wooden chests of drawers had arrived in their flat from his Draga villa complete with a new telephone set which appeared to be a genuine miracle of technology in Arma's eyes, plus two old-fashioned Draga Villa chairs the consultant did not like.

"We'd better give them the chairs, the chests of drawers, the carpet and the telephone," Di said.

"Yes," her mother said.

Arma had sold their old chairs to a used furniture dealer then spent the money on a gorgeous blouse she'd dug up in her favorite second-hand "Chic-Chic" store. The gentleman Arma went to book launch parties with admired her new very fashionable line and gave Arma a present to celebrate the fact that he adored her new second-hand garments: a plastic coat stand — that was his present. The Greek businessmen that rented one of the book lover's apartments had bought a new stand and had thrown the old one in the street. The book lover had taken it and, declaring he did not need such "a tasteful object," came to install it in Arma's flat. All the while the man cursed Di's indolent father who had not whitewashed the walls since Di was born.

Arma's book premiere boyfriend turned out to be an orderly and efficient fellow; he bought second-hand tiles from some shady company dirt cheap and began to glue them onto the walls in the corridor. In the evening, he ate dinner with them, occasionally reaching out across the table for her mother's hand, dropping hints like, "Arma, my love, thank God you met me," to which Arma lowered her eyes, and the book lover's hand climbed up her elbow slowly advancing towards her shoulder. Di felt embarrassed for her mother's sake. Arma was perpetually at a loss for words; she wanted to tell the man she didn't have enough money to buy meat. He understood her silences perfectly well and patted Arma's knee assuring her he could solve any problem. He constantly removed imaginary specks of dust from her face, shoulders, and lapels announcing he could take care of the food. Then he really produced ham, sausages and sweets, which smelled of his cheap deodorant and tobacco.

On Friday, at 10 pm sharp, the time for the romantic comedy on the TV, he told Arma, "We'd better go, love. We don't want to miss the last bus."

"Where are you going, mom?" Di had asked her, but it was the book lover that took the floor.

"Di, I'm taking your mother to my place," the literary connoisseur went on, overcoming his embarrassment.

However, "embarrassment" seemed to Di incompatible with the man. She listened.

"Well, Di, there's no other place in town where you can spend the night, is there? Your mother and I respect your right to privacy. On the other hand we need to be alone. She means a lot to me, your mother. Similar interests in literature, similar tastes in arts, you know."

On Sunday, her mother's civilized admirer fixed the kitchen sink.

"The massage exerts a salutary effect on me." Di gave a violent start. The plump lady's skin had become rosy under her hands from the heels of the small, soft feet to the last square inch of her neck. Her client's face looked very healthy. "You work well," she added, her eyes studying Di's face.

"Thank you, Ma'am," Di answered in her safe, standard way. She felt it was about time she was paid her fee. "Would you prefer to pay me after your massage is over or at the end of the month?"

The plump young woman made no reply. Di's question floated like a solitary parachute in the air.

"Go on, please," her client said. "I'd like you to repeat the whole series more slowly. I'd like a glass of mineral water as well. Anything for you? You will get your fee, do not worry about that."

"A glass of mineral water, please," Di said, but her client had forgotten about her.

Di sighed with relief.

"Mrs. Aneva informed me that you are an excellent student," the new client's voice sounded flat and self confident, a voice capable of making mountains quake, a voice of a provincial ruler that controlled dairies, factories, wheat fields, houses, the soil and the sky. However, Di had become accustomed to potentates a long time ago.

"I make every endeavor to complete my education successfully, Ma'am," Di answered, maintaining the speed of the smooth easy spirals of her palms on her client's satisfied skin.

"I would be grateful if you could quote excerpts from the works of famous French poets and writers while you work. I'd love it if the poems or the short stories belong to the world classics. I am interested in period pieces by contemporary French authors as well. It would be a pleasure to admire the beauty of French literature. I assure you that your efforts will be rewarded."

"I will do my best, Ma'am."

"Mrs. Aneva told me you knew poems by François Villon by heart. *The Ballad of Fat Margot*, for example."

Di had recited the ballad when she had given Becky Aneva a neck massage. After the massage was over, Becky had asked her to a small beautifully furnished room where Tchaikovsky's *Swan Lake* was in the air, and Di had tried to recite other ballads by the French poètes maudits. She had forgotten the exact words of the poems and had awkwardly stopped the recitation, Mrs. Aneva's eyes following her dark face.

"You can say absolutely anything in French," Mrs. Aneva had whispered. "I will not mind if you say something wrong. I will not understand anything. I don't speak a word of that language."

"Can you start with *Ballade de la grosse Margot?*" the new client asked.

Di went on working diligently, carefully, as if her life depended on adapting her movements to the rhythm of the poem.

"Could you speak slower?" the plump young woman asked. "I cannot grasp the meaning of the words."

As Margot's carnal desires inflamed Villon's mind beyond control, Di's hands followed the well known route: the vertebrae of the neck, then the shoulders, the chest reaching the final destination: the indistinct line of the waist. Di had worked on her client's back for about half an hour when a very attractive man entered the room. Di did not flinch at his exceptionally good looks; she had broken this harmful habit of her facial muscles. Trick number one of her trade was "the only item a masseuse should see is her clients' backs," so she concentrated on the plump woman's body.

"My dearest," the man started enthusiastically, his eyes hopping from her client's neck to her pretty plump face. "My dearest." The man approached the naked shoulder glowing rosily under Di's fingers and kissed it passionately. He poised his fingers above the plump shoulder ready to gently caress the woman's warm skin for at least an hour.

"Mr. Anev has already arrived, my love. He's been waiting for ages hoping your massage will come to an end soon. We have to discuss the opportunities for the implementation of our joint project..."

Di's client did not budge. Di had stopped reciting *Ballade de la grosse Margot*, but the plump lady waved her to go on. Di didn't obey right away, glancing at the enthusiastic gentleman. He was tall, perfectly groomed, fashionably dressed, and had an expensive haircut. In short, he was so refined that the only item Di remembered of him was his dazzling suit.

"Please, do not interrupt the massage and do not stop reciting the poem unless I explicitly ask you to do so," the client said, her green eyes momentarily noticing Di.

It was the first time she had looked Di in the eye. "Gallantine," her head crowned with thick red hair slowly turned to the man, her green eyes showing no interest in him.

"Gallantine, my love, my massage will be over in one hour and twenty minutes." It was a lie and Di wondered what she was supposed to do in the course of an hour and twenty minutes. She felt exhausted, incapable of pressing her client's soft arms and legs. Furthermore, she had already drunk all her mineral water and her throat felt sore on account of the *Ballade de la grosse Margot.*

"Please, Moni," the man pleaded, abruptly changing his approach. "Mr. Anev cannot wait a whole hour... you know he is a busy man. Please," the man said as he kissed again her client's round rosy shoulder.

"My massage will be over in one hour and twenty minutes," the young lady repeated. "However, I need a bath. Therefore, Mr. Anev should to do some sightseeing around town for at least two hours. Actually, he might visit some of my breweries if he thinks it's not too cold for him. You know I need time to put on my make-up..."

Di guessed her client's voice had made people freeze in their tracks since she was five years old. Perhaps at that time she already possessed the breweries and dairies around the town with old, battered blocks of flats.

"Let me introduce you to my new masseuse. Mrs. Aneva recommended her to me."

"How do you do, my name is Lawyer Gallantine, Ph.D.," the man said without casting an eye over Di. "Please, Moni," he said, resting his hands on her client's pearly arm.

"Well, if you want me to look my best, I have to admit that making up may take some time," she smiled. "I'll talk to Mr. Anev in two hours."

The man looked dejected, his face turning into a molehill out of which an uninvited, discourteous sentence could erupt any minute. However, his behavior proved Di's judgment wrong.

"Mr. Anev asked after a girl called Nora. You probably know her or might have heard things about her. She's said to be very attractive."

The molehill on the man's face winked at Di's client. "Mr. Anev sounded very interested. He said he'd very much like to have a word with that young woman."

The plump lady did not say anything and the issue remained poised between life and death.

"So you don't know Nora?" the man asked after he kissed his lady's fat neck.

Di concentrated discreetly on her client's calves, the man paying no attention to her as if she was on another planet. This was only natural: Di was one of numerous staff, a broom in the corner, a fly on the wall, and her task was to raise her plump client's heart through massaging her buttocks. Di should not expect anything else and she knew it.

"Please, go on."

The client turned to Di, her eyes stronger than Di's.

"Let's not waste precious time. My love," she spoke politely to the man, "I adore Francois Villon's poetry and I'd prefer it if I was all by myself. Thank you for dropping in."

The blue-eyed fellow nodded, caressed her client's soft hand, and said very sincerely, "Enjoy yourself, my love."

Di wondered what she would do during these two interminable hours. She didn't have to wait long: the plump lady promptly enlightened her on this issue.

"I will watch *Sound of My Voice*. It is a two-hour feature film. You are not obliged to watch it with me, so you can read the magazines on the small table in the corner. I'd be grateful if you could stay in this room till the end of the movie. Of course, I am prepared to pay for your patience and understanding."

Her voice had some rest as Di took care of the lady's back giving it a series of short percussive strokes.

"I approve of your work," her client said after a while. "I can send my chauffeur for you next Wednesday at 7 pm. Will you agree to come?"

"I'd love to, Ma'am."

*** *** ***

NORA

THE WEATHER WAS RAINY AND COLD; thunderstorms struck and hailstorms broke. One could see few passers-by and fewer cars in the streets. The Struma River, the old gossip, flowed near the blocks of flats, its two steep banks overgrown with rough grass, nettles, and thistles, a pack of stray dogs sniffing at chunks of bread thrown under the bridge.

Nora saw them through the window as she sat up in bed. Her mother went to work at 4:30 am and wouldn't be back before 9 pm. Her mother was a tough woman. A quiet one. Nora smiled.

"Two goons looked for you at The Greasy Café," said a thin, tall man in soiled overalls smelling of glue. Countless drops of gooey yellowish substance had landed on his hair, chest and face. "They said Anev had sent them to look for you."

"They probably wanted to bite my head off," Nora murmured. "Well, we'll wait and see."

"I don't think they were after your head," the man said, hanging wallpaper in the living room.

He was an efficient worker and his hands moved nimbly as he

spoke to Nora. "They left eight hundred dollars and said you were to take the money."

"Leave the wallpaper on the floor," Nora said. "Come here." He hesitated. "Come on! Leave it on the floor!" she repeated.

"I've been working here for a week and the room is not ready yet," the man muttered. "It's a shame. Your mother will laugh at me."

"Listen, when my stomach grows bigger I won't ask you to come on." Nora took a couple of steps toward him yanking on the pot of glue in his hands. "Come quickly when I tell you."

"I think I might hurt you…I might hurt the baby, too," the man said.

"Petko, you're not a great thinker, you know."

"Here they are, eight hundred dollars," the man said producing the money from his pocket. "Gozo told me Anev had sent him to your place. 'Tell Nora I want to see her,' Anev had said. 'I want to see her as soon as possible. Tell her to come to The Greasy Café on Thursday at 6 pm.'"

"How come the money's with you?"

"Gozo brought it in the morning. I didn't want to wake you."

Nora was about to kiss him when she felt the baby kick.

"Petko, take the money and run to the farmers market, please. Buy whatever you like, okay? These are Anev's dollars. Bring me three pounds of cherries, three pounds of strawberries, three pounds of everything. Do you understand?"

"Will you go to see Anev on Thursd…" he tried to ask, but Nora did not let him finish.

She kissed him, the baby kicked again, and that was only natural for a baby in his mother's stomach.

"Well, it might be dangerous… Are you going to see Anev on Thursday?" The tall thin man said, still hesitating.

"I will unless you come to bed with me straight away," Nora declared.

A thunderstorm broke, the black clouds spouted rain, lightning kicked the sky, torrents thrashed the roofs, but Nora enjoyed storms. The meteorologist said on TV there was no rain in Spain. It was hot there; one could buy cheap things from the stores and she hoped her brothers had enough bread. She could see the Struma River through the window of the gray block of flats; the water in the whirlpools under the old willow-trees was now black and angry. The twins had called. They were okay. They were washing dishes all day long. They'd send enough money for Nora's baby.

"Mom is okay, don't you worry," Nora had said. "Everything's okay. I'm okay, don't you worry."

Petko had mended their broken bunk beds, fixed the leaking tap in the kitchen and replaced the broken windowpanes. Petko was an orderly fellow. He swept Nora's room every day. In the beginning he felt awkward in her mother's presence, but one Saturday he stayed for the night and after that gradually brought all his clothes and things to Nora's room.

"So you won't go to see Anev on Thursday?" he asked.

Nora ignored the question.

"If you say one more word about Anev I can't promise you'll be safe here. You can count on that," she whispered, kissing him.

*** *** ***

Moni

THE RICKETY HOUSES were very close to the river, just below the medieval Slavonic Krakra Fortress, at the very end of the town. The neighborhood was known by the name Karama: shacks covered with odd pieces of sheet iron, puny narrow backyards with taut copper wire clothes-lines on which dozens of washed clothes hung, appearing dirty. Hens and dogs squeezed freely under the clothes-lines which served as fences between the shacks; scraggy pigs ran in the streets that during the early wet summer were potted by deep muddy puddles. Some inventive people had put sandstone slabs or rubble in front of their homes, items they had pilfered from different construction sites, so that their wives and kids would not sink to the waist in the mud. Indeed, there were white marble slabs in the mud, too: some of the Karama men worked at the Central Railway Station in Pernik. They unloaded the wagons full of precious white marble from the village of Simit and stole some of the slabs if they could. A flock of children usually sat under the roofing iron of the dilapidated houses in the neighborhood. Sometimes the kids were bored and threw stones at the International Express

Train Sofia – Athens; at other times they fought or argued over green apples and feathers or simply played, pretending they were cops and robbers. Even if it was raining cats and dogs the children gathered together under the big sheet iron roof of the only café in Karama, the Lena Café.

Their fathers sold to Dan, the café owner, the scrap iron they had stolen. Dan sold the scrap to a hunch-backed guy, who in his turn sold it to a gent called the Sponge. The Sponge was a genius. He sold the scrap for three times its worth to that lousy bitch ... what was her name? Bloody Rayo's daughter. People said she had money to burn. Rayo got shot last year and he well deserved it, if you ask anybody if this neighborhood. His lousy daughter had taken over her father's business and wallowed in money. Well, that didn't stop her from skinning young and old in town. She gave a hell of a time to all honest guys who stole scrap iron to eke out a living. All they wanted was to buy bread for the kids who sat under that rusty roofing iron while the rain came down in torrents. It was so cold one could hardly recognize if it was summer or autumn. Rain made scrap iron rusty very quickly and Dan, the owner of Lena Café, paid you half its price.

It was Thursday, so the guys did not unload marble from the wagons at Pernik Railway Station. That day Simo had invited them all; all folks from Karama were gathered in front of his house. Well, the house didn't exactly belong to him; its owners were his two married sisters who had nine children between them, very beautiful children with black eyes, darker than the nights in January, the best looking kids in this neighborhood. If these kids started playing football and you watched them it would be a sight to delight your heart in case you were a guy who loved and knew about the game. If some decent coach came here, to Karama, he could choose a dozen lads like the famous football player Stoichkov, and if the coach were clever enough to teach the children of Simo's sisters well, oh, my God!, they'd make young and old speak about Bulgaria! Everybody from Brazil to Germany, from Poland to Japan and the UK would know them. For they were no ordinary children, they didn't go without food as you might imagine or, if they did, this happened very rarely.

The roof of Simo's house was white marble. Simo had stolen it under the very nose of the Chief of the Station at the risk of getting caught, beaten, and sacked. Well, who could catch Simo stealing white marble from Pernik Railway Station? Nobody could, of course. Fatma was one hundred percent convinced of that. Most people knew her Bulgarian name was Natasha, the Bulgarians sent for her saying, "Please, Aunt Natasha, come home to make a lucky charm for my boy. If he sees a big truck he cries his lungs out and I think this should end. His father's a driver, you know."

So Natasha made lucky charms, told the lad's or lassie's future and saw many good things in it. She was a very decent lady and everybody recognized that. She introduced Simo to the snow-white beautiful girl whose eyes were as green as Vitosha Mountain, which towered over the town. The girl's eyes looked even greener than the mountain; you could take Natasha's word for it!

Simo had gathered young and old in front of his house, the only building with a marble roof in the neighborhood. He had bought twenty-five cases of beer — such a beautiful girl was going to arrive in Karama for the first time. Simo had spent all his salary on twelve bottles of brandy; not the fake sleazy swill you bought from Dan's Café Lena. No, Sir, he'd give you first-class plum brandy. Well, he bought some swill, of course, for what difference did it make what alcohol you'd be boozing if you were stone drunk? You wouldn't differentiate between the swill and the gorgeous plum brandy, would you? He had bought Coca-Cola, Pepsi and Sprite for the kids; he had bought each lassie a hairpin but not the cheap trash, which cost twenty-five cents apiece. The hairpins Simo chose cost one lev, fifty cents, and you could only find them in the posh shops in the center of Pernik. Simo bought each lad a penknife and even the youngest toddler of Karama would know when Simo brought his pretty girl to the house with the most beautiful marble roof in town.

Simo said he'd arrive at 3 pm and everyone was waiting for him; his mother was chatting with Natasha, both of them smoking expensive cigarettes. So did Simo's father and his married sisters. They all usually smoked the cheapest possible gaspers, but that day they made an exception to the rule, for it was Thursday. There was no marble from the village of Simit at the railway station and the space around it looked desolate, but everybody guessed it was perfectly all right and even the babies in swaddling clothes were ready for the feast.

It was past three and Simo still hadn't shown up. The men waited and waited, then shyly and gradually made a decisive move. They started opening the bottles, not the ones with the gorgeous brandy; they'd crack them open the minute Simo brought his young bride. They opened the flasks of swill; they all had got accustomed to it and it tasted delicious, like any normal brandy in their mouths. The children, too, could not endure that long waiting; kids like Stoichkov, the football player, were a very impatient lot. They opened their bottles of Coca-Cola, Pepsi and Sprite and looked very secretive indeed. Then they started arguing over one exceptionally beautiful piece of glass and after that about whose penknife was the sharpest.

"Where's that son of yours, Nadi? It's a shame, he's late." Fatma said.

That day she had put so much rouge on her face that her cheeks shone like the sun itself.

"He'll show up any minute now," Nadi answered.

She had borrowed three hundred levs from Dan, the café owner, and had bought pork chops with them. She had four daughters and only one son; a wonderful chap, her son Simo: slim and tall, with a handsome face, serene like the moon. A very smart chap he was,the only guy capable of dragging out so much marble under the very nose of the Station Chief!

At last the exhaust smoke of an ancient car mixed with the rain and a green boneshaker belonging to one of Simo's numerous cousins roared and spluttered, climbing the hill of Karama. It was surely bringing Simo's young bride! Then the men switched on simultaneously three old cassette-recorders, and *You Are My Everything*, the Gypsy love hymn, rang blaring up to the Krakra fortress, to Vitosha Mountain and perhaps even to Athens in Greece. The women and the children knew that song very well too, so they all sang it at the top of their voices. That song always brought you happiness and if you sang it to a pretty girl, she was positive to give birth to strong sons and beautiful daughters with warm brown eyes.

The green boneshaker crawled along the only street in Karama that was covered with asphalt. The three cassette-recorders sang *You Are My Everything*, the women and the kids joined in vigorously, and everybody was itching to catch a glimpse of Simo's girl first, although Natasha had described her to them in minute detail

— a girl with green eyes like the hill overgrown with thick pine trees. The girl's skin was very white like an iceberg or whatever Fatma thought an iceberg looked like.

The car stopped in front of the house and everybody stood on tiptoe bating their breath. The door opened and Simo showed up dressed in a brand-new T-shirt, the best one in the most fashionable sports store in the Main Street of Pernik. He had paid a juicy twenty lev bill for it. He had put on a pair of black corduroys as well, a wonderful chap and you could take Fatma's word for it.

No girl got out of the car.

"He's hiding her," the men laughed in their beards. "He's not ready to show us his bride."

"None of your tricks, boy," the women laughed as well. "We've been hidden in exactly the same manner, you know."

"Where's she? Where's she?" the children shouted craning their necks, on tiptoe, the girls with the expensive hairpins in their hairs, the boys squeezing tightly the penknives in their hands so no one could extricate them from their fingers in the hustle and bustle.

"Where is your bride, son?" Fatma asked. She looked so pretty with her new rouge that the young women would better take care! "Simo, don't hide her. Let us see her."

Simo looked down at the holes in the street unable to raise his head.

"What's wrong with you, son?" his father asked.

The air was clean and it was cold although it shouldn't be at that time of the year. It was June, the wind blew and the drizzle was slowly turning into a steady rain. There were few trees in Karama but above the shacks the green woods started — not much of a forest anyway, bushes, prickly shrubs, and thorns, but they all had a lot of green leaves. The forest was near the Krakra fortress and the people could easily bring their goats there to graze the soft leaves.

"Where's the girl?" Simo's mother asked.

Simo looked very handsome in his yellow expensive T-shirt. His black corduroys were excellent, too, although they were spattered up to his belt with splashes of dry mud.

"She..." he muttered his eyes glued to the holes in the asphalt. "She won't come."

Everybody shut up. One could hear the clouds move in the sky and the stones wobble in the ancient walls of the fortress. Not even the little kids said anything.

They surely thought there was no girl with green eyes. How could a girl in her right mind lie to Simo, how could she refuse to come over and live with him below the Krakra fortress? It was so beautiful there; one hour by the express train and you reached Sofia, three hours and you'd wake up in Greece! You could go to Portugal or Spain, you'd only have to catch some train and beat it. Why should you stay in Karama if you didn't have a girl? It was not worth it.

"Why isn't she coming?" Fatma asked. "I know her. She wouldn't lie to you."

Simo didn't say anything. He stood silent staring at the asphalt and it was a pity he was in such a yellow T-shirt, so bright and ostentatious that everybody stared at him.

"Well, she will come next Thursday," Simo's eldest cousin said. "Cheer up, guys. Let's drink bottoms up. For Simo!"

"Cheers," all men and women muttered and started crooking the elbow or sipping at the delicious brandy which had nothing to do with the swill; the children ate the pork chops thinking they could swallow them all at one gulp. Even the grown-ups were of the same opinion because the broiled pieces of tender meat tasted so good and melted in their mouths.

"Don't get upset, man," the youngest sister's husband consoled him. "She'll come some other day."

Simo did not hear him. He stood silent, a tall, slim guy, who looked suddenly very thin and could not understand it was raining, and could not feel it was cold in June. The rain became heavier, but he did not go under the roofing iron where all the rest had gathered together.

He stood alone, immobile in the rain, unable to think, unwilling to hide in his house, the only one with a marble roof in the whole neighborhood.

*** *** ***

Fomite
Burlington, VT

A fomite is a medium capable of transmitting infectious organisms from one individual to another.

"The activity of art is based on the capacity of people to be infected by the feelings of others."
Tolstoy, *What Is Art?*

Flight and Other Stories - Jay BoyerIn *Flight and Other Stories,* we're with the fattest woman on earth as she draws her last breaths and her soul ascends toward its final reward. We meet a divorcee who can fly with no more effort than flapping her arms. We follow a middle-aged butler whose love affair with a young woman leads him first to the mysteries of bondage and then to the pleasures of malice. Story by story, we set foot into worlds so strange as to seem all but surreal, yet everything feels familiar, each moment rings true. And that's when we recognize we're in the hands of one of America's truly original talents.

Loisaida - Dan ChodorokoffCatherine, a young anarchist estranged from her parents and squatting in an abandoned building on New York's Lower East Side, is fighting with her boyfriend and conflicted about her work on an underground newspaper. After learning of a developer's plans to demolish a community garden, Catherine builds an alliance with a group of Puerto Rican community activists. Together they confront the confluence of politics, money, and real estate that rule Manhattan. All the while she learns important lessons from her great-grandmother's life in the Yiddish anarchist movement that flourished on the Lower East Side at the turn of the century. In this coming-of-age story, family saga, and tale of urban politics, Dan Chodorkoff explores the "principle of hope" and examines how memory and imagination inform social change.

Improvisational Arguments - Anna Faktorovich
Improvisational Arguments is written in free verse to capture the essence of modern problems and triumphs. The poems clearly relate short, frequently humorous, and occasionally tragic stories about travels to exotic and unusual places, fantastic realms, abnormal jobs, artistic innovations, political objections, and misadventures with love.

Carts and Other Stories - Zdravka Evtimova
Roots and wings are the key words that best describe the short story collection *Carts and Other Stories,* by Zdravka Evtimova. The book is emotionally multilayered and memorable because of its internal power, vitality and ability to touch both your heart and your mind. Within its pages, the reader discovers new perspectives and true wealth, and learns to see the world with different eyes. The collection lives on the borders of different cultures. *Carts and Other Stories* will take the reader to wild and powerful Bulgarian mountains, to silver rains in Brussels, to German quiet winter streets, and to wind-bitten crags in Afghanistan. This book lives for those seeking to discover the beauty of the world around them, and will have them appreciating what they have — and perhaps what they have lost as well.

Fomite
Burlington, VT

Zinsky the Obscure - Ilan Mochari

"If your childhood is brutal, your adulthood becomes a daily attempt to recover: a quest for ecstasy and stability in recompense for their early absence." So states the 30-year-old Ariel Zinsky, whose bachelor-like lifestyle belies the torturous youth he is still coming to grips with. As a boy, he struggles with the beatings themselves; as a grownup, he struggles with the world's indifference to them. *Zinsky the Obscure* is his life story, a humorous chronicle of his search for a redemptive ecstasy through sex, an entrepreneurial sports obsession, and finally, the cathartic exercise of writing it all down. Fervently recounting both the comic delights and the frightening horrors of a life in which he feels — always — that he is not like all the rest, Zinsky survives the worst and relishes the best with idiosyncratic style, as his heartbreak turns into self-awareness and his suicidal ideation into self-regard. A vivid evocation of the all-consuming nature of lust and ambition — and the forces that drive them.

Kasper Planet: Comix and Tragix - Peter Schumann

The British call him Punch; the Italians, Pulchinella; the Russians, Petruchka; the Native Americans, Coyote. These are the figures we may know. But every culture that worships authority will breed a Punch-like, anti-authoritarian resister. Yin and yang — it has to happen. The Germans call him Kasper. Truth-telling and serious pranking are dangerous professions when going up against power. Bradley Manning sits naked in solitary; Julian Assange is pursued by Interpol, Obama's Department of Justice, and Amazon.com. But — in contrast to merely human faces — masks and theater can often slip through the bars. Consider our American Kaspers: Charlie Chaplin, Woody Guthrie, Abby Hoffman, the Yes Men — theater people all, utilizing various forms to seed critique. Their profiles and tactics have evolved along with those of their enemies. Who are the bad guys that call forth the Kaspers? Over the last half century, with his Bread & Puppet Theater, Peter Schumann has been tireless in naming them, excoriating them with Kasperdom....*from Marc Estrin's Foreword to Planet Kasper*

The Co-Conspirator's Tale - Ron Jacobs

There's a place where love and mistrust are never at peace; where duplicity and deceit are the universal currency. *The Co-Conspirator's Tale* takes place within this nebulous firmament. There are crimes committed by the police in the name of the law. Excess in the name of revolution. The combination leaves death in its wake and the survivors struggling to find justice in a San Francisco Bay Area noir by the author of the underground classic *The Way the Wind Blew: A History of the Weather Underground* and the novel *Short Order Frame Up*.

Short Order Frame Up - Ron Jacobs

1975. America as lost its war in Vietnam and Cambodia. Racially tinged riots are tearing the city of Boston apart. The politics and counterculture of the 1960s are disintegrating into nothing more than sex, drugs, and rock and roll. The Boston Red Sox are on one of their improbable runs toward a postseason appearance. In a suburban town in Maryland, a young couple are murdered and another young man is accused. The couple are white and the accused is black. It is up to his friends and family to prove he is innocent. This is a story of suburban ennui, race, murder, and injustice. Religion and politics, liberal lawyers and racist cops. In *Short Order Frame Up*, Ron Jacobs has written a piece of crime fiction that exposes the wound that is US racism. Two cultures existing side by side and across generations--a river very few dare to cross. His characters work and live with and next to each other, often unaware of each other's real life. When the murder occurs, however, those people that care about the man charged must cross that river and meet somewhere in between in order to free him from (what is to them) an obvious miscarriage of justice.

Fomite
Burlington, VT

All the Sinners Saints - Ron Jacobs
A young draftee named Victor Willard goes AWOL in Germany after an altercation with a commanding officer. Porgy is an African-American GI involved with the international Black Panthers and German radicals. Victor and a female radical named Ana fall in love. They move into Ana's room in a squatted building near the US base in Frankfurt. The international campaign to free Black revolutionary Angela Davis is coming to Frankfurt. Porgy and Ana are key organizers and Victor spends his days and nights selling and smoking hashish, while becoming addicted to heroin. Police and narcotics agents are keeping tabs on them all. Politics, love, and drugs. Truths, lies, and rock and roll. *All the Sinners Saints* is a story of people seeking redemption in a world awash in sin.

Loosestrife - Greg Delanty
This book is a chronicle of complicity in our modern lives, a witnessing of war and the destruction of our planet. It is also an attempt to adjust the more destructive blueprint myths of our society. Often our cultural memory tells us to keep quiet about the aspects that are most challenging to our ethics, to forget the violations we feel and tremors that keep us distant and numb.

When You Remember Deir Yassin - R. L. Green
When You Remember Deir Yassin is a collection of poems by R. L. Green, an American Jewish writer, on the subject of the occupation and destruction of Palestine. Green comments: "Outspoken Jewish critics of Israeli crimes against humanity have, strangely, been called 'anti-Semitic' as well as the hilariously illogical epithet 'self-hating Jews.' As a Jewish critic of the Israeli government, I have come to accept these accusations as a stamp of approval and a badge of honor, signifying my own fealty to a central element of Jewish identity and ethics: one must be a lover of truth and a friend to the oppressed, and stand with the victims of tyranny, not with the tyrants, despite tribal loyalty or self-advancement.
These poems were written as expressions of outrage, and of grief, and to encourage my sisters and brothers of every cultural or national grouping to speak out against injustice, to try to save Palestine, and in so doing, to reclaim for myself my own place as part of the Jewish people." Poems in the original English are accompanied by Arabic translations.

Roadworthy Creature, Roadworthy Craft - Kate Magill
Words fail but the voice struggles on. The culmination of a decade's worth of performance poetry, *Roadworthy Creature, Roadworthy Craft* is Kate Magill's first full-length publication. In lines that are sinewy yet delicate, Magill's poems explore the terrain where idea and action meet, where bodies and words commingle to form a strange new flesh, a breathing text, an "I" that spirals outward from itself.

Visiting Hours - Jennifer Anne Moses
Visiting Hours, a novel-in-stories, explores the lives of people not normally met on the page — -AIDS patients and those who care for them. Set in Baton Rouge, Louisiana, and written with large and frequent dollops of humor, the book is a profound meditation on faith and love in the face of illness and poverty.

Fomite
Burlington, VT

The Listener Aspires to the Condition of Music - Barry Goldensohn

"I know of no other selected poems that selects on one theme, but this one does, charting Goldensohn's career-long attraction to music's performance, consolations and its august, thrilling, scary and clownish charms. Does all art aspire to the condition of music as Pater claimed, exhaling in a swoon toward that one class act? Goldensohn is more aware than the late 19th century of the overtones of such breathing: his poems thoroughly round out those overtones in a poet's lifetime of listening."

John Peck, poet, editor, Fellow of the American Academy of Rome

The Derivation of Cowboys & Indians - Joseph D. Reich

The Derivation of Cowboys & Indians represents a profound journey, a breakdown of the American Dream from a social, cultural, historical, and spiritual point of view. Reich examines in concise detail the loss of the collective unconscious, commenting on our contemporary postmodern culture with its self-interested excesses, on where and how things all go wrong, and how social/political practice arely meets its original proclamations and promises. Reich's surreal and self-effacing satire brings this troubling message home. *The Derivation of Cowboys & Indians* is a desperate search and struggle for America's literal, symbolic, and spiritual home.

Views Cost Extra - L.E. Smith

Views that inspire, that calm, or that terrify — all come at some cost to the viewer. In *Views Cost Extra* you will find a New Jersey high school preppy who wants to inhabit the "perfect" cowboy movie, a rural mailman disgusted with the residents of his town who wants to live with the penguins, an ailing screen-writer who strikes a deal with Johnny Cash to reverse an old man's failures, an old man who ponders a young man's suicide attempt, a one-armed blind blues singer who wants to reunite with the car that took her arm on the assembly line — and more. These stories suggest that we must pay something to live even ordinary lives.

Travers' Inferno - L.E. Smith

In the 1970's, churches began to burn in Burlington, Vermont. If it was arson, no one or no reason could be found to blame. This book suggests arson, but makes no claim to historical realism. It claims, instead, to capture the dizzying 70's zeitgeist of aggressive utopian movements, distrust in authority, escapist alternative lifestyles, and a bewildered society of onlookers. In the tradition of John Gardner's *Sunlight Dialogues*, the characters of *Travers' Inferno* are colorful and damaged, sometimes comical, sometimes tragic, looking for meaning through desperate acts. Travers Jones, the protagonist, is grounded in the transcendent — philosophy, epilepsy, arson as purification — and mystified by the opposite sex, haunted by an absent father and directed by an uncle with a grudge. He is seduced by a professor's wife and chased by an endearing if ineffective sergeant of police. There are secessionist Quebecois involved in these church burns who are murdering as well as pilfering and burning. There are changing alliances, violent deaths, lovemaking, and a belligerent cat.

Entanglements - Tony Magistrale

A poet and a painter may employ different mediums to express the same snow-blown afternoon in January, but sometimes they find a way to capture the moment in such a way that their respective visions still manage to stir a reverberation, a connection. In part, that's what *Entanglements* seeks to do. Not so much for the poems and paintings to speak directly to one another, but for them to stir points of similarity.

Fomite
Burlington, VT

The Empty Notebook Interrogates Itself - Susan Thomas

The Empty Notebook began its life as a very literal metaphor for a few weeks of what the poet thought was writer's block, but was really the struggle of an eccentric persona to take over her working life. It won. And for the next three years everything she wrote came to her in the voice of the Empty Notebook, who, as the notebook began to fill itself, became rather opinionated, changed gender, alternately acted as bully and victim, had many bizarre adventures in exotic locales, and developed a somewhat politically incorrect attitude. It then began to steal the voices and forms of other poets and tried to immortalize itself in various poetry reviews. It is now thrilled to collect itself in one slim volume.

My God, What Have We Done? - Susan Weiss

In a world afflicted with war, toxicity, and hunger, does what we do in our private lives really matter? Fifty years after the creation of the atomic bomb at Los Alamos, newlyweds Pauline and Clifford visit that once-secret city on their honeymoon, compelled by Pauline's fascination with Oppenheimer, the soulful scientist. The two stories emerging from this visit reverberate back and forth between the loneliness of a new mother at home in Boston and the isolation of an entire community dedicated to the development of the bomb. While Pauline struggles with unforeseen challenges of family life, Oppenheimer and his crew reckon with forces beyond all imagining. Finally the years of frantic research on the bomb culminate in a stunning test explosion that echoes a rupture in the couple's marriage. Against the backdrop of a civilization that's out of control, Pauline begins to understand the complex, potentially explosive physics of personal relationships. At once funny and dead serious, *My God, What Have We Done?* sifts through the ruins left by the bomb in search of a more worthy human achievement.

As It Is On Earth - Peter M. Wheelwright

Four centuries after the Reformation Pilgrims sailed up the down-flowing watersheds of New England, Taylor Thatcher, irreverent scion of a fallen family of Maine Puritans, is still caught in the turbulence. In his errant attempts to escape from history, the young college professor is further unsettled by his growing attraction to Israeli student Miryam Bluehm as he is swept by Time through the "family thing" — from the tangled genetic and religious history of his New England parents to the redemptive birthday secret of Esther Fleur Noire Bishop, the Cajun-Passamaquoddy woman who raised him and his younger half-cousin/half-brother, Bingham.The landscapes, rivers, and tidal estuaries of Old New England and the Mayan Yucatan are also casualties of history in Thatcher's story of Deep Time and re-discovery of family on Columbus Day at a high-stakes gambling casino, rising in resurrection over the starlit bones of a once-vanquished Pequot Indian tribe.

Love's Labours - Jack Pulaski

In the four stories and two novellas that comprise *Love's Labors* the protagonists, Ben and Laura, discover in their fervid romance and long marriage their interlocking fates, and the histories that preceded their births. They also learned something of the paradox between love and all the things it brings to its beneficiaries: bliss, disaster, duty, tragedy, comedy, the grotesque, and tenderness. Ben and Laura's story is also the particularly American tale of immigration to a new world. Laura's story begins in Puerto Rico, and Ben's lineage is Russian-Jewish. They meet in City College of New York, a place at least analogous to a melting pot. Laura struggles to rescue her brother from gang life and heroin. She is mother to her younger sister; their mother Consuelo is the financial mainstay of the family and consumed by work. Despite filial obligations, Laura aspires to be a serious painter. Ben writes, cares for, and is caught up in the misadventures and surreal stories of his younger schizophrenic brother. Laura is also a story teller as powerful and enchanting as Scheherazade. Ben struggles to survive such riches, and he and Laura endure.

Fomite
Burlington, VT

Suite for Three Voices - *Derek Furr*

Suite for Three Voices is a dance of prose genres, teeming with intense human life in all its humor and sorrow. A son uncovers the horrors of his father's wartime experience, a hitchhiker in a muumuu guards a mysterious parcel, a young man foresees his brother's brush with death on September 11. A Victorian poetess encounters space aliens and digital archives, a runner hears the voice of a dead friend in the song of an indigo bunting, a teacher seeks wisdom from his students' errors and Neil Young. By frozen waterfalls and neglected graveyards, along highways at noon and rivers at dusk, in the sound of bluegrass, Beethoven, and Emily Dickinson, the essays and fiction in this collection offer moments of vision.

The Housing Market - *Joseph D. Reich*

In Joseph Reich's most recent social and cultural, contemporary satire of suburbia entitled, "The Housing market: a comfortable place to jump off the end of the world," the author addresses the absurd, postmodern elements of what it means, or for that matter not, to try and cope and function, and survive and thrive, or live and die in the repetitive and existential, futile and self-destructive, homogenized, monochromatic landscape of a brutal and bland, collective unconscious, which can spiritually result in a gradual wasting away and erosion of the senses or conflict and crisis of a desperate, disproportionate 'situational depression,' triggering and leading the narrator to feel constantly abandoned and stranded, more concretely or proverbially spoken, "the eternal stranger," where when caught between the fight or flight psychological phenomena, naturally repels him and causes him to flee and return without him even knowing it into the wild, while by sudden circumstance and coincidence discovers it surrounds the illusory-like circumference of these selfsame Monopoly board cul-de-sacs and dead ends. Most specifically, what can happen to a solitary, thoughtful, and independent thinker when being stagnated in the triangulation of a cookie-cutter, oppressive culture of a homeowner's association; a memoir all written in critical and didactic, poetic stanzas and passages, and out of desperation, when freedom and control get taken, what he is forced to do in the illusion of 'free will and volition,' something like the derivative art of a smart and ironic and social and cultural satire.

Still Time - Michael Cocchiarale

Still Time is a collection of twenty-five short and shorter stories exploring tensions that arise in a variety of contemporary relationships: a young boy must deal with the wrath of his out-of-work father; a woman runs into a man twenty years after an awkward sexual encounter; a wife, unable to conceive, imagines her own murder, as well as the reaction of her emotionally distant husband; a soon-to-be-tenured English professor tries to come to terms with her husband's shocking return to the religion of his youth; an assembly line worker, married for thirty years, discovers the surprising secret life of his recently hospitalized wife. Whether a few hundred or a few thousand words, these and other stories in the collection depict characters at moments of deep crisis. Some feel powerless, overwhelmed — unable to do much to change the course of their lives. Others rise to the occasion and, for better or for worse, say or do the thing that might transform them for good. Even in stories with the most troubling of endings, there remains the possibility of redemption. For each of the characters, there is still time.

Fomite
Burlington, VT

Signed Confessions - *Tom Walker*
Guilt and a desperate need to repent drive the antiheroes in Tom Walker's dark (and often darkly funny) stories:
A gullible journalist falls for the 40-year-old stripper he profiles in a magazine.
A faithless husband abandons his family and joins a support group for lost souls.
A merciless prosecuting attorney grapples with the suicide of his gay son.
An aging misanthrope must make amends to five former victims.
An egoistic naval hero is haunted by apparitions of his dead wife and a mysterious little girl.
The seven tales in *Signed Confessions* measure how far guilty men will go to obtain a forgiveness no one can grant but themselves.

Raven or Crow - Joshua Amses
Marlowe has recently moved back home to Vermont after flunking his first term at a private college in the Midwest, when his sort-of girlfriend, Eleanor, goes missing. The circumstances surrounding Eleanor's disappearance stand to reveal more about Marlowe than he is willing to allow. Rather than report her missing, he resolves to find Eleanor himself. *Raven or Crow* is the story of mistakes rooted in the ambivalence of being young and without direction.

The Good Muslim of Jackson Heights - *Jaysinh Birjépatil*
Jackson Heights in this book is a fictional locale with common features assembled from immigrant-friendly neighborhoods around the world where hardworking honest-to-goodness traders from the Indian subcontinent rub shoulders with ruthless entrepreneurs, reclusive antique-dealers, homeless nobodies, merchant-princes, lawyers, doctors, and IT specialists. But as Siraj and Shabnam, urbane newcomers fleeing religious persecution in their homeland, discover, there is no escape from the past. Weaving together the personal and the political. *The Good Muslim of Jackson Heights* is an ambiguous elegy to a utopian ideal set free from all prejudice.

Meanwell - *Janice Miller Potter*
Meanwell is a twenty-four-poem sequence in which a female servant searches for identity and meaning in the shadow of her mistress, poet Anne Bradstreet. Although Meanwell herself is a fiction, someone like her could easily have existed among Bradstreet's known but unnamed domestic servants. Through Meanwell's eyes, Bradstreet emerges as a human figure during the Great Migration of the 1600s, a period in which the Massachusetts Bay Colony was fraught with physical and political dangers. Through Meanwell, the feelings of women, silenced during the midwife Anne Hutchinson's fiery trial before the Puritan ministers, are finally acknowledged. In effect, the poems are about the making of an American rebel.
Through her conflicted conscience, we witness Meanwell's transformation from a powerless English waif to a mythic American who ultimately chooses wilderness over the civilization she has experienced.

Alfabestiario
AlphaBetaBestiario - Antonello Borra
Animals have always understood that mankind is not fully at home in the world. Bestiaries, hoping to teach, send out warnings. This one, of course, aims at doing the same.

Fomite
Burlington, VT

Four-Way Stop - Sherry Olson

If *Thank You* were the only prayer, as Meister Eckhart has suggested, it would be enough, and Sherry Olson's poetry, in her second book, *Four-Way Stop*, would be one. Radical attention, deep love, and dedication to kindness illuminate these poems and the stories she tells us, which are drawn from her own life: with family, with friends, andt wherever she travels, with strangers – who to Olson, never are strangers, but kin. Even at the difficult intersections, as in the title poem, *Four-Way Stop*, Olson experiences – and offers – hope, showing us how, *completely unsupervised*, people take turns, with *kindness waving each other on*. Olson writes, knowing that (to quote Czeslaw Milosz) *What surrounds us, here and now, is not guaranteed*. To this world, with her poems, Olson brings – and teaches – attention, generosity, compassion, and appreciative joy. — Carol Henrikson

Dons of Time - Greg Guma

"Wherever you look...there you are." The next media breakthrough has just happened. They call it Remote Viewing and Tonio Wolfe is at the center of the storm. But the research underway at TELPORT's off-the-books lab is even more radical -- opening a window not only to remote places but completely different times. Now unsolved mysteries are colliding with cutting edge science and altered states of consciousness in a world of corporate gangsters, infamous crimes and top-secret experiments. Based on eyewitness accounts, suppressed documents and the lives of world-changers like Nikola Tesla, Annie Besant and Jack the Ripper, Dons of Time is a speculative adventure, a glimpse of an alternative future and a quantum leap to Gilded Age London at the tipping point of invention, revolution and murder.

Body of Work - Andrei Guruianu

Throughout thirteen stories, Body of Work chronicles the physical and emotional toll of characters consumed by the all-too-human need for a connection. Their world is achingly common — beauty and regret, obsession and self-doubt, the seductive charm of loneliness. Often fragmented, whimsical, always on the verge of melancholy, the collection is a sepia-toned portrait of nostalgia — each story like an artifact of our impermanence, an embrace of all that we have lost, of all that we might lose and love again someday.

Screwed – Stephen Goldberg

Screwed is a collection of five plays by Stephen Goldberg, who has written over twenty-five produced plays and is co-founder of the Off Center or the Dramatic Arts in Burlington, Vermont.

My Father's Keeper – Andrew Potok

The turmoil, terror and betrayal of their escape from Poland at the start of World War II lead us into this tale of hatred and forgiveness between father and son.

Fomite
Burlington, VT

Unfinished Stories of Girls – Catherine Zobal Dent

The sixteen tales in _Unfinished Stories of Girls_ are framed by the quiet yet violent towns, fields, and riverbeds of Maryland's Eastern Shore. The reader is invited inside the lives of people who are trying to figure out the gleaming, marshy world. A girl in the tiny town of Cordova believes she is receiving holy instructions to save men through sex. An Oxford housekeeper serves time in prison for forging employers' signatures. A jewelry clerk and an undercover cop from Cambridge live in a doomed TV marriage. The tidewater community stews in its guilt over a hit-and-run accident that leaves a child dead. In this extraordinarily powerful debut collection, each character's deep love of the region shines. But the landscape continually shifts around them: giving so much, and taking so much away.

Rafi's World – Fred Russell

Rafi's World is a hard-hitting novel that takes an unflinching look at the brutal realities of the Other Israel and its emerging criminal class. Set in the late 1980s as the country undergoes its final transformation into a Western-style consumer society, it tells the story of those left behind in the ruins of the Zionist dream. Rafi Cohen, a smalltime hood, moves through the mean streets of the urban jungle in an Israel rarely before seen. Driven by hatred and alienated from the world around him, he hurtles toward his inevitable end in a gripping story that illuminates the darker corners of Israeli society

Sinfonia Bulgarica – Zdravka Evtimova

Sinfonia Bulgarica is a novel about four women in contemporary Bulgaria: a rich cold-blooded heiress, a masseuse dreaming of peace and quiet that never come, a powerful wife of the most influential man in the country, and a waitress struggling against all odds to win a victory over lies, poverty and humiliation. It is a realistic book of vice and yearning, of truthfulness and schemes, of love and desperation. The heroes are plain-spoken characters, whose action is limited by the contradictions of a society where lowness rules at many levels. The novel draws a picture of life in a country where many people believe that "Money is the most loyal friend of man". Yet the four women have an even more loyal friend: ruthlessness of life.

.

Writing a review on Amazon, Good Reads, Shelfari, Library Thing or other social media sites for readers will help the progress of independent publishing. To submit a review, go to the book page on any of the sites and follow the links for reviews. Books from independent presses rely on reader to reader communications.

CPSIA information can be obtained at www.ICGtesting.com
Printed in the USA
LVOW08s1114310716

498493LV00002B/457/P